Guardian Spirit

To Annette,
Hope you enjoy and feel
the magic of the mountains.

Sarah
October 12, 2013

Guardian Spirit

SARAH MARTIN BYRD

Sarah Martin Byrd

Guardian Spirit

Printed in the United States of America

This book is a work of fiction. Names, characters, locations, and events either are the product of the author's imagination or are used fictitiously, and any resemblance to actual persons (alive or deceased), places, or events is entirely coincidental.

ISBN: 978-1-62020-127-5
eISBN: 978-1-62020-179-4

Author's photograph by Jerry Byrd
Cover Design by Matthew Mulder
Page Layout by Janice Phelps, LLC

INKSWIFT
427 Wade Hampton Blvd.
Greenville, SC 29609, USA
www.inkswift.com

The colophon is a trademark of Inkswift

~ In Memory of ~

BILLY THOMAS MARTIN
*Here's to you, Daddy. You were, like me, far from perfect,
but I've always loved you anyway.*

VERLIE PRUITT MARTIN
*Grandma Verlie, thank you for showing me
there really are spirits among us.*

~ Acknowledgments ~

First of all, thank you Estes and Thelma Wagner for sharing your enchanted cabin in the woods. The first time I saw it, I knew there was magic there.

My sincere thanks goes to Jo Martin Harris, who quickly transformed from acquaintance, to editor, to friend. I am forever indebted to you for sticking with me through all the red marks and side notations. Your insight and expertise pushed me to make this the best book I possibly could. I will always hold you in the highest regard.

To the first reader of *Guardian Spirit*, my daughter, Wendy, thank you for being the guinea pig for my original words, I wouldn't have trusted them with anyone else.

To Emma, my granddaughter, I hope you'll always remember your time with Gi-Gi. You are so very special to me.

To Jerry, my friend and husband, I know you totally don't understand what I do, yet you have been patient with me while I live my dream, thank you.

To Kay Martin, my friend and best cheerleader, thanks for taking the time to read my stories. I loved seeing genuine enjoyment in your eyes as you told me how much you enjoyed my books.

To all who have suffered the sting of a hand, been degraded by words spoken in hate, or treated un-justly, *Guardian Spirit* is for you. Sometimes nothing can help, lest a miracle…so close your eyes and believe.

And to the One who has been performing miracles since the beginning of time, whose spirit abides among us, I dedicate this book to You, the One from whence I came, and to which I shall someday return.

I close in peace, and in great hope of healing for all.

~Sarah Martin Byrd

But ask now the beasts, and they shall teach thee:
and the fowls of the air, and they shall tell thee.

~Job 12:7

~ Chapter One ~

*A*n elderly woman wearing a soft apron sits in the porch swing of a lilac Victorian house. The early May breeze through the mountains lifts a wisp of her gray hair from the long braid at her back. She brushes it aside absentmindedly as she loses herself in the fading afternoon sun.

Down the stem of a bent daffodil to its bulb, her mind travels like electricity across the roots to those of a nearby hickory tree. Down from there and even farther into the earth's core, the roots mark her path to the old cave where she meets her guides for another of many similar encounters.

"We are glad to see you," says one.

"As always, I am honored to be here," she says. "And soon?" she says, "Is it soon? All the signs seem . . ."

"Yes," says the elder, "and your part is written and told to the heavens."

He nods to the bear at the cave entrance. The woman takes a deep breath, smelling the smoke of the fire inside the circle. All the elders are silent. All are ready. The bear disappears.

❖ ❦ ❖

"Where are we going, Mama?" twelve-year-old Sadie Madison asked. "We've been driving for two days now. You said it would take two days. Aren't we about there?"

Millie Madison looked over at her headstrong oldest child, and then peeked at the curled up form of Sammy, her five-year old son, who lay in the back seat. Overwhelming love stirred inside her and hot tears threatened to flow down her cheeks. She couldn't let Sadie see any of the emotion she held deep inside: fear, pain, and worst of all the uncertainty.

Millie felt the place where the growth was removed from the back of her neck. Every time she turned her head, the grinding of scar tissue vibrated through her ears. How long would it take? Two months, two years? No one could tell her exactly when. They were just sure it would eventually sprout new growth just like a seed potato, the new taking over and the old left to rot away.

Millie forgot to watch the highway for just a second. She was as tired as she had ever been in her life.

God, she silently pleaded, *please let this work. I know you're leading me back to the cabin, but what then? What am I going to find? It's been over twenty years since my last trip up this mountain. What if it's not even there? What if it is? Has Grandma sold it to someone else? Will she be there? How old would she be now? Grandma was almost twenty years older than Mama who would have been fifty now, so Grandma should be almost seventy.*

Millie vaguely remembered that day all those years ago when her mama had packed up their clothes one rainy morning and told her they were going away for a while. That while had been everlasting—forever until now. But today she was going to be home, her home-away-from-home those first seven years of her life.

Millie's mother told her it was for the best that she didn't see her daddy and grandparents, and as time passed Millie had almost forgotten what they looked and smelled like, except for Grandpa. He always smelled like a freshly opened pack of chewing tobacco. Millie found out that Grandpa passed away more than ten years before. That day before her mother died, she found out a lot more. Millie had always thought her daddy had sent them away, but before her mother went to sleep forever, she cleared her conscience. She said she'd left Jonathan, Millie's father, because she had fallen in love with Luke Turner, the man with whom she spent the rest of her life. Luke had been a good stepfather to Millie, and their lives had been okay, except for the times her mother would get really sad. Sometimes it would last a few hours and sometimes several days. She would lock herself away in her room with the shades pulled tightly closed. Millie would hear her praying over and over for God to grant her peace.

Now as an adult Millie understood. She imagined that her mother never got over the guilt of taking her away from her daddy, a father who died before she could find him again.

Millie's mind traced too many deaths, too much pain.

"Mama . . . Mama, are you going to answer me?" Sadie asked.

"I'm sorry, Sadie Girl. I don't know where my mind was." Millie said.

Sadie Girl was what her mama called her sometimes. It made Sadie feel a special closeness to her mama, like she was her special girl and nobody else's.

"Yes, we're almost there. We should be pulling in within the hour."

"In where?" Sadie asked. "Where are we going?"

"Look around. What do you see?"

Sadie gazed out the front windshield. In front of her loomed a big wall of mountains.

"I see hills."

"Those aren't just hills, those are the Blue Ridge Mountains and they hold magic in them."

"Magic, what kind of magic?"

"Oh, Sadie. That is something I can't explain. It's a sensation you'll have to feel for yourself. I was very young when I left these hills, but I haven't forgotten their enchantment. Now as I get closer I can almost sense it as strongly as the day I left."

Up that winding mountain road they drove, jostling through the curves woke Sammy.

"I'm hungry. When can we stop and eat?"

As Sammy sat up, he rubbed his eyes and looked out the window up ahead at the mountains and then down through the valleys. He could see for miles, both ways.

"What is all that stuff down there? Where are we?"

"Those are houses and barns and land. It's the same way it would look from the sky if we were up in an airplane."

"I'm not going up in any airplane. I saw that picture in the newspaper when one fell out of the sky. I'm never going to do that, never."

"No, honey. We're not going to fly in an airplane, we're going home."

A terrified look crossed Sammy's little face, his eyes misted and he caught his breath. "Home? But I thought we didn't ever have to go back there again. You promised." Sammy's voice was soft and shaking.

Millie stopped the car at the next pullover. She turned around and looked into her son's eyes, bright with fright. The cut beneath his eye was healing nicely, but the whole side of his face was still a dark purple.

"Come here, Sweetie."

Sammy crawled over the seat and snuggled up next to his mama.

"No, we're not going back to Texas. We are far, far away from there now. Look at me, both of you. I promise you as long as there is breath in me your daddy will never lay another hand on any of us ever again, especially you two.

"Let me tell you about the home we're going to. Many years ago when I was a little girl, I stayed with my grandma and grandpa. They would pack up the old Ford truck with food and supplies, and we'd head off to the cabin. I can't wait for you to see it. It's the most extraordinary place in the world—small with two bedrooms and a kitchen. The living room has a big, old fireplace with a hand-looped rug in front of it. We used to sit in front of that fire at night and eat popcorn. Grandma read me books until I fell asleep. All the while she made fun of the silly noises coming out of Grandpa as he slept in his chair. But the best part was the sounds. On warm nights, we sat out on the side porch and listened to the creek ripple or sometimes roar when it had rained a lot. In the mornings we'd be wakened by the animals."

"Animals? What kind of animals?" both children asked at once.

"Well, mostly birds and turkeys. There are huge, gigantic oak trees all around the cabin. Their enormous limbs hang down almost touching the roof. Those limbs are also the roosting place for all the local game. Grandpa always used to fuss, and try to run them off, so they wouldn't wake us up every morning. But occasionally when they would roost somewhere else, he'd go in and out of the door a dozen times every evening looking for them. 'I wonder where they are, Ann,' he'd say. He'd tell us they were our guardian angels looking down and watching out over us. I can almost hear them now—gobble, gobble, gobble—and the loud swishing of their wings as they took flight."

"Mama, you're fibbing. Turkeys are raised in big houses. They don't live out here in trees," Sammy said, giggling at his mama's attempt to sound like a turkey.

"Now . . . have I ever fibbed to you?"

"No," Sammy said, hanging his head a little.

"What other animals live there?" Sadie asked.

"Oh gosh, kids, you're just not going to believe it. You can look out the kitchen window every evening and again at sunrise and see the deer running and playing in the bottoms below. Young bucks will stand on their hind legs and paw at each other trying to see who is the stronger of the two. And the ornery old does will bunt the sides of another weaker one if she comes too close to something she is eating. They seem quite selfish, but it's really just their instinct to survive."

Survive? Yes, that was exactly what she would do. She was determined to bunt heads with anyone who stood in her way. She would be like that strong female deer as she stands against the elements protecting her young. Millie had been the weaker one for way too long. From this day forward no one would ever hurt her family again.

"What else is there?" Sammy asked, wide-eyed.

"There are twitchy little squirrels scampering all about, rabbits hopping around, and noisy old raccoons and opossums. I know there are bears, too, even though I never saw one. Grandpa and I saw tracks down by the spring creek one day. But the most special to me of all the animals were Heidi and Hannibal."

"Who were they?" Sammy asked with his eyes all big and shining.

"Why, they were our outhouse chipmunks."

"What are outhouse chipmunks?" Sadie asked with a roll of her eyes.

"First of all, do you guys know what an outhouse is?"

"It's a house that is outside," Sammy chimed in.

"No, silly," Sadie corrected him, "it's a toilet outside in a little building."

"A toilet outside? How does that work?"

"You'll just have to see it, Sammy, to understand. You both have seen pictures of chipmunks haven't you?"

"Yes," they said.

"Well, Heidi and Hannibal lived behind a board inside the outhouse. They were black and white and fluffy. Every spring they'd have their babies behind that board. As the babies grew, they'd come and go out of a hole between the rafters until one day when they would all go their different ways making homes of their own. But every winter our furry friends would come home to the outhouse. They would gather up papers, twigs, and leaves to rebuild their little nest behind the board. They would stay all winter, and come spring, the whole cycle would start over again.

"The first winter we met them, they almost gave Grandpa a heart attack. It was just before Thanksgiving and we had gone up to get everything ready for the family get-together. As usual,

Grandpa took the broom up to the outhouse to sweep and clean it out. Grandma and I heard him holler and ran out of the cabin to see what was the matter. There Grandpa stood, holding the broom up like a weapon at four glowing little eyeballs huddled up in the corner. Who was the most afraid that day, the chipmunks or Grandpa? We'll never know, but Grandma and I always said Grandpa was.

" 'What are them things?' Grandpa said. 'Them varmints almost jumped on my head when I opened that door.'

" 'Look, Millie, it's just a couple of cute little chipmunks,' Grandma told him.

" 'Cute my eye!' Grandpa said. 'I'm going to kill them pests. Just look there, they've shredded that whole roll of toilet paper. Take in all this mess!' he roared. Grandma calmed him down by saying, 'Leave them alone, they'll probably run off now since you've scared them half to death.' But they didn't leave, they stayed right through the winter and were back again the next fall and the next and the next. From that day on, going to the outhouse was an adventure.

"I believed Heidi and Hannibal could hear and understand me when I talked to them. They became my best friends, other than Grandma. We had to be real careful though and make sure we kept the toilet paper done up tight in a bag with a twisty tie, because if you left it even a little bit open, the chipmunks would dig the paper out and add it to their nests."

Sadie noticed her mama's face glowed remembering the good things. She hoped she and Sammy would find that kind of happiness up here in these mountains.

Millie leaned her head back on the seat for a minute, letting all the fond memories fill her thoughts. She hadn't even known she'd had all these things in her head. Recollection after recollection came flooding back. Again she prayed. *Please God, give me time to share the magic with my children.*

"Are you all right?" Sadie asked.

"Yes, I'm fine, just remembering . . . Are you ready?

"Oh, one more thing kids: I'm not sure what we'll find when we get there. Someone else may be living there, but I want you to at least see it, even if we might not be able to stay."

"Why haven't we ever been here before?" Sadie asked. "How could you have gone this long not seeing your grandma since she was your best friend when you were little?" So many things just didn't make sense to Sadie.

Cranking the car, Millie answered her inquiring young daughter the best way she knew how. "Some things are better left unsaid, especially when the dead are not here to defend themselves."

This didn't satisfy Sadie, but she dropped it for now anyway. As Sammy crawled to the back seat, the Suburban turned back onto the highway.

"Here we go, kids. Next stop Skunk Cabbage Bog."

"Where and *what* is Skunk Cabbage Bog?" Sadie had taken about all the mystery she could stand for one day.

"That's the name of the road the cabin is on. Grandma christened it after the green, leafy stuff that grows in the creeks coming out of these mountain springs. It is light green with big leaves and it tastes awful, or at least that's what I remember. Grandma would pick it in the springtime and cook it for Grandpa. It would stink up the whole cabin for days. Grandpa loved it. I never could understand how anyone could love to eat a weed, especially one that smelled so bad. The good part was when Grandma cooked the greens she heated me up a can of tomato soup and fried hushpuppies with lots of catsup, probably the best meal in the whole world. Maybe the cabbage will still be there and I'll show it to you."

"Mama, I want some hushpuppies. I'm hungry."

"We'll put that on our first grocery list, Sammy, when we're settled in," Millie said.

It was early May and everything was coming to life in the mountains—plants, baby animals—and the maples were budding red, setting the hills on fire. Millie's chest grew tight with anticipation and hope.

"What does bog have to do with skunk cabbage!" Sadie asked.

"Oh yeah, the bottomland has bogs," Millie said.

"What is a bog?" Sammy asked, a bit of concern crossing his face. Bog sounded scary to him.

"A bog is very low, wet, spongy mountain land. In fact the bogs are a dangerous place to go. Grandpa never let me wander far from him. He always said the bogs would suck me up if I stepped into one of them."

"Do monsters live there?" Sammy asked, his eyes getting bigger by the minute.

"No, silly," Sadie said. "There's no such thing as monsters."

Millie wasn't so sure about that, for they'd just left one in Texas.

"Well, Mama said something would suck you up. What would it be but monsters?" Sammy's eyes grew moist with fright.

"Mud. Really, you will just sink up in it; it won't suck you up. It's just mud, not something alive," Millie said, trying to calm Sammy's fears.

"Does anything live in the bogs?" Sadie asked.

"Yes, as a matter of fact—little tiny turtles and, of course, snakes and lizards and such."

"Little tiny turtles? How tiny?" Sammy asked.

"Very tiny. They are called bog turtles, and I believe they are the smallest turtle in the world. They are also very special. I remember men in uniforms with high boots coming up here to the bogs a couple times a year to try to find them. They would count each one they saw and compare the numbers to the time before. They are almost extinct. I only saw one. It was perched on the edge of a rock close to the bank one day when Grandpa and I were walking in the pine grove. Grandpa said it was a very special thing to get to see one. They like to hide from humans, and not many people ever get a glimpse.

"I remember it wasn't any larger than a quarter. It was black with yellow on its shell. We stood very still and just watched it sitting there doing nothing. I squatted down and looked right in its eyes, and it looked into mine. I wanted to pick it up, but Grandpa said that it was wild and touching it might hurt it. So I just sat there on the ground, me watching the bog turtle and the bog turtle watching me. I sat doing that until Grandpa got bored and said, 'Let's go.' I wanted to stay longer, but it was almost suppertime.

"As I walked off, I looked back. The turtle was still there. It had turned around and was watching me leave. I never really thought about it until now, but it was as though he was trying to tell me something with his eyes. Oh well, I guess I'll never know what it was."

"I miss Grandpa Luke," Sammy said. Talking about Grandpa had stirred up thoughts in his head.

"I know you do, but we can't see Grandpa Luke. He lives too close to Daddy. Maybe he can come and visit us sometime when we get settled."

"Can he? Oh boy! Can he?"

"I hope so, Baby, I hope so."

"Do you think Grandpa Luke will always be sad now that Grandma Lindsay is in heaven?" Sadie asked.

"I don't think so, Sadie Girl . . . Time has a way of healing our hurts and worries."

~ Chapter Two ~

*T*ime had helped Millie. Her mother Lindsay had died from an automobile accident almost a year ago. She had been a good mother and grandmother. Millie would never let her children know the things her mama had told her the day before she died. Children didn't need to know about how lives and families are torn apart because of the weakness of the flesh.

Mama had stripped her away from her daddy and grandparents because she had been selfish. She thought life with Luke would be better than it was with her daddy. That day almost a year ago, Lindsay shared her soul with Millie and told her daughter that she had made a huge mistake all those years ago. Even though Luke was a devoted husband, Lindsay had never stopped loving Millie's daddy Jonathan. Lindsay Turner had begged her only child Millie to forgive her, to pardon her for taking her away from her daddy, to exonerate her for not helping her leave Brad years ago.

Lindsay hadn't wanted Millie to take the kids away from their father, as she had. But, Lindsay had no idea of the torture Brad Madison put Millie and the children through. No one knew but Sadie, Sammy, and her, for most of the bruises, burns, and cuts were hidden by clothes, and their battered spirits were tucked deep inside away from the world's eyes. After Lindsay passed away, Luke didn't come around too often. He had heard Lindsay tell Millie everything, and he also shared in the guilt. Meanwhile Brad became bolder and crueler once no one was popping in on them.

Sadie's arm being pulled out of the socket was "an accident"; she'd "fallen off the bed." Candle burns on Millie were hidden, especially from her children. Every day Brad added some new kind of persecution, until three days ago when Millie felt sure Brad was finally going to kill one of them. Sammy had been Brad's punching bag that day. If Millie and Sadie hadn't come in when they did, Millie wasn't sure Sammy would be sitting in that back seat right now. They had both jumped on Brad's back and some- how pulled him off the little boy. That evening Millie knew her marriage was over. Brad had looked at them with the eyes of a madman or devil—Millie couldn't decide which one he was—and vowed to put them in a place away, far away. She knew he was not going to stop until he had killed one or all of them.

That night Millie finally admitted to herself that she and her chil- dren had to escape. She fell asleep behind the locked door of her children's room with her arms locked tightly around each of them. Under her pillow lay the long two-pronged fork she used to flip chicken on the outside grill. She had never killed anything more than a fly, but as she felt up under her pillow, her fingers rested on the coldness of the stainless steel. She'd do whatever she had to do. She'd had enough and her children had born wit- ness to way too much. In a fitful doze, Millie dreamed of a little cabin way back in the woods. By morning it was clear to her. She knew where to go.

She got up and tiptoed out of the bedroom with the fork in her hand. All was quiet. Brad would occasionally leave and not wake her to fix his breakfast. Thankfully this was true of that morning. She threw everything she could into paper sacks and cardboard boxes and loaded the children into her five-year-old Chevy. With one stop at the bank, Millie cleaned out their savings account. Thankfully Brad was a tightwad, so there was plenty of money to tide them over for quite a while.

* 🌿 *

Millie slowed the car. "I think it's just around this next curve."

So many years . . . maybe she wasn't even on the right road? At her last visit she had only been seven. But fortunately there had been many trips in those seven years. Sure enough as they rounded the bend there was a small green rectangular sign that read: SKUNK CABBAGE BOG. It wasn't the same sign her Grandma had hand-painted. It was more official as if the county or state had put it up. Either way, it was there and this was the right road.

As Millie steered into the narrow dirt drive, a feeling of peace overwhelmed her. It was a comfort that surpassed anything she'd felt in a long time.

The confined road was barely wide enough for the vehicle. Tree limbs overhung the roadway. Years of rain had washed deep gullies making for a bumpy ride. It was obvious no one had traveled this cabin road in many years. Millie was glad, but judging by the condition the road was in, there was no telling in what shape she'd find the cabin, if it were even still standing. The denseness of the woods made it seem darker and more mysterious than it actually was. Millie took a deep breath and felt her grip tighten on the steering wheel.

~ Chapter Three ~

*D*r. Lewis Townsend excused himself from his patient. "I'll be back in just a minute, Mrs. Henderson."

A cold sweat popped out on his forehead and the familiar roaring began in his ears. This was the usual routine when the pictures in his minds eye appeared. This started when he was a young boy. He should be used to it, but he wasn't.

"I'll be right back, Laf," Lewis called to his secretary as he walked into the bathroom. He sat down on the shut lid of the toilet and closed his eyes, listening as the voices came alive in his head.

> *"Please, won't you stop? I know if I have just a few minutes, I can find the root to make the fever tea. It will help my people." Tomeka says.*
>
> *His answer is a hard blow to the left temple from the soldier's heavy rifle.*

Lewis cradled his aching head in both hands. Giving himself a minute, he finally stood. Running his fingers across his forehead, he fully expected to feel the knot. Then as always, the pain subsided and he saw a flash of the huge black bear.

The bear trudges up an oak-spiked hillside and between the rhododendron thickets until he reaches a rock outcropping, stops, and unfurls slowly upright on his hind legs revealing his broad shoulders. He swats at the left side of his face with his paw and releases a faint moan.

At the end of the day Lewis finished his paperwork, as always he added the date, May 8, 1968. He had many strange days in his forty-eight years, but this one so far was at the top of the list. Flashes of the black bear had appeared to him all afternoon.

❋ ❦ ❋

"I'm scared, Mama," Sammy said.

"Scared of what?"

"Those bog monsters you told us about."

"Not bog monsters, just little tiny turtles. There's nothing to be afraid of. You're going to love this place."

Sadie sat up on the edge of the seat and took in every detail of the narrow dirt path. She could see nothing but trees. They were in the middle of a giant forest of mostly white pine. Looking sideways, she crooked her neck up to the sky and could barely see the tops of some of the trees.

"Oh, no . . ."

"What's wrong?" Sammy asked, a little bit of fear still shining in his eyes.

"The log chain is still across the road."

As Millie looked in front of her, she saw the great big hoops of the rusted logging chain. She also saw that it was still securely fastened with the familiar lock. She remembered the many times when Grandpa would stop and Grandma would open the glove compartment to pull out the set of keys that always stayed there. Grandma would jump out of the old truck, go to the lock, insert the key, and just like magic, it would pop open and the chain would plop to the ground. All the while Millie sat beside Grandpa on the edge of the seat, watching Grandma. But today there was no magic key in the glove compartment; Millie pulled it open anyway just to check.

"What are we going to do now?" Sadie asked.

And then as if something had flipped a switch on in her brain, Millie spoke out loud, "Knothole."

"Knothole? What are you talking about?" Sadie asked.

"Grandpa used to leave a key in a knothole of a tree for his brother Stan to use when he came up here hunting, but which tree? Okay kids, we're going on our first adventure, a key-in-the-knothole hunt. I believe it was on the driver's side of the road. Let's go find a key."

Sadie was pretty sure her mama was going a little crazy. All Sadie could see were giant trees. While most of them were white pine, there were also some humongous oaks and tall, skinny poplars. Last fall she did a scrapbook of all of the tree leaves around their house for school, so she was pretty good at identifying what species they were, even though the trees did look a bit different here in North Carolina. Sadie reached down, pulled open the door handle of the car, and walked around the front to where Millie and Sammy were standing.

"I can vaguely remember the day I watched Grandpa hide that key. I was sitting in the truck right here, but I can't remember if I was looking ahead or behind me. Anyway I know it's here close. Let's start searching."

Millie grabbed the hands of her children. They went behind the car and walked back the way they came. They weaved back and forth searching every tree for close to an hour.

"We're never going to find it. There's no way to get around, the trees are too big and close together on each side of the chain. And I'm hungry," Sadie said.

Millie led the way to the car and opened up the back. Inside she lifted the cooler lid. She took out three colas and handed one to each of them.

"Okay, what will it be? Bologna or peanut butter and jelly sandwiches?" she said.

"Peanut butter and jelly!" Sammy said, acting excited even though Sadie couldn't imagine what there was to be excited about. Sandwiches were all they'd eaten for three days.

"Again?" Sadie said. She couldn't help but admit to herself that she was becoming a bit nervous about this adventure stuff.

"For now, it'll have to do until we get settled in somewhere and buy supplies."

Working from the tailgate of the Suburban she made them all PB&Js. She helped Sammy jump up on the gate to sit, and then started to help Sadie.

"Lord, Mama, I believe I can handle it by myself. I'm not five, you know."

"Okay, sorry." Millie admired her independent daughter as she released the grip she had on her arm and watched her hop up on the makeshift seat. Sometimes she forgot the things Sadie had seen and been through her entire life. She had never been allowed to be a child. Sadie seemed more like twenty than twelve.

Leaning against the side of the car, Millie ate without tasting. She was beginning to get a little anxious. It would be dark in a few hours and she had to get them settled in for the night somewhere. About that time she heard a noise in the underbrush to the right of her. She looked over and saw a squirrel scamper up an old dead oak, its branches long past bearing any acorns.

"That's it! That's the tree! It's dead now. That's why I didn't recognize it."

She put down the remainder of her sandwich and ran to the backside of the tree. There the hole was! She reached up and let her fingers examine the inside. She felt around everywhere—no key. By this time Sadie had helped Sammy off the tailgate and they were standing beside her.

"It's got to be here. I *know* this is the tree."

Millie fell to her knees and put her hands over her eyes. She would not cry, she couldn't scare the kids. They'd seen enough tears. She lowered her hands and started to rise and saw it. Right at the base of the trunk it lay. It wasn't shiny and new anymore; in fact it was brown and rust covered. Millie picked it up ever so gently as if she'd found a precious diamond.

"Let's go try it," Millie said as she held the key tightly in her hand.

All three headed for the locked gate. Millie knelt down and took the lock in her hand. Flipping it upside down, she put the key to the hole. She wiggled and worked, but it wouldn't go in.

"Sadie, go and get my nail file out of my pocketbook."

Running, Sadie was back in a flash with the file in her hand. Millie set to work, rubbing away at the built up rust. When she thought it was enough, she stopped, picked up the lock again, inserted the tip, and then the entire key into the hole. A twist to the right and the lock flung open as if brand new.

"Yes!" Millie shouted as she jumped up and down.

The kids joined in the celebration. Their first hurdle had been mastered, and hopefully this would be one of many accomplishments. Millie slipped the key safely into the pocket of her jeans.

"Let's go. Nothing to stop us now."

Away they went back to the car, mother, daughter, and son, hand in hand. It was sad that something so simple had made them so happy. They'd known very little joy these past years. It wouldn't take a whole lot to keep them content as long as they were safe and had each other. Millie could only pray for a miracle.

After gathering up the picnic, Millie cranked up the car. She only pulled forward far enough to get passed the fallen chain, and then stopped.

Stepping out of the car, Millie said to Sadie, "Will you help me put the chain back up? It's unlikely anyone will come this way, but we'll lock ourselves in just in case."

Sadie picked up the heavy chain and handed the end around the tree to her mama. Millie slid the lock through two links and used the heel of her hand to hit the bottom as the top was wedged against the tree. Snap, it was locked.

Sammy was hanging out the car window. "Did you get it?"

"Got it, Sammy, with the help of your sister."

Sadie had been Mama's helper all her life. Millie would tell Sadie, "I've got to go do these errands for your daddy. Sammy's asleep. Will you please sit by him, and as soon as he wakes, play with him, so he doesn't get in your daddy's way?" Sadie had learned a long time ago to stay as far from him as possible. He wasn't always mean, but you never knew when he would be, and it seemed he was getting viler more and more often. Helping her mama tiptoe around him had always been a way of life for her.

Sadie had tried her best to help. She had often lain awake at night when her daddy was on a rampage, listening for any sign of him trying to hurt her mama. Thankfully she was listening a few months ago. By the time Sadie got into her parents' bedroom, her mama's lips were turning blue from his overpowering fingers clasped tightly around her throat.

Sadie would never forget that night for as long as she lived. Jumping onto the bed, she beat her father with her fists. He let go his hold on Millie's throat as he backhanded Sadie across the mouth. The blow flung her small body off the bed and onto the floor.

"What the hell do you think you're doing, you little weakling? I swear you get more like your mama every day. You're going to wind up just as useless and pitiful as she is."

With that he slapped Millie, stepped off the bed, and kicked Sadie in her side on his way out the door. At that moment what little love she'd managed to have for him died, never to be reborn. She knew it wasn't right to hate someone, and that the Bible says children should honor their mother and father, but she didn't care. God would just have to punish her. Right then she didn't really care, she just knew she hated him and she was anything but a weakling. From that night on, Sadie prayed that she and her brother and mama could go far, far away from him, and then she'd pray for God to forgive the way she felt.

With her window down, Sadie felt the stirring of the cool mountain breeze blowing through her tangled red hair. She knew her prayers had been answered. God wasn't mad at her. He understands because He had seen it all, yes, all of it. Everything was going to be okay, she just knew it.

Pulling the cranked car into gear, Millie lightly stepped on the gas. What would they find? Butterflies fluttered around inside her. She was anxious and happy and scared all at the same time.

"It's just around this bend in the road, kids. Do you see it? There it is!"

Millie stopped a short distance from the cabin. She just sat there and stared. Nothing yet everything had changed. She couldn't help it—tears poured down her cheeks. She was home, and a peace she'd not known for two decades welled up inside her.

"Do you think your grandma Ann still lives here? It is so grown up. It looks like a fairy tale dream I have often. Mama, I just love it. May we go in?" Sadie spoke in an almost whisper.

Sammy on the other hand just kept leaning over the front seat looking at this strange new place.

"Mama, may we?" Sadie whispered again.

Snapping out of her reverie, Millie coasted down the weed-grown driveway and came to a stop right at the front door. She opened her door, and motioned out the children.

"Do you hear it kids?"

"Hear what?" Sadie asked, stepping out.

Sammy crawled over the seat and slid out the door to the ground. He folded his hand into Sadie's, listening.

"What is it?" Sammy asked.

"That's Brush Creek and it sounds like it is running full. It winds all around the side of the cabin and up through the bottom. Come on, I'll show you."

Grabbing Sammy's other hand, the three strolled toward the rippling sound. In just a few steps, they were past the enormous tree stump. Millie ran her hand over it. The last time she saw it, it had been a magnificent white oak. Then they spotted the glistening waters of the creek down the steep bank below, rushing from all the spring rains.

"May we stick our feet in?" Sammy asked.

"You'll have to wait till it gets a little warmer. If I remember correctly, it's pretty cold even in the heat of summer, and since it's only May eighth, it'll be extremely cold."

Sadie was taking it all in. In the growing dusk of the late afternoon, it was getting really dark in the thick woods. The huge trees that surrounded them were cutting off what little sunlight remained. Over to the left a movement caught Sadie's eye. As she fixed her gaze toward the sound, all she saw was a flash of white. Millie saw it at the same time.

"A deer . . . kids, look."

Sammy jumped. He wasn't used to seeing wild animals unless they were behind a fence at the zoo.

"It's all right. It won't hurt you. We must have scared it. I'm sure it's not accustomed to visitors."

Sadie wasn't scared. She started walking toward where the deer had been, hoping she'd spot another one.

"Come on, Sadie. Let's go check out the cabin," Millie said.

Convinced there wasn't another deer, Sadie turned and followed her mama and brother toward the overgrown cabin. Bushes and vines had grown up past some of the windows, and the roof was covered in green spongy moss.

Millie didn't go to the door but confidently walked to the first window on the right side of the cabin. It all felt familiar, except this time Millie didn't need her grandpa to boost her up so she could reach the door key. It was always hidden on the top of the shutter. Stretching up on her tiptoes, she quickly wrapped her fingers around the cold metal. Then she made her way to the front door. Millie touched the handle of the screen door. Slowly she opened the wooden frame. A fluttering overhead made her step back and let the handle go. She almost knocked Sammy down. After all, he was clinging to her.

"What the heck?" Looking overhead, Millie realized she had disturbed a nest of birds that had found a home over the frame of the door. She stepped back upon the step, so she could see it clearly now, and in it were three little speckled heads.

"Come here, Sammy."

Millie picked him up and landed him on her hip.

"Can you see them? Sadie, do you see?"

"Oh . . . baby birds. What kind are they? They're so cute," Sadie said.

"Will they peck us?" Sammy asked, still scared of yet another wild creature.

"No, they won't peck you. They're way too small for that. Anyway we can't touch them. If we get our scent on them, their mama and daddy won't take care of them."

They stood watching what Millie determined to be baby wrens. But really the children couldn't agree since they certainly weren't used to identifying baby birds in the wild.

"Let's go in the side door so we won't bother them."

With that, Millie reached down, taking her wide-eyed children by the hands. Three steps up and they were on the back porch. A few more steps and Millie put her hand on the screen door's rusty handle. This time she looked overhead: no feathery friends this time.

With the key still safely in her hand, she moved the tip into the hole. After a bit of wiggling and prying, it finally went all the way in. Someone might have tried to jimmy the lock, but Millie wouldn't voice her concern out loud. Sammy was spooked enough.

"Are you ready, kids?"

Sadie quickly answered, "Yes," and Sammy looked to be on the verge of tears.

As she turned the key to the right, Millie heard the lock click and knew they were in. She placed the door key with the chain key in her pocket. Her hand on the knob, she willed herself to turn it. Why was she holding back now? Why was there a fine bead of sweat on her upper lip? Why, because this was their future, their haven of safety and peace.

"Open the door. I want to see inside," Sadie said.

Millie slowly turned the lovingly worn brass knob and the door squeaked open. Wider and wider it parted. With both children standing behind her peeking around, she finally gave it one more shove, and it flew all the way open. The first thing they all noticed was the musky smell of old.

"Yuck, what is that stink?" Sammy asked, taking a step back and holding his nose.

"Smells like stinky socks, doesn't it?" Sadie said.

"Well, I guess it does a little bit, but I believe it's just musty because it's been closed up for many years. I really don't think anyone has stayed here since I was a little girl."

Stepping in, Millie adjusted to the semi-darkness and scanned inside the small room. Late afternoon shadows washed away what little sunlight that was left. In a minute, she transfixed on an object over in the corner behind the kitchen table. It was her little red wagon, and in it sat Teddy. She remembered that she always left him at the cabin, so she'd have something to sleep with when she was here.

She was given the brown teddy bear for her first Christmas by her grandma Ann. Walking toward it, she was oblivious to the cobwebs that clung to her as she made her way across the room. She reached down and took the bear lovingly in her arms.

The children heard her ever so quietly say, "Oh Grandma, where are you? I need you so badly."

Sadie held Sammy's hand as she watched her mama rock the stuffed animal back and forth. It was several minutes before Millie snapped back to reality and the tasks before her.

~ Chapter Four ~

*A*nn Hampton threw her legs over the side of the bed just like she had every morning at six-thirty for as many years as she could remember. She didn't need an alarm clock. Her aging body was used to the routine. Ever since she and Jake had closed down their little country store close to twenty years before, that's the time she got up. She always felt a bit guilty for sleeping later. When they were working, they'd be up by five and opening the store by six-thirty.

Now there really wasn't any use getting up at all. Every day was the same—dress, eat, read the paper, straighten the house, eat again, do some outside chores and of course, her daily walk. Strolling down the road was her favorite thing to do. It was one of the few pleasures Ann had left in her life. She set out almost every morning usually the same route. Taking a left at the mailbox took her a mile down the road to her grandparent's old home-place and the springhouse. Here she would stop for a minute, sip a little water out of the aluminum dipper that hung on a nail, then start back up the hill toward home. Just like every day Ann's mind wandered back in time, before Jake her husband died, before Millie disappeared, and before Jonathan her son had left her too.

For the better part of the last twenty-three years, Ann's thoughts had been tormented. With a few written words of farewell from her daughter-in-law, Lindsay, back in 1945, Lindsay was gone and with her Millie, Ann's only grandchild. Ann would never forget that blessed spring day April 22, 1938, when Melissa Ann Hampton entered the world. It was love at first sight, not because it was her grandchild and she was supposed to love her, but it ran deeper than that. Millie was her only son's flesh and blood, and Ann didn't know how she could possibly love anything or anyone more than him, but she could tell it was going to be a close race. Of course, she wasn't worried because she believed you could never love too much. Little Millie had Ann's heart strings tied all up in knots right from the beginning.

During those precious seven years before they vanished, Ann and her granddaughter had spent so many happy hours together. Ann sometimes wondered if that was one of the reasons Lindsay had run off with Millie. Was she envious that Millie always wanted to stay at Granny Ann and Pappy Jake's? Was Lindsay upset that Millie would rather run off with her and Jake to the mountains, and spend the weekend at the cabin, than stay home?

Ann's walk was the same every day, with the same unanswered questions.

Lindsay's note had been short and to the point. Ann had it word for word in her memory:

Dear Jonathan,

I am going away today. I need to sort some things out in my head. I don't know what's wrong with me. I know I should be happy but I'm not. When I get settled I'll let you know where I am and you can visit Millie.

Lindsay

That was the last her husband and his family ever heard from Lindsay. She never let Jonathan know where she went. For the next three years he searched every waking moment for them, running to the mailbox the second he heard the brakes squeak to a stop on the postman's car, praying there would be a letter from Lindsay. He spent every dime he had, and Jake and Ann gave him every cent they could spare. Jonathan hired a man who was supposed to be real good at finding people, but nothing turned up.

He slowly but surely drank and mourned himself to death. His wife and child had fallen off the face of the earth; he had no reason to live. Ann tried to help him get through it by consoling him, telling him they were out there somewhere and would turn up, but they never did. Jonathan never quit trying to find them.

Lindsay's hand didn't hold a sharp-edged knife to Jonathan's heart; but she'd killed him just the same. She just did it from the inside out.

Jonathan had been gone for three days, and as usual Ann and Jake knew where to find him. They loaded up in their old '47 Ford pickup and headed to the mountain. They'd found him at the cabin before and that's where they found him this time. As they pulled in sight they saw his car, but no smoke rose out of the cabin's chimney. Ann said nothing as her heart swelled with dread. She felt sure it would explode any minute. When they stepped out on that frigid January morning, they both had that foreboding feeling even before they opened the door. Sometimes Ann hated the intuition that had been passed down to her by her grandma, and sometimes she wished she had more of it.

Jake turned the knob on the front door, and it opened easily. It wasn't locked. He hesitated before slowly pushing it open. As the door swung in, he and Ann stepped across the threshold. The sunlight streamed in the kitchen windows that were facing east, but the couple didn't feel the warmth. Their eyes scanned the room, nothing. As they walked through the sitting room they stopped in front of the first bedroom door. Their eyes found him at the same time. The release of Ann's held breath broke the silence.

"Oh God, Jake!" Ann whispered.

They didn't have to touch Jonathan to feel the cold. His eyes were wide open. He was curled in a ball facing the door. Fingers on one hand gripped around the whiskey bottle. Lying in the circle of his other arm, he held Teddy, Millie's special bear, tightly to his heart.

Ann's knees threatened to buckle as she made the long few steps to her only child's side. Kneeling beside the bed, she laid her head on the teddy bear that lay on Jonathan's heart. There she stayed for a long time crying softly, trying to believe she'd feel the beating of his heart. A thud brought her back to reality. She saw Jake crumpled on the floor clutching his chest.

"Jake, what's wrong?" Ann rushed to him.

"I just had an awful pain here in my chest, took my breath away."

Jake started to get up, but a rush of queasiness overtook him, and he threw up on the floor before he knew what had hit him.

Ann ran to the kitchen and was thankful there was a bucket of water in the sink. She took the rag from the countertop and tried to dip it into the bucket, but there was a frozen layer of ice on top. Reaching into the drawer, she grabbed a big butcher knife and chopped into it, breaking it into large hunks. Dipping the cloth into the freezing water, her hands barely felt the stinging cold as she pulled the cloth out of the bucket, wringing it out. She made her way back to Jake and laid the cloth over his face.

"We've got to get you to the hospital. Go slow. I'll try to help you stand."

Leaning down, Ann looped her arm under his armpit. Together they got him on his feet. Near the door, Jake turned back to Jonathan.

"We can't leave him here by himself."

"It's okay. He's not alone anymore. We've got to get you to the hospital. I won't survive another loss today."

The force of sheer willpower got Jake loaded up into the old truck. Ann ran to the driver's side door, flung it open, and jumped in. As the motor turned, she looked up and realized she hadn't shut the front door.

She ran to the door. She couldn't leave it open for animals to get in. Standing on the top step, she reached in and grabbed the knob. All of a sudden a warm breeze blew through the house and out the door. The warmth of it brought a flush to Ann's face, and then she saw an animal through the kitchen window: a giant black bear running down the hill toward the creek. Never had she seen a bear here, even though they'd seen the signs. Now she didn't have time to dwell on it. She closed the door and ran to the truck. Going past the chain gate, she didn't stop to lock it.

Twenty minutes later they were at the little community hospital in Spartan. Jake had experienced the first of several heart attacks he was to face over the remaining five years of his life.

After he was stable, Ann called the police and gave them the address of the place they would need to send the coroner to pronounce her thirty-three-year-old baby dead.

Since that day Ann had returned to the cabin only once. After getting Jake home and after Jonathan's funeral, she went back. The chain gate was still down and the door unlocked. As she entered, Ann whiffed the smell of dried vomit. She took the same bucket of water from the sink and another rag from the cabinet and set out cleaning the floor. When she was done she walked through the little cabin. The laughing sounds of Jonathan and his little girl were gone forever now. Reaching down, she picked up Teddy from the bed where it had been pried from Jonathan's stiff fingers. She drew it to her and rubbed its furry softness against her cheek. Memories and grief mixed as tears flooded her cheeks. How could she live without them both?

After a long time, Ann became aware of the darkening shadows in the room. Late afternoon had given way to evening. She walked to the kitchen and placed Teddy in Millie's little red wagon. That was where she'd look for it if . . . when . . . she came back.

Ann made one more study about that precious place of remembrances. At the side door, she threw her hip against the wood to make sure the lock had caught. Then she went to the front door, mashed the button on the door knob to lock it, pulled it closed, and walked head hung and heart heavy to the olive green truck. She had to get home to Jake. He was all she had left.

Up the long path of a driveway Ann stopped past the chain gate, knocking the truck out of gear and setting the emergency brake. She stepped to the back of the truck. Then she reached down and picked up the chain, stretching it around the tree, and put the lock through two links and snapped it shut with the heel of her hand, hitting the bottom of the lock as the top rested against the tree, just like she'd seen Jake do a thousand times. Back in the truck she released the brake and pushed the gear stick up into first.

As she looked up, that same bear she'd seen earlier ran right in front of the truck. Ann watched as bulks of fat flopped on the sides of the black bear as he lumbered his way through the thick woods. Ann watched until he was completely out of sight. She hadn't realized it, but all of a sudden it had gotten real hot in the truck. She took off her thick wool jacket and stroked the fibers, wondering if the bear's coat was just as coarse.

Ann drove away and did not go back to the cabin for eighteen years. Sometimes she would come to the gate and sit. Over the years, especially after Jake died, it was as if she needed to make sure it was still locked, holding all the wonderful times and memories on the inside, safe but not forgotten. She would remember and pray just as hard as the first day Millie was gone that she'd find her. She'd never stopped searching; that's how, the sheriff's department came to know Ann by name.

❧ ✦ ❧

This morning as she pulled her slippers on, she knew she had to go to the gate. Overwhelming urges to ride to the mountain enveloped her consciousness. Today just might be the day she'd unlock the gate, just maybe today . . . .

~ Chapter Five ~

I'm scared," Sammy said as he clung tightly to Sadie's jacket sleeve.

Millie lay Teddy back down in the wagon and went back to her children. Kneeling, she wrapped an arm around both of them hugging tight. At that moment a warm breeze came through the door and lifted Sadie's hair. They all three noticed it was warmer than the early May air should have been.

"Maybe it's going to be summertime tomorrow," Sammy said.

"Maybe so. Come on, kids, we've got some cleaning to do."

As Millie looked around she saw the light fixtures on the walls in every room. She knew it would be too much to ask, but she went toward the one at the side door and pulled the string at the bare bulb, nothing.

"I knew that would be too good to be true. We'll think of something," Millie said as she leaned against the wall.

Sadie walked toward the bedrooms. As she pulled the string in the first room, she saw a shadow move past the window just as the bulb made a hissing sound and then popped. Startled, Sadie went to the window. In the distance she could only make out movement, no shape, in the now-darkening woods.

Millie was so excited that the power was still on that she didn't notice Sadie's movements. Walking quickly to the other bedroom,

Millie ever so gently pulled the string, and there it was: blessed light. The one in the sitting room worked too.

"Hey, kids, two out of four isn't bad, is it? Sadie, what are you looking at?"

"Nothing, Mama, just thought I saw something. It was probably just the flash of the light bulb as it popped." Sadie knew she saw something but didn't want to scare Sammy more than he was already, so she kept her thoughts and worries to herself.

"Sadie, if you'll get the broom and start knocking down these cobwebs, I'll go to the spring and get us some water," Millie said.

"What do you mean, go to the spring? What's a spring? I want to go too!" Sammy squealed.

"Come on, it's just right down the hill. Let's all go," Millie said.

At the cabinet under the sink, she reached in and took out two buckets. They were white galvanized with a red ring painted around the top. There was a piece chipped off the bottom of one of them. Millie hoped it didn't leak.

"Why don't we just turn the handle?" Sammy asked.

Millie pointed to the holes where knobs should have been on the double cast iron sink.

"Grandpa never piped water to the cabin from the spring, so we have to carry it in these buckets from the spring to the house."

Sammy, as well as Sadie, looked a little puzzled, but started following Millie out the door anyway.

"I want to carry a bucket," Sammy said.

"Okay, here you go. Sadie, do you want the other one?"

"Sure, Mama, why not," Sadie said, rolling her eyes.

Out the door and down the back porch steps they went. As Millie pulled her jacket a little tighter, she saw the piece of tin that was attached to the backside of the house, and under it the mountain of wood Grandpa always kept cut. Hopefully it wouldn't be too old and rotten because they'd surely need a fire tonight. Turning back to the path that led down the hill, she saw the big green leaves in the spring creek before she saw the springhead.

"Look, there's the skunk cabbage I was telling you about."

"You really ate those big weeds?" Sammy asked.

"I tasted it, but remember I didn't like it."

"I think we should try it. You said your grandpa Jake liked it. Maybe I will too," Sadie said.

Millie was a little surprised by her daughter's response. This was coming from a child who could live on chocolate and cereal. She smiled broadly as she put an arm around Sadie.

The spring was a dug out hole in the side of the steep bank. They all leaned into the opening at the same time. Way before Millie was born Grandpa had built a roof over it and placed rock on the sides of the hole, so the water would stay clear and fresh.

"Why's that wire covering up the hole?" Sammy asked.

"That's so animals can't get to the water and contaminate it."

"What does 'contaminate' mean?"

"It means poop in it, silly," Sadie said, looking more that a little annoyed by all her brother's questions.

"We also don't want them drinking out of it and slobbering all in it. Some animals have rabies." Millie didn't want to scare them, but wanted them to know the danger.

Millie reached and slipped the wire over the nail heads; laying the grate to the side, she turned back to the clear water and stuck her hand in. "Whoa, that is cold." Shivering, Millie quickly removed her hand.

"I wanna feel, I wanna feel," Sammy said.

"Okay, come here. Let me hold your hand so you can lean down and touch it."

Millie lowered her son toward the pool of water. When his fingers touched the iciness, he pulled back with a shout.

"What's that crawling around down there?"

Millie could see a colossal, old granddaddy crawfish slowly making his way along the bottom of the spring. "Oh that's just a crawfish. They live here in the water. They won't hurt you as long as you keep your fingers away from their pinchers."

"What pinchers? I want to see," Sammy said, getting more excited by the minute.

Patiently Millie explained that they'd go crawfish and spring lizard hunting one day, but right now they needed to get settled. Skimming her hands across the surface of the water, Millie lifted out the filth of dead leaves. When it was clear, she dipped the buckets one at a time into the water to fill them up.

"Let's get to work, kids."

As they made their way back up the path, Millie remembered all the rocks she and Grandpa had flipped over in that little creek. Crawfish and lizards, oh yeah, Sammy would love the lizards, so much to do, so many things to share with her children. She prayed for God to please give her time, *God, please.*

"I've got to go to the bathroom," Sadie said.

Millie looked up the hill at the aged but familiar outhouse. "Let me get this water inside and find the broom so we can clean out the bathroom."

Sadie knew what her mama was talking about as she stared at the small, weather-beaten board structure, but she couldn't say she was overly excited about it. *How bad could it be anyway?* She rationalized. *But to call it a real bathroom . . .* Sadie didn't think so!

Millie went to the place where her grandma had always kept the broom, and right there it was beside the stove. She then reached up on a top shelf above the kitchen counter and grabbed a dingy roll of toilet paper.

Together again, the three made their way up the hill to their next adventure. Millie hesitated at the door before turning the whittled-out wooden knob.

"Watch out for those varmints, Mama," Sammy said.

"I will. I believe it is too late in the spring for the chipmunks to still be nesting, but I'll go slowly just in case."

Cracking the door, Millie peeked inside. No movement, so she opened it a little farther. As the inside darkness gave way to light, she could see the mess—tattered paper and leaves were everywhere. Spider webs entangled the floor, walls, and rafters.

"Are they in there?" Sammy questioned, as he sneaked a peek around his sister into the toilet house.

"Nothing in here but a mess. Let me get it cleaned up."

Millie started at the top knocking down the cobwebs, sweeping the walls, and finally the floor. The only thing she left was the chipmunk nest behind the board. When they returned this fall, she wanted their home to still be there just like hers had been here at the cabin for her.

The plastic bucket still set in the corner. Millie told Sadie and Sammy that Grandma kept lime in it.

"You just sprinkle a little in the hole and it covers up the smell," Millie told them.

"We'll have to start ourselves a list of things we need. Lime will be the first thing I put on it, that is, after lightbulbs and the hushpuppies."

Sadie had been standing back taking this all in. She saw all the spiderwebs her mama had swept away and she knew that where there were webs, there were spiders. She saw her mama twirl the broom around down in the hole making sure no bugs, bees or spiders were down there, but Sadie still wasn't convinced.

Unsure she could do this, she stepped up and pulled the door to, leaving a little crack to let light in. She knew she'd have to get used to this. She loved everything else about this place so far. Surely she could learn to at least tolerate this too.

Sadie wasn't sure if it had warmed up outside or if it was her nerves, but all of a sudden she felt hot again. When she stepped out, her mama called back to her, "Bring the toilet paper back with you in case the chipmunks decide to visit."

As Sadie strolled back toward the cabin, she heard a rustling behind the outhouse. She stared into the distance not really seeing anything, and surveyed the woods a long while. In fact she stood there so long that Millie came looking for her.

"What are you looking at?"

"Nothing, I guess. Just heard something."

"Well, come on inside. We've got lots to do before bedtime."

Inside, Sadie picked up the broom and started her attack on the cobwebs. Millie got Sammy busy with a cleaning rag dusting the tops of everything he could reach. Then Millie went to work on the chimney. With a flashlight from the car she laid on her back on the floor shining light up the flue. All she could see was darkness. She reached up and pulled away a thin sheet of metal that was being used as a damper to keep the rain out in the summer and the cold out when the fire was not burning in the fall and spring. She could see the sky, so she felt pretty good about building a fire. She'd been afraid it was full of birds' nests like over the front door.

Up and out the side door, Millie reached the woodpile, gathering her arms full of the lengths of logs. Back in the house she knelt in front of the brick-and-mortar funnel. After placing three sticks of wood on the iron dogs, she felt in her pocket for a pack of matches. Twisting up a crumpled tissue from her other pocket, she stuffed it partially under the top log.

Sadie and Sammy came to look over her shoulder. Millie struck the match and put the tip to the tissue. It flamed up, sputtered, and sparked as the flames lit the bark of the very dried-out logs. At first the smoke came out into the room and all three stood back, fanning their faces with their hands.

Millie said, "I don't remember this much smoke."

A loud whish sounded, and it was as if someone were on the roof holding a powerful vacuum at the top. The smoke not only drew up the chimney, the suction was clearing most of it from the room too. And in no time, with both doors open, the foggy haze disappeared, and the room became cozy. The early May evening was getting quite cool, so the new cabin dwellers welcomed the warmth from the flames.

"I'm going to unpack the car and carry more wood up on the back porch," Millie said.

With the cobwebs down and the floors swept out, Millie set Sadie to work on the beds.

"There are probably old sheets on these beds. Will you take them off and dust down the springs and mattresses?"

"Sure, Mama," Sadie said. "Come on, Sammy you can help." Sadie tugged at her brother's hand.

Together they stripped both beds, wiped and swabbed down the metal springs. Struggling, they maneuvered the heavy mattress back on top of the springs. As Sammy took the yellowed pillowcases off the flat pillows, a few feathers drifted in the air.

"There's been a bird in here. Look, there's feathers!"

"No, that's what the pillows are stuffed with. Those are goose feathers. Wait till you lie your head down on them tonight. You've never felt anything so soft."

Sammy again didn't understand. *Goose feathers in a pillow?* He still wasn't sure about the outhouse and no running water. But he didn't question all these strange things. Even in his young mind, he knew being here sure topped being at home in Texas.

Millie had the good sense to pack clean sheets from home. She knew she had forgotten many things in her haste, but she'd piled everything she thought they might need into that car.

Sadie took the sheets from Millie. She and Sammy smoothed them over the blue-and-white-striped ticking on the mattresses. Meanwhile Millie brought in the last of their belongings. Plopping down the cardboard box filled with their clothes, Millie felt relieved. She looked at her children, and then around the little cabin. The fire popped and cracked in the hearth. Its light, along with the glow of the two bulbs, set off a more than cozy atmosphere in the wee confines of the rooms. Sammy and Sadie sifted through their belongings, a look of ease on their faces. She had seldom seen such serenity in Texas. Peace relaxed her tired body and she took a deep breath so she wouldn't cry.

"Kids, I'm going after more water before it gets pitch dark. Sadie, will you look under that cabinet and find two of the biggest pots in there?"

"Okay, but for what?"

"We've got a couple more things to do before bedtime: eat and take a bath. We'll use the pots to heat water."

"How are we going to take a bath?" Sammy asked.

"You'll see, just be patient," Millie said as she leaned into him rubbing their foreheads together, a bucket swaying in each of her hands.

With three trips to the spring, Millie filled four pots and arranged them on the stove to be heated. One more trip and she replenished the buckets again and set them on the counter.

"Okay. Keep your fingers crossed that this old stove will work."

Millie turned the first burner to high, then the second, third, and finally fourth. In a few minutes, all burners but one glowed.

"We can live with that, can't we kids?"

When they first arrived Millie opened the door to the ancient refrigerator and found it just as it had been left all those years ago. The food inside was black and crusted, unrecognizable but still cold. Cleaning that would be tomorrow's project.

In no time steam was rolling off the water. Millie went to the back porch and found the number three washtub she'd taken baths in many times as a girl. Hauling it inside, she set it in the middle of the floor. Sammy squealed when he realized that was his new bathtub. Sadie wasn't quite that excited but was looking forward to a good scrubbing.

Taking two pots of the boiling water, Millie poured it in the tub. Next she added most of a bucket of cold water. It was still pretty warm but not too hot.

"Okay, Sammy, you're first—strip off those yucky clothes. Sadie, will you find his pajamas and our towels and washcloths?"

In a second, Sammy was stepping over the side of the tub and into the water. "Oh, it's too hot!"

"Okay, let me pour a little more cold in." She poured the mountain water over Sammy's feet.

"That's cold!"

"Sorry, Sammy. Stir the water with your foot and see how it feels."

Swirling the water with his foot, it didn't take but a minute for him to plop down. "This is fun. May I play for awhile?"

"Let me get you washed, and you can for a minute. But we've got to be quick, so the water doesn't get too cold for Sadie and me."

Sadie grimaced. "We're going to use the *same* water?"

"We are this time because it's too dark to go to the spring again."

Sadie didn't protest. She could see the dark circles under her mama's eyes and how she slumped over the tub as she scrubbed behind her little brother's ears. She wasn't sure her mama had slept at all in the three days they were on the road. Sure, they pulled over at a rest stop both nights for a few hours, but every time she woke up, her mama had been wide-eyed, standing guard.

"It's okay, Mama," Sadie said. "It's just you and Sammy. It's not like we haven't shared each other's germs before."

Millie stared up at her little girl. Sadie was responsible beyond her years. She'd always been serious and shy, always on guard, ever watchful for trouble since she was old enough to know that there was danger in their home. Millie saw the skinny arms and legs of her red-haired, blue-eyed baby girl. She looked younger than her twelve years, but her mind was aged, far more advanced than her body. Millie prayed this was all going to change and that her children could for once be just that, children.

Sadie handed her mama one of their towels from home as Sammy stood up after his good scrubbing.

"Step out on the towel and I'll dry you," Millie said.

Sammy leaned into his mama's arms. She gently picked him up and stood him on the towel. Luckily the heat of the fireplace had made the room fairly warm. Sammy lay his little head over on his mama's shoulder. As Millie dried his little frame, too bony, she was overcome with guilt. *Why did I stay so long? Why didn't I take them away from Texas years ago?*

"Sadie, round up your gown, and I'll warm up the water for you as soon as I get Sammy into his pajamas."

Sadie got her things and headed for the tub. She watched her mama pour another pan of hot water in the galvanized pool.

"As soon as I warm up Sammy a grilled cheese, I'll help you wash your hair. Sammy is worn out. I don't believe he'll stay awake much longer." Even as she spoke, she watched her son's little head droop over on the arm of the couch. "Sammy, try to stay awake for a few more minutes. You need something warm to eat."

In minutes Millie warmed the sandwich and carried Sammy to the table.

"Here, honey. Eat this all gone for me while I help Sadie."

Sadie had scrubbed herself and was waiting for help with her hair. Millie mixed some of the remaining hot water with some of the cold.

"Get your head wet with the dirty water; here, use this cup to pour water over it. Then after it's soaped up, I'll rinse it with this warm clean water."

Sadie did as her mother asked even though it wasn't that easy. She was skinny but fairly tall, so fitting into the tub wasn't the easiest thing she'd ever done. Head scrubbed, she held it back as her mama poured the warm liquid over her soapy curls.

"There, all done. That wasn't too bad was it?"

"No, it felt good."

"Get dried off, wrap up your hair, and I'll fix you a warm cheese sandwich too."

Millie turned to her son. His head was lying on his arm on the table, and he was sound asleep. Thankfully he'd eaten about half of his sandwich. In the front bedroom Millie turned down the freshly made bed. Back to the kitchen she wrapped her arms around Sammy and lifted him to her. Hugging him to her tightly she carried him to the bed where she had lain as a child. She put him in the middle of the mattress where she always slept between Grandma and Grandpa. She reached down and pulled the sheet up under his chin and then the heavy homemade quilt that had always been on the bed. It still smelled a little musty, but that was such a small thing, a thing she could live with.

With Sammy all tucked in, Millie headed back to the kitchen. Sadie had on her long pink gown and was getting bread out of the loaf to fix her sandwich. "I can fix this, Mama. You get cleaned up now."

Millie looked at her little girl's head wrapped in a towel, big eyes shining above her freckled nose. She walked over to her and hugged her tightly. "Are you okay with all of this?"

Sadie paused for just a second, then looked at her mama and nodded. "Yes, I can't explain it, but it feels like home. I've dreamed of this place. I love it here. I never want us to leave."

A single tear rolled down Millie's cheek as she watched Sadie's eyes dance as she talked. She couldn't remember the last time she saw that twinkle of happiness in her eyes, or had she ever? Again Millie thought, *I waited way too long, way too long.* Millie embraced her young daughter again, and then went to the table and picked up the rest of Sammy's sandwich.

"Do you want me to fix you one?"

"No. I'll just eat what's left of Sammy's." With that she took a bite of the now cold cheese and bread, and by golly, it was the best thing she'd tasted in what seemed like years. She ate it all.

❦

Millie dipped out some of the tepid water from the tub before she poured in the rest of the hot. She stripped off her clothes of three days and stepped in the warm water. It felt so good to her war-torn body. She was too big to sit, so she kneeled in the tub. Millie tried to be discreet and turn her back to Sadie as she bent and washed. She tried to hide the cigarette burn scars, but in such tight quarters it was hard to hide all the marks on her stomach and chest. She knew in the past that Sadie heard her whimpers behind the locked door even though she'd tried not to cry out. Sometimes the torture had just been too painful to remain quiet.

Tonight Millie had really seen her gaunt children, and for the first time in a long while, she looked down and realized she, too, was dangerously thin. It's going to get better now. It's going to be okay. She squeezed water out of the cloth and let it trickle down her beaten-down body.

Millie wet her head by pouring a few cups over it. She lathered it up well with the shampoo she packed. Realizing she used all the hot water, Millie called to Sadie, "Will you bring me that bucket that's about empty?"

From the counter Sadie took the handle and lifted it down and over to her mama. "Mama, don't you want me to warm this up for you?"

"No honey, it'll be fine. Would you use the cup and pour it over my head? I am so tired I don't know if I can raise my arms to do it."

Sadie rinsed the soap out of her mama's hair. Millie shivered as she wrapped her arms around herself, more to hide the scars than for warmth.

"There, I believe it's all out. Here's your dry towel. I'll go find your gown."

Sadie laid another log on the fire before she walked into the back bedroom where they put their clothes. Searching through the sack that held her mama's belongings, she found the gown with the green frogs on it. This was her mama's favorite, the one she first reached for when it was clean. Taking it along with the socks and underwear into the kitchen, she handed them to her mama.

"Thank you. Did you see our toothbrushes anywhere in all that mess?"

"Yes, I'll get them."

Back she came with her purple one, Millie's green one, Sammy's blue one, and toothpaste and mouthwash. Her mama was at the sink rinsing out their milk glasses and the pan. Once finished, she and Sadie stood together at the sink and brushed their teeth, rinsing their mouths in the fresh mountain spring water.

Millie knew they had another big day ahead tomorrow. There was more cleaning to do, and she had to find a grocery store.

She walked to the front door and made sure the button was clicked in to lock it. Then at the side door she not only checked the button, she threw her hip against it to make sure it had caught well. She didn't even realize she did it. That was just something she'd seen Grandma Ann do before bedtime every night.

Then she went to the fire and put the rest of the wood from the hearth into it. This time she set the rusted, old fire screen in front of it all. Reaching up she took the towel from around her brown hair. Sadie handed her mama the wide-toothed comb she'd just finished running through her own curly top. They both stood in front of the fire for a few minutes until their hair was almost dry.

"Let's go to bed," Millie said, glancing at the watch she always wore, seeing that it was almost eleven o'clock. She was too tired to count how many hours she'd been up.

As they walked past the kitchen table to the front bedroom the stuffed brown bear caught Sadie's eye. "Mama, may I sleep with your bear tonight?"

"Yes, I think Teddy and I would both like that."

Picking him up, Sadie crawled in the bed on one side of Sammy as her mama got in on the other side. They always slept together unless her daddy came in and dragged her mama away. On those nights she snuggled up to Sammy and lay awake listening for any sign her mama might need her.

No lying awake tonight. No book reading. They had barely told each other goodnight before all three were sound asleep. Not one bad dream greeted them. There was nothing to be afraid of. They were safe and together in their new home in the woods.

~ Chapter Six ~

*L*ong before daylight, Lewis rose from a restless night in bed. The day before haunted him: his great-great-grandfather's pleas for help, all those poor Indians sick and shivering in the cold. A chilling to the bone sweep through him as he felt their numbness.

He needed coffee. Throwing on his flannel robe, he headed down the steps, toward the rich aroma of fresh perked coffee. Grandmother was up already.

By the time Lewis entered the kitchen, she already had his cup filled and was waiting for him at the bar.

No words were needed. He knew she could feel his torment. He didn't understand why, but she always knew what was going on in his head. She spoke only a few words before leaving the room.

"You will feel much more pain before the healing comes. Be brave, my grandson. Many will need your strength."

* ❋ *

Sadie rolled over for the first time since she laid her head on the pillow the night before. She opened her eyes and saw daylight breaking. Something had awakened her—what was it? She looked over at Sammy and her mama. They were still sound asleep.

There it was again. *What's that noise?* Sadie eased out from under the covers. When her feet hit the floor, she noticed the chill in the cabin. She went to the side door, gently opened it, stepped out to the pile of wood Millie had stacked there, and grabbed a piece. She heard the noise again. It was like metal scrubbing against metal. She laid down the wood and walked to the edge of the porch. This alerted the nesting birds: a couple dozen wild turkeys took flight, their large wings fanning the air as they left their roosting place . . . Grandpa Jake's guardian angels?

Back at the woodpile, she loaded up her arms. Inside, she gently placed the wood on the hearth and with the poker stirred the few remaining embers. Then she laid a small scrap of bark on top of the coals. In a minute it caught up, and Sadie crossed three sticks on top of the hot sparks the same way she'd watched her mama do the night before.

She tiptoed back over to the bedroom door. Peeking in, she noticed Sammy had rolled over, but Mama was still in the same position. Sadie gently pulled the door closed and stepped into the other bedroom. There she found a pair of socks in the heap of clothes. After slipping them on, she headed back to stand in front of the fire which was now blazing nicely. With her back to the flames, she could see out the kitchen window onto the bottom below. A dense fog was rising from the damp creek soil. Sadie watched it slowly lift, revealing the lush spring grasses underneath. Thinking she saw movement, she stepped away from the warmth and walked closer to the window. In just a minute or two, the fog revealed a mama deer with a fawn trailing behind, and then another quickly appeared. All of a sudden, the mama stopped and stomped her right front foot against the soft ground several times. This alerted her offspring to gather close; when she had their attention, she, along with her young, turned and ran back in the direction they came from near the creek.

Still standing watch at the window wondering what had scared the beautiful deer, Sadie saw him. Slowly on all fours, a bear wandered through the rising mist. She watched, mesmerized by the greatness of him. He swayed and twisted his heavy body moving at a snail's pace across the bottom's clearing. For a minute he was out of sight as he entered the woods, resurfacing in an old roadbed two hundred yards behind the cabin. Then he stopped. Sadie couldn't help but gasp as he rose on his hind legs and looked straight at the cabin window, peering at Sadie through the transparent glass. He stood there for a long while. One frail with a wounded spirit, the other a mighty warrior—neither beast nor maiden moved. Sadie could see steam coming from his nostrils as he breathed in the cool morning mist. His stance never tottered. His eyes did not shift. Sadie knew he was reading her, checking out this new pilgrim who had invaded his stomping ground.

For some reason Sadie wasn't scared, even though her heart pounded and she dug her nails into the palms of her hands. Her stare at him never wavered either. It was as if they were dueling, seeing who would back away first. Neither moved, not even an eye twitch. Sadie wasn't sure how long she stood there, but it was long enough for her legs to ache from being locked into the same position for so long.

Finally, the giant bear dropped back down on all fours and, without a sound, turned and made his way up the hill behind the outhouse, through the woods, and out of sight. Sadie watched till she could see no sign of him. She sighed loudly. She'd held her breath, not knowing if he was going to try and get closer or leave her alone.

She was relieved but sort of sad at the same time. There was something about the way the bear stared at her that made her feel he wouldn't hurt her, that maybe he was hurt himself and needed her.

Pulling out one of the kitchen chairs, Sadie sat at the table until her tensed legs stopped aching. She looked over at the fire and wondered how it had gotten so hot in there. She was wet with sweat. She would tell Mama about her visitor, but not when

Sammy could hear. He was already terrified of the strange sights and sounds of the wild.

* 🐾 *

As dawn was breaking through the gray morning sky, Lewis closed his eyes. The roaring in his head had started anew. Sometimes he would fight it, but this time he simply gave into it.

> *The bear stands on his hind legs looking up through the meadow. He sees a shack, and in the window a young girl stands staring back at him. Her hair is the color of a fresh, new copper pipe. She is as thin as a new sapling pushing up through the ground after winter. Her eyes are strong, looking straight ahead at him.*
>
> *In those eyes, he sees hurt and pain, but no fear, only respect.*
>
> *The bear's heart aches for her.*

When the roar stopped, Lewis could only wonder who the girl was and why his guardian spirit had revealed her to him. He knew the answers would come, but when?

* 🐾 *

In a minute, Sadie moved from the window and went to the second bedroom, found clean clothes, and put them on. Knowing she needed to go to the outhouse, she laced up her sneakers and eased out the side door, making her way. Halfway there she remembered the toilet paper, so she retraced her steps to the back door, opened it, reached to the shelf above the cabinet, got the tissue down and headed back to the door.

Millie's voice stopped her. "Sadie? Where are you? What are you doing?"

"Just going to the bathroom. I'll be right back."

As Sadie made her way back to the cabin, she realized she hadn't been worried about Blackie at all. In fact that was the first time she'd wondered about him while she'd been outside. Blackie, yes, that was a perfect name for him. That's what she'd call him.

Sadie eased in the side cabin door. Not a sound came from inside. Her mama probably went back to sleep. Sadie knew she was exhausted. She also knew something was very wrong with her mother. She'd been going to doctors for over a year now, and those few days she spent in the hospital, she also had to take pills every day. The pills . . . Sadie could still hear her daddy's words, crude and ugly.

"Where's your pain pills, you sick old hag? You don't need them. There ain't nothin' wrong with you except laziness."

How many times had she watched her mama hand him the pills? He quickly swallowed them down while Sadie later watched as her mama tossed and turned, moaning in her restless sleep. She asked her mama about it all one day, but was told there was nothing to worry about. She was fine. All Sadie could do was to hope and pray her mama was right.

All Millie could do was guard her children from the awful alien that had invaded her body . . . cancer. She didn't even want them to hear the word.

Sadie walked around the small cabin, quietly picking up last night's towels and hanging them over the backs of the kitchen chairs to finish drying. The tub was still full of water in the middle of the floor, but she'd make too much noise if she emptied it, so she just sat down on the couch, her head on the armrest. The next thing she knew Sammy was tugging on her sleeve.

"Sadie, Sadie. Wake up. I've got to pee."

Rubbing her eyes, she swung her feet to the floor. The sun was now high in the sky. It wouldn't surprise her if it weren't close to noon.

"Okay, Sammy. Let me just check on Mama, and then I'll take you. Go find your shoes."

Sadie tiptoed the few steps to the bedroom door and saw that her mama was still asleep. She could see the gentle rise and fall of her breathing underneath the patchwork quilt.

Turning back to Sammy, she helped him lace up his shoes, and then took his hand and headed out the door. This time she remembered the toilet paper.

"Sadie, what if I fall down that hole?"

"I'll hold your hand. You'll be fine. There's nothing to it. I've used it twice already."

Sadie stepped inside the outhouse first. She took a handful of toilet paper and wiped around the inside of the seat rim. She didn't want Sammy to know, but she was just making sure no new spider had made his home there.

"Here you go, Sammy. Are you sure you just need to pee?"

"Yes." Sammy was not the morning person Sadie was. It always took him awhile to wake up and he was usually pretty testy until he did.

"How far is it down there?" Sammy was listening to his pee hit the earth below.

"I don't know. We'll have to bring the flashlight back next time and look."

"Yeah, neat. Can we go get it now?"

"We'll see. Right now I'm starving. Let's go see what we can find to eat."

Hand in hand they skipped back to the cabin. The sun was bright and had warmed up the morning air. It was going to be a great day.

Sadie pulled the box of corn flakes out of their bag of food. Maybe there was enough milk left for them both. Reaching into the cooler, she found it and split what little there was between the two bowls, giving Sammy a touch more than herself. Today they would wash all the dishes on the shelves, and then they wouldn't have to use plastic. Food just wasn't as good out of plastic.

They ate silently until Sammy started asking questions: "What are we going to do today? Do you think Mama will let us go down to the creek? Where's my big yellow dump truck? We brought it, didn't we, didn't we?"

"Yes, it's still in the car. We'll get your toys out when you get dressed."

Looking toward the sound of a creaking floor board, they saw their mama propped against the doorframe.

"I'm sorry I slept in, kids. Have you been up long?"

Looking down at her watch, Millie saw it was eleven thirty-two. She probably could have slept longer, but that familiar ache at the base of her neck had awakened her. From the top of the refrigerator, she took down her pocketbook. She took the bottle of aspirin, shook two into her hand, walked over to the water bucket, and dipped the cup they used last night to rinse their hair. She popped in the pills and swallowed them. Turning back to her purse, she took out another bottle. This time she took one of the little green pills. She looked at the label, four refills. Millie wondered how much trouble she'd have filling a prescription from another state? She didn't know, but she'd have to find out soon. One, two, three, four, five more pills. . . Today was Saturday; she'd need more by Thursday. Millie would do whatever it took to get them. The medicine was the one thing buying her time; hopefully they would keep her cancer in remission for many years . . . if she was lucky.

"You're not going to believe what woke me up," Sadie said between bites. "Turkeys! They were everywhere. It was barely daylight. When I scared them, I've never heard such a noise. Their gigantic wings churned the air and made a terribly loud noise. I can't believe you slept through it."

"I believe I would have snoozed through a tornado last night. I know that was the best sleep I've had since I was seven years old."

"Oh yeah, the deer were in the bottom just like you said they'd be until Bla—" Oops, she'd almost let it slip about Blackie in front of Sammy.

"Until what, Sadie Girl?"

"Nothing, they just ate for awhile then ran off."

"I want to see. Where are they?" Sammy asked as he got up and went to the window.

"Maybe they'll be back this evening. If not, you'll have to get your lazy behind up early in the morning," Sadie said.

Millie listened to her children banter back and forth as she dipped some water into a pot. Heating it up, she searched in their food bag for the instant coffee. She took down the tan mug with the brown stripe around the top and washed it out at the sink. As she ran the cloth around the top, she felt the little chip. She remembered the morning that had happened.

"Look, this is my grandma Ann's coffee cup. When I was little, she'd always let me have the last of her coffee. She'd spoon in a half-teaspoon of sugar and let me sit right there where you and Sammy are, and stir it up until the sugar was all melted. One morning I was really stirring, and the side of the spoon hit the edge too hard. The little bit of chip flew in the floor, and I froze. I knew this was Grandma's favorite cup, just like the plate with the rooster painted on it was Grandpa's favorite."

She took the plate off the shelf and held it up for Sadie and Sammy to see. It had a small crack on the edge and it was covered with stains.

"It looks so old. Doesn't it need to be thrown away?" Sammy asked.

"No, I want to use it. Can it be mine now?" Sadie asked. She loved the way the bright colors of the rooster still stood out.

"Sure, why not? Anyway, Grandma never said a harsh word to me. She just took the cup from me and said, 'Here, Millie, let me have that. There might be some glass in it. I'll have to fix you some more,' and that's just what she did."

"Mama, do you think Grandma Ann will come to see us?" Sadie asked.

"I don't know. We'll have to figure all that out, but for now let's get dressed, do some more cleaning, and go to the store."

Millie and Sammy dressed while Sadie started the cleanup. They all helped make the bed, dump the bath water, wash dishes, clean the refrigerator, and mop the floor. In a few hours, things were looking really good. They even washed the windows. Taking down the ratty, old sun-scorched curtains, they threw them away. Millie knew they'd fall apart if they were washed.

"We'll buy new ones in some bright cheery colors and maybe some bedspreads that match."

Millie was so excited. She hadn't been this much at peace in so long. Just watching the children be children, not having to worry about them being too loud, blessed her heart beyond measure.

"Come on. Let's go find some groceries."

Grabbing the two-page-long list they compiled, they headed out the door. Before Millie mashed the button to lock the side door, she felt in her jeans pocket to make sure she put both keys in the clean pair.

"We'll need to be pretty quick. I want to be home before dark," Millie said. What a beautiful word "home" had become.

At the gate, Millie stopped, handed the key to Sadie and said, "Unlock it and I'll drive through. Then I'll get out and help you fasten it back."

Sadie jumped out and did just that. After they locked it, Millie noticed their tire marks on the other side.

"Wait a minute." Reaching up into a poplar tree, Millie broke out two limbs. "Here—swish this around over the tire tracks. I don't want anyone to know someone's been down to the cabin." Then they laid their branches off the road a bit, so no one would notice and they could use them again.

"Can I help do that next time?" Sammy asked.

"You sure can. You and Sadie can hide us safely inside when we get back."

They left the same way they came in, only at the stop sign Millie took a right. She knew there was a town only a few miles up the road where she used to shop with Grandma.

~ Chapter Seven ~

*I*n no time they were pulling in at the A&P Grocery Center. As they filled their buggy, Sadie checked the items off the list: light bulbs, hushpuppies, flour, sugar, flavored drink mix, coffee, potatoes, bacon, hot dogs, bread, buns, shortening, soap, toilet paper, a pack of cookies, dried beans, bananas, more cereal, hot chocolate mix, popcorn, and the list went on and on. Seventy-seven dollars and twenty-two cents later, they were out the door. The only thing still on the list was the lime for the outhouse.

Looking across the road, Millie eyed the hardware store. "Come on kids. Let's finish this list."

Hand in hand, they crossed the street. The sun had set behind the downtown buildings, and it was getting cool again. Millie opened the door and the bell chimed overhead.

"Come in. Come in. What can I help you with this afternoon?"

Millie stopped and stared at the old man behind the counter. She knew she'd seen him before but couldn't remember his name. He was the same man who had run the store years ago. A touch of fear caught in her throat. Then she realized that even though he looked much the same, she was indeed quite different. She wasn't that seven-year-old little girl anymore.

When she'd found her tongue she answered, "Yes, we're needing a bag of lime."

"It is getting gardening time, isn't it? Already sold three bags today. Where you livin'? I don't believe I've seen you 'round these parts before."

Taken aback, Millie struggled for something to say. "I'm, I'm—"

"Oh Mama, look at the cute kitties!" Sammy squealed. He had puttered around the side of the counter. There a box on the floor had the words **FREE KITTENS** written on the side. Millie looked his way just as he stepped around the corner of the table with a kitten under each arm.

"They are just adorable," Sadie said, walking toward Sammy.

Two more little ones were scampering around Sammy's feet, and Sadie knelt down and reached for them. Sammy sat down in the floor beside his sister; they were both very busy stroking the little one's heads.

"That's just what you need, young'uns. Been trying to give them away for two days, but this time of year everybody's got a barn full of their own kittens. These right here are kind of special. Gladys and me had to help raise them after a darn old coyote or something tore their mama up. The vet patched her up, but Daisy was just too weak to take care of her babies, so we fed them with medicine droppers. Used that evaporated milk full strength, and look how it fattened them up. They're almost eight weeks old now and eating on their own.

"Gladys thought about keeping one or two of them, but she knew Daisy would probably have another batch on the way by fall of the year."

Millie listened while the elderly storekeeper rambled on. Sadie and Sammy were in total bliss with the kittens crawling around all over them. Brad had never allowed them to have any pets—no dog, no cat, not even a goldfish. He said they carried diseases, and that's all he needed, to have sick, whiny kids around him giving him the worms or something.

Millie snapped back to the present as the friendly gentleman stuck out his hand to her.

"My name's Romy, Romy Taylor. Where'd you say you were staying?"

Millie thought he was distracted by the kitten story, but she wasn't so lucky.

"Well, we're looking to buy something if we like the area. My husband died and we need a new start. Just renting a cabin down the mountain a bit till I decide what to do. Maybe we'll be somewhere permanent by the end of summer."

This seemed to satisfy Romy, but then he asked, "Didn't catch your name . . ."

"Mi . . . Mildred, and this is Lydia and Thomas."

Millie hated to lie and had to hope Sammy would remember the names they decided to call themselves when they had to come into town. She'd almost slipped herself and told him her real name.

"Mama, may we have them? Can we take them home?" Sammy stood up with the two cats still under each arm.

"I don't know, Honey. You've never had animals before. They are a lot of work and responsibility. You have to keep them fed and clean and safe."

"Just like you do us," Sammy said.

"Yes, that's right."

"Are we too much work?"

Well, that just about did it for Millie. "Now you know you're not. Maybe we could take two of them."

"No." Sadie had been silent up until then. "We can't separate them, Mama. They're brothers and sisters. They should stay together, and if we can't take them all, we should leave them."

Millie watched her defiant young daughter and was very proud of her.

"Please, may we take them, *pleeaasse*?" Sammy pleaded.

"I'll even throw in a litter box and a couple bags of food if you take them all," Romy said.

Millie thought for a minute. How could she refuse anything

that would bring her children happiness? And besides, they were awfully cute.

"Okay, load them up. What else will we need for them, Mr. Taylor?"

"Yea! Yea!" Sadie and Sammy hollered and jumped up and down.

As Romy walked around the store with Millie gathering up cat supplies, Millie spotted something else she had to have. It was a twenty-five-gallon plastic barrel with a spout that turned on and off at the bottom. She could fill that up with water from the spring every few days and not have to run down there every time they needed water.

"Mr. Taylor, I need that green barrel too."

"All righty, what else now?"

"Surely that will do us for a while, but I was wondering if you have a coin laundry in town and a drugstore?"

"Drugstore's in the back of Abernathy's Soda Shop just down the street, and on past that Mr. Dixon has a half dozen washing machines in a building beside his gas station, even has a couple of them fancy dryers. Thought about buying Gladys one, but she says she wants her clothes to smell like the sunshine."

"Oh, that reminds me. I'll need some clothesline cord and clothespins."

He fetched those too.

"Here you go, Mildred."

Romy looked at all the supplies piled on the counter and floor. He hit the cash register button only four times. He charged them seventy-five cents for the bag of lime, a quarter each for the bag of clothespins and roll of cord. As he hit the key the fourth time, he said, "That barrel's a little pricy, cost me five dollars."

Millie saw the sticker with six dollars and ninety-five cents written on it and thought it would be worth every penny.

"That will be six dollars," Romy said, not looking Millie in the eye.

"Mr. Taylor, you couldn't have counted all this stuff. Here, I want to pay you what is fair." Millie handed him a twenty-dollar bill.

"Now I told you, I'm giving them young'uns that cat stuff, so there you go. Don't argue with an old man 'cause we're always right. Lived long enough to earn it."

Taking the twenty-dollar bill, he counted her back fourteen dollars in change. A happy little glint sparkled in his eye, so Millie couldn't feel bad and take away his blessing.

"Lydia, Thomas?" No response. They hadn't recognized their fake names. "Come on, kids." Millie walked over to where they were still playing with the kittens. "Now come over here and thank Mr. Taylor. He's been very generous with us."

Sadie and Sammy walked to the counter and at the same time said "Thank you, Mr. Taylor, for the kittens and everything."

Then Sadie said, "We'll take very good care of them."

"I'll just bet you will. Have fun! Now let's get you loaded up."

Romy noticed the Texas license plate right away, but didn't question Mildred any further. Seemed like a good family, and he liked them, no matter from where they hailed. Romy had always been a decent judge of folks' natures. But he did think they'd sure come a long way just to choose their small little town.

Headed back to the cabin, Millie noticed a Ben Franklin Store on the left. "We'll shop there for curtains when I go to the drug-store the first of the week," Millie said.

She dreaded yet another encounter with people and all their questions. The high school girl who checked them out at the grocery store couldn't have cared less who they were though, and Mr. Taylor hadn't been too nosy. She'd just have to keep her stories straight and make sure the kids remembered their pretend names.

Back at the gate Sadie jumped out to unlock it and then waited for Millie to pull through. This time she drove down past the curve, and she and Sammy walked back up the road to Sadie. First they locked the gate, and then Millie picked up the two branches she broke off earlier that day and handed one each to the children.

"Here you go kids. Wipe our tracks away."

Millie walked ahead as Sadie and Sammy walked backward, swishing the leafy branch over the tire marks. In no time they were back at the car, tracks gone.

"Good job, guys. Here, give me the branches and I'll carry them back to their hiding spot at the gate. We'll need them again."

When Sadie opened the car door, one of the kittens jumped out. They had them in the tall box with FREE KITTENS written on the side, but the black one with white feet had somehow gotten out.

"Here kitty, come here. You'd better get back in the truck. You'll get lost out here," Sadie called to the kitten.

It stopped, looked around, and then ran as fast as it could right to Sadie's feet.

"Got scared didn't you, little one?" Sadie said as she reached down and scooped up the kitty. As she stroked its head, she could hear its purring motor start to wind up.

Millie was back from hiding the swishing branches. "Did he almost get away from you?"

"No. I believe when he saw how big everything is here in the woods he got scared. I told him not to be frightened, everything would be okay, and that I'd take care of him. Listen to him purr, Mama."

Millie leaned down and heard the happy sound of his motor running.

"He's a loud one, isn't he?" Millie said.

"I'm going to name him Spook 'cause he's black and the woods spooked him," Sadie said.

"Okay with me if it is with Sammy."

"We'll let him name two and I'll name two."

"That should work. What do you think, Sammy?" Millie asked.

"That's okay with me. I like this gray one with the orange splotches, and this one with gray stripes loves me already, so you can have this smoky gray one. Okay, Sadie, okay?"

Sammy kneeled on the back seat, taking one kitten after the other in and out of the box.

"That's good with me," Sadie said as she hopped in the car. Spook was now asleep in her arms.

As Millie cranked up she looked back at Sammy. "What are you naming yours?"

"I don't know. I'll have to see what they act like."

"Oh, is that how you'll name them?"

"I don't know. I guess I've never named anything before, have you, Mama?"

"Yes. I named you and Sadie, and remember the outhouse chipmunks Heidi and Hannibal? I also had a hound dog named Red. Not the most original name since he was red, but it suited him. He made me feel safe."

Red was another thing that had been left behind when Lindsay took Millie away from her daddy.

"My daddy gave Red to me on my fifth birthday. He was the gentlest animal there ever was, with me, that is. But if a stranger approached, the hair on the back of his neck would rise and he'd snarl, curling his lip up to show his teeth. He softly but fiercely growled, and nobody, and I mean nobody, would come close to him or me if Red was around."

"May we get a dog too?" Sammy asked.

"We'd better see how we get along with cats first."

"Okay," Sammy said, content with his furry friends.

Pulling up close to the cabin's side door, they all three jumped out. First they took the kittens inside and put them in their box in the second bedroom, shutting the door so they couldn't get out. They all three made several trips until finally the car was empty.

"May I go play with my kitties now?" Sammy asked.

"Yes, but why don't you get them set up on the back porch? We'll fix them a nice warm bed and fill up their litter box. You'll need to fill up the water and food bowls Mr. Taylor gave you. Sammy, that will be your job from now on, making sure they're fed and have water. Sadie, sorry, but you'll be in charge of the litter box."

Sadie wasn't overjoyed but didn't fuss. She was just so happy to be here in this special place with her mama and little brother, far, far away from her torturous father.

That night Millie fixed their first good meal in several days: fried chicken, gravy, mashed potatoes, biscuits, and banana pudding. Before dark they had filled the big water barrel, so Millie just went to the back porch and turned the spigot, filling her pan with water to heat to wash dishes. Millie washed while Sadie dipped the dishes into clean water to rinse and piled them on a towel to dry while Sammy played with his cats.

"I know what I'm going to name them." Holding up the gray one with orange splotches, he said, "This one is going to be Sonny 'cause he's orange like the sun, and this one is Stripy 'cause he's got stripes."

Millie and Sadie looked at each other and grinned at the little boy's logic.

"Those are wonderful names, don't you think, Sadie? And by the way, have you thought of a name for your other one?"

Looking at the smoky gray kitten chasing the newly dubbed Sonny she answered, "Well, he's gray like smoke, so I guess I'll have to call him Smoky."

So there they were: Spook, Sonny, Stripy, and now Smoky. Who knew if they were boy or girl and if the names fit, who really cared? Millie also thought it odd that all their names started with an S just like Sadie and Sammy.

"Okay guys. Time to get the kittens out for the night and take your bath. Come on, let's put them on the porch, so they can go night-night."

"May I sleep with Sonny and Stripy? Please, please."

"No way, son. No cats in my bed. Now outside on the porch they go."

After getting them settled, Sammy walked over and picked Teddy up out of the wagon where Sadie had put him that morning.

"May I sleep with your teddy bear tonight, Mama?"

Millie looked over at Sadie who was coming through the door with an armful of wood. It had been a warm day, but the spring night air was getting cool, so they needed a fire.

"Sadie, is it okay if Sammy sleeps with Teddy tonight since you did last night?"

Sadie felt a little tug of jealousy, but quickly pushed the feeling out of her heart.

"Sure. We can take turns. You can sleep with him tomorrow night. He is, after all, your bear."

So that was the way it went, each night Teddy slept in the embrace of first Sadie, then Sammy, and lastly Millie. Millie found herself on her nights hugging Teddy just as closely as Sadie and Sammy had.

"Tonight we're going to have pan baths." Moving to the stove Millie took the kettle of hot water and poured it into a white galvanized pan. It, too, had a red stripe around the rim. After mixing in some cold, she carried it to the table.

"Come here, Sammy. Let's get you cleaned up and in your pajamas."

Millie lifted her wafer thin little son onto the table proceeding to soap the rag, wash the child, then rinse the rag, wiping over him again to get the soap off.

"That feels good," he said as she slipped the top on.

Sadie had been warming his pajamas in front of the now blazing fire.

"Go snuggle up on the couch, and if you'll look in the box of toys we brought, you'll find our storybook. Get it and we'll read a little before bedtime." Millie said.

Sammy dug out the tattered book of stories. It held a mixture of fables and fairy tales. It had been in Millie's possession for as long as she could remember. Jumping onto the couch, Sammy told them to hurry up so they could read.

"Okay, Sadie. Here's a fresh pan of water for you. Can you handle this new-fangled bathtub?"

"Yes, I believe I can." She took the rag and bathed herself.

"I'm going to turn our bed down and bring in another armful of wood while you finish up."

"I've got to go to the bathroom and I don't want to go outside. It's dark and those bog monsters might get me." Sammy whined when he was scared.

"Okay, time for one more surprise." Millie walked into the second bedroom, reached under the bed, and pulled out a pot with a lid on it. She found it there when she mopped the floor that morning. "Come here. You can use the chamber pot."

"The what?" Sammy asked as he ventured into the bedroom.

"It's called a chamber pot. It's just like a toilet except you have to wash it out yourself every day."

Looking down at the ivory bucket, Sammy was a little doubtful of this new bathroom twist, but he didn't have much choice. It was either use the pot or go face those bog monsters.

"Just sit on it like you did the toilet at home. Holler when you're finished, and I'll help you clean up."

Millie and Sadie left the room and reluctantly Sammy sat down, in a few minutes he hollered that he was done.

"Now that wasn't so bad, was it?"

"No, it was kind of fun. May I use it all the time instead of that outside one?"

"Just at night. During the daytime, we use the outhouse."

Even Sammy's young mind understood this. Millie carried the used pot to the back porch. She hadn't yet taken the bag of lime to the outhouse, so she pulled the top apart to open it. She scooped up a handful, opened the chamber pot lid, and threw it in. In a second the odor was gone; nevertheless, she left the pot on the porch.

Sadie was glad her mama dug out the pot for Sammy because even though she wasn't afraid of Blackie, she knew they should be cautious. If Blackie was out there, then so could there be other bears.

Finishing up her bath, she slipped her nightgown over her head and went to the sink to throw out the water.

"Mama, do you want me to fix your water for you?"

"Sure, that would be wonderful."

After finishing up, Millie turned off all the lights except for the lamp with the newly purchased bulb. She sat on the couch by the glow and snuggled her children securely to her. She sat quietly for a minute watching the dried up wood spark, spit, and spew, the warmth of the flames calming her after their very busy day.

"Read, Mama, but not about the Three Billy Goats. I'm afraid of that troll that lives under the bridge," Sammy said while rubbing his eyes.

It was only nine-fifteen, so they hadn't been up that long, but they were all tired. Or was it that they were all finally peaceful?

Sadie didn't care what story her mama read. She'd heard them all many times. She just loved to listen to her mama's voice as she made each page come alive.

"How about *Hansel and Gretel*? You both like that one."

"Yea, yea," Sammy said hugging Millie tightly. "I am so happy when the *good* daddy finds Hansel and Gretel. He reminds me of you, Mama. And that mean old witch and step-mom is like Daddy."

By the time Millie got to the part where the old witch had locked Hansel in the cage, both her children were asleep. Sadie's head lay on the couch arm and Sammy's was on Sadie's tummy with Teddy tucked up snugly under his chin. Millie needed to be reassured of the happy ending, so she finished the story even though no one but she heard it. Millie then eased off the couch and went and stood by the window. All she saw was the pitch darkness of the night. The clouded sky camouflaged the moon's brightness into nothing more than a blackened orb. Thoughts she'd not had time for the past few days clouded her head. How long could they stay here? Would Brad look for them or be glad they were gone? She'd have to eventually look for a job, get the kids in school, and find herself a doctor she could trust.

Her prescriptions would last through the summer. She'd worry about that then. Yes this would be the best summer of their lives, and Millie also knew it could very well be their last together. With that thought, she reread the end of *Hansel and Gretel* . . .

> Here are two children, mournful very,
> Seeing neither bridge nor ferry;
> Take us upon your downy white back,
> And row us over, quack, quack, quack!
> Thus all their troubles were ended, and they
> all lived happily ever afterward.

Where are you, oh great white duck? Millie could only pray her children would have as happy an ending.

Outside in the dark of night, breath from the great black bear's nostril's clouded the children's bedroom window. . . .

~ Chapter Eight ~

*A*fter praying she went to her clothing bag in the second bedroom. Digging down deep, she felt the box with her notebook in it. The ink pen was still clipped to the hard cover. She took it, went back to the couch, and gently sat back down under the glow of the lamp. She penned the events of the past five days. She started to flip back through all the pages but knew better. She didn't want to remember all the things Brad had done to her and the children. She wanted to forget, but it was all in there: every slap, punch, burn, spit in the eye, and cruel word. She hoped she never saw or heard tell of him again, nor would she ever need to use this journal. But deep down, she reasoned it might come down to a battle, a conflict she couldn't lose.

For now she sat with her children in the middle of the woods in the little cabin with the fresh pitter-pattering of rain coming down on the moss-covered shingled roof. Millie laid down her notebook, put her head back, closed her eyes and prayed, first of all thanking God for this haven of hope.

By eleven o'clock, Millie had carried Sammy and Teddy to bed and gently nudged Sadie awake enough for her to stumble to bed. She went back to the living room, took the journal and safely delivered it back in the box, putting it in the top drawer of the dresser in the second bedroom. She checked the kittens on the back porch, loaded the fireplace with wood, and she herself used the chamber pot. She might have gone outside had it not been pouring rain.

She checked the door locks. It would be a long time or maybe never before Millie was without fear.

She rubbed the back of her neck and took one of the three pain pills she had hidden from Brad. The pain wasn't severe but was bad enough to keep her awake. She flipped off the lamp and felt her way to the bed, curling up the way she always slept with her knees up to her chest. Listening to the rain hit the window over head she waited for the pill to ease the ache.

❧ ❦ ❧

"Mama, what is that noise?"

It took Millie a minute to wake from her deep slumber to realize Sadie was whispering to her. She heard the rain still falling on the roof but nothing else. "I hear the rain."

"No, it was something different, a squeaking noise, like something scratching."

"Where?" Just as Millie's words came out, she heard it. Flipping her legs over the edge of the bed, she felt in the windowsill for the flashlight. She flashed it on her watch: eight minutes past five. Then she heard it again. Creeping to the fireplace hearth, she grabbed the poker. Sadie was right on her coattail, creeping to the side door where the noise had come.

"What do you think it is?" Sadie asked.

"I don't know, but we're going to find out."

Tiptoeing to the door, Millie willed herself to be brave. She had to protect her children no matter how scared she was. Taking the knob in her hand, she gently turned it. She heard the lock unclick and pulled the door open only a crack. But it was open enough for four fuzzy kittens to come barreling through. They almost scared Millie and Sadie to death as they scampered between their legs.

Then they heard it again. Shining the flashlight toward the noise, she saw a set of eyeballs high on the porch screen glowing in the light. The eyes slowly descended while the sound of sharp claws scraped the screen. The creature lowered himself and with a final plunk, hit the ground.

Millie and Sadie exhaled together and at the same time said, "Raccoon."

Flashing the light around the porch, Millie saw what the bandit-eyed intruder had been after. The bag of cat food was now spilled out across the floor. The black-eyed outlaw was stealing the kittens' food.

Flashing the light up the screen, Millie saw where it had come loose from the wooden strip to which it fastened.

"I'll have to fix that tomorrow. We'll need to be careful not to leave food out here to tempt any more animals." Millie didn't say it, but they were lucky it was only a raccoon.

Walking back into the house, they didn't see the kittens. Sadie checked the second bedroom and Millie looked in the front one. There, curled up completely surrounding Sammy, were all four kittens. All five were fast asleep.

Sadie stood by her mama watching their even breaths. "Do you want me to put them back on the porch?"

"In a minute. They look so peaceful. I'll put them out when I get the porch cleaned up. Why don't you go curl up with them? It's awfully early."

"I'm not sure I can go back to sleep, but I might just lie with Spook and Smoky for a little while."

Sadie climbed back up in bed, the old springs squeaking and swaying down with her weight. She reached over and took her two kittens and laid them beside her in the crook of her arm, stroking their little heads and talking quietly to them.

"Mama, are you coming back to bed?"

"In a minute, maybe after I clean up the porch."

"If you're up at daylight, you might see Blackie."

"Blackie, who's Blackie?"

"He's the bear I saw yesterday morning. He came up out of the foggy bottom almost all the way to the cabin. Didn't want to tell you in front of Samm . . ." Sadie's voice got fainter and fainter with each word. Before she finished her tale, she had drifted off to sleep.

Sadie must have dreamed about a bear. Millie made her way to the messy back porch. Taking the broom and dustpan, she swept and scooped up all the food and poured it into the bag. This time she set it inside behind the door just in case the raccoon came back before she could fix the screen.

When she went back and peeked in on the kids, the scene caused an ache in her heart. Millie saw childhood innocence in her children who slept so peacefully. How much damage had Brad caused to their young psyches? Sammy was so young, he might forget, but Sadie would remember well the hand of her father. Why God had blessed her with another child was a mystery to her. She had a very hard labor with Sadie. Then after only two weeks, Brad beat her up late one night, after which he had to call an ambulance to come and get her because she was hemorrhaging so badly. That was the first time he was physically abusive to her.

Later examinations proved she probably had too much scar tissue to ever get pregnant again, but seven years later she did, and the result was Sammy. She remembered that things with Brad got worse after Sammy was born. Brad's already possessive nature went out of control when Millie had to spend even more time with yet another child.

Millie glanced at her watch, two minutes after six. She'd never be able to go back to sleep, so she fixed herself her first cup of coffee for the day. Waiting for the water to boil she looked out the window as the dark gave way to light. It wasn't raining very hard now; just a fine mist fell on the already soaked earth. Millie suddenly felt a chill, but noticed she was sweating and suddenly hot.

It wasn't the coffee. She hadn't drunk it yet. It wasn't the fire being too hot. All she could think was . . . *cancer.*

With her cup of coffee in hand, she went to the second bedroom and found the Bible she brought. It lay under the journal. Taking it out, she held it to her. How many times had she turned to its pages for strength the past twelve years? There was no telling how many million tears had fallen between its folds. She could see the spots on the thin, flimsy pages before she even opened it. Today was Sunday—what should she read the children? Brad never allowed her to take them to church, so she had her own devotion time with them at least twice a week. Sadie was quite knowledgeable of the Scriptures, but all Sammy wanted to hear about was Noah, Jonah and the whale, and his latest hero, David, killing the giant Goliath.

Millie went to the couch. Switching on the lamp she let the pages fall open; they were indeed tattered with many of the corners turned down. The first verse she saw was 2 Kings 5:3. She said to her mistress, *"If only my master would see the prophet who is in Samaria! He would cure him of his leprosy."*

Millie was encouraged as always when she read the Word, especially this verse. Yes, God was capable of curing her. She could only pray it would be His will to do so.

She studied and read until it was as light as it was going to be on this dreary day. She got up and started their breakfast—bacon, eggs, and toast—Sadie's favorite.

Millie had been so into her own thoughts that she hadn't even noticed the two deer as they jumped and played in the field behind the house. Neither did she see the huge black shadow that had been lingering at the edge of the woods, but she did hear the turkeys as they flew from their perch high above the rafters. Their screeches could not be ignored.

Sadie wasn't sure if the birds woke her or the clatter of pans and the smell of bacon frying. No matter, she was awake but still snuggled up with Spook and Smoky snoozing between her and Sammy.

"What was that racket?" Sammy softly asked, as sleepiness overcame him. Barely opening his eyes, he saw the kittens.

"Kitties! I thought Mama said we couldn't sleep with them. Hey, Sonny and Stripy," Sammy said as he gently rubbed their sleepy heads.

"They got scared by a pesky raccoon last night, so I guess Mama felt sorry for them and let them stay in. That racket you heard was the turkeys taking off for the day."

"Will they wake me up every morning?"

"I hope so. They're our guardian angels just like Grandpa Jake said." Sadie was only partially right.

They ate breakfast, fed the cats, got dressed and cleaned up, and then all three sat down on the couch for Sunday school. It was still drizzling rain, so they were happy to be inside, warm, dry, and together. The kittens snuggled in a ball in front of the fire on the hand-looped, once-white rug.

"I thought we'd read about Jesus healing a man with leprosy today."

"What's leprosy?" Sammy asked.

As Millie explained, she opened her Bible to Matthew 8.

* * *

Lewis lay in bed awhile longer than usual since it was Sunday and especially since he was restless yet another night. He dreamed of being outside the shack, the same one where he saw the girl standing in the window yesterday. In the dream he saw only the shadow of someone taller than the girl moving around. He could sense the deep sadness in her soul, and there was something else . . . pain. . .real physical pain.

Lewis had always been insightful, ever since that day all those years ago when his guardian spirit revealed himself. His grandmother explained that a true medicine man has a magic that not many others possess. What he still didn't understand after all these years though was why could he see all these things that happened years ago and feel people's pain but not be able to help them? What did it all mean? What was he supposed to do? And why did the dead need rescuing?

~ Chapter Nine ~

*A*nn looked out her bedroom window, the one that faced the Blue Ridge Mountains. She couldn't see the outline of the peaks for the fog and rain. It was just plain crazy for her to try and make that drive this morning. She knew the smoky mist would be so thick she'd have to creep to find her way.

Pulling her faded purple fleece wrapper tighter around her thin frame, she stepped out in the hall and headed to the kitchen. She puttered around, fixing herself a cup of coffee. Then just like always she sat down and watched the birds swoop and hover around the feeder outside the kitchen window. There he was, that nuisance of a woodpecker, scaring her little yellow finches away. She walked over to the window and tapped on it. The woodpecker didn't seem to notice.

Ann fixed herself two hard-boiled eggs and poured a glass of cranberry juice. She kept thinking she'd eventually talk herself out of going to the mountain if she stalled long enough. But an hour later, dishes washed and clothes on, she took her purse from the hall closet, grabbed her brown jacket, and headed out the door. She wondered again what in the world she was doing as the stinging rain pelted her face. Running the short distance to her 1962 Black Ford Pickup, she jumped in. All she and Jake had ever owned had been pickups, so the two times she'd traded since Jake died, she didn't think twice on what to get. She had, however, upgraded to an automatic this last time. She wasn't getting any younger, and it was much easier to drive with no more clutches to stomp in.

As Ann started up the mountain, the rain steadily fell, but there was no fog. This lifted her spirits, and the forty-five minute drive was over in no time. As Ann pulled into the familiar little drive, she thought something looked different. Was the grass in the routes mashed down? Had someone been down the road? The rain had washed away any evidence of tire marks, but Ann was sure a vehicle had been down the lane. She steered the truck to a halt in front of the gate. Putting it in park, she sat looking ahead.

There was no grass growing in the deep woods, so Ann couldn't tell if anyone had come this far or not. It didn't look like anything had been through the gate; there were no signs on the opposite side. Someone must have just ridden down here, and seeing the locked gate, backed out.

She sat there for a long while, staring ahead, listening to rain fall through the leaves and drop on top of her roof. Her thoughts ran wild. Visions of sunny days, laughter and smiles flooded her memory. There they were, she and Millie racing to the spring to fetch water . . . letting Millie win . . . jumping into a pile of leaves Jake had just raked up . . . sitting around the fire at night telling stories . . . roasting those hot dogs, the ones that were linked together that Millie had always loved to pull apart. . . . . . and then Jonathan.

As she sat there for over an hour, tears streaming down her face, Ann's heart ached. She knew she'd see Millie again. She felt it deep down in her soul, but when? She leaned over and opened the glove compartment. Reaching into the corner, she felt the keys. Taking hold of them, she looked at the two—one for the gate, one for the cabin—then she reached down and pulled up the door handle.

Down the familiar but much-neglected path only a few hundred yards away was her Millie, and unbeknownst to Ann, two more children, actually great-grandchildren. They all three lay on the bed napping the afternoon away, Millie in the middle this time, one child snuggled in the crook of each arm.

Walking to the gate, Ann's hand shook so badly it took her a while to get the key in. Was she really going down there this time? Could she stand to be that close again? Wiggling the key, it just wouldn't seem to go in the hole.

She looked at both keys, knowing she was using the right one. Sliding the tip to the hole, she was ready to push it in. A snap made her look up. Away in the distance between her and the cabin, she saw movement. She stood up, letting the key drop back into her hand and away from the lock. Her eyes stayed focused as the snapping of underbrush got closer. It was raining a little harder now, so she wiped her face with the backside of her hand.

When she looked back up, there he was. She could see him clearly now, just as big maybe bigger than he'd been eighteen years ago. But it couldn't be the same bear, surely not. She'd been up here, stopping at the gate, dozens of times and hadn't seen him again until today. How many years did bears live anyway? She didn't know.

Frozen, Ann watched him. He was still far enough away, so her heart was only slightly pounding. She knew he was watching her, but didn't seem to be agitated by her presence. He didn't come any closer but didn't back away either. He stood between her and the past . . . or perhaps her unknown future.

Ann wasn't sure what to do. If she went on down to the cabin, would he rush her? Would he pound the cabin door down and tear her to pieces? This place had already witnessed one too many tragedies. She didn't know what to do, torn between her family pulling her down the path and something called a big black bear pushing her away.

She'd let the animal have his way this time. Odds were she wouldn't see another bear around here for another eighteen years. She'd gotten this close to going all the way this time. Maybe she could do it after all . . . next time.

Getting back into the truck, Ann laid the keys back in the corner of the glove compartment on the left side. She then took off her brown jacket. Probably just nerves. She felt smoking hot. Cranking the truck, she backed up the lane to the turning-around place. Glancing down the trail, she saw the huge black bear had disappeared. *See you later, Blackie.* She had no idea why she called him that. It just seemed right. Going back down the mountain, she decided to stop by the police station in town before she went home. It never hurt to ask about Lindsay and Millie one more time.

❀ ❦ ❀

As Lewis sat in his study reading the paper, the sweat and roar started at the same time.

> *There stands a woman, an older woman, another new face. Now she is moving away from the black truck toward a chain gate. The gate locks the entrance to a narrow path. She wants to move, to go through the barricade, but the lock is a hindrance, she can't get it open. The woman is wiping rain from her eyes. She tries once again to open the latch. Does she really want it open? There's resistance, but not from the lock. Lewis feels her thoughts and sees her memories. So much good . . . but oh, so much bad.*
>
> *Lewis feels her need. Her fear. Her pain is so deep like his own that he senses it with all his being. Who is this woman and why is she so important? Of what is she afraid? What indeed is Lewis's own fear?*
>
> *Then up ahead he sees the bear. Their eyes meet, an intention forms in the animal before it comes through the man's lips as a chant.*
>
> *"You can't come through . . . it's not time. No, not yet. Go away."*

Lewis chants the same words over and over. He can't let the woman through, not yet.

His grandmother stood at the door listening in respect, for she'd seen him like this before . . .

~ Chapter Ten ~

*M*onday morning dawned clear and crisp. Millie put a stick of wood on the fire before heading to the stove to heat her coffee water. She dreaded today because she knew she had to go back into town and have her prescriptions filled. She could only hope there wouldn't be any problems, and that she wouldn't have to see a doctor. That would be way too personal, and she'd have to give out more information than she was ready to reveal. She needed to take all the dirty clothes and linens to the laundry, too, and get a few more supplies. She really didn't want to venture out more than once every couple of weeks.

As she fixed coffee, she glanced out the kitchen window. Pulling the fog from the moist ground, the sun painted a beautiful picture especially of the turkeys when they took flight out of the trees and flew into the shafts of light.

"Mama?" Sammy called.

Walking to the bedroom door, Millie answered, "What's wrong?"

"Was that those turkeys again?"

"Yes, it sure was. I'll bet there were forty or fifty this time. You'll get used to them, and they won't wake you up."

"I don't know how, but I hope so." Snuggling back into the covers, Sammy was back asleep in no time.

Sadie was also awake. She took Teddy and laid him beside Sammy, pulling the covers up around both their necks. Throwing the quilt off, she got up and came into the kitchen.

"Do you want some hot chocolate?"

"Yes, that sounds good."

Mother and daughter sat at the silver-speckled aluminum-legged table and talked about their day.

"Can we look for curtains today while we're in town?" Sadie asked.

"If it doesn't take too long at the laundry, yes. We've got several loads to wash. I'm going to dig out Grandma's bedclothes and wash them. Maybe they won't fall apart since they've been in a drawer away from the sun."

After Sammy got up, they ate oatmeal with raisins, dressed, loaded up the car and headed out again, Millie's medicine bottles in her pocketbook. On the other side of the gate, they went through their track-covering routine. In town they passed Mr. Taylor's hardware store, and there on the right was Abernathy's Soda Shop. Millie parked in front, and they all got out. Hand in hand, they went through the front door, passed the soda counter and on to the back where large letters read PHARMACY above the high countertop. There was a man standing behind there, head down, concentrating on his work. He glanced up and saw the strangers waiting. Sweat dampened Millie's palms. *God*, she prayed, *let this go smoothly.*

"Good morning. Hope you didn't wait long. Didn't hear you come up. What can I help you with?" His voice sounded pleasant enough.

"Yes, I need two prescriptions filled."

"Sure thing, ma'am. What you got?" Stepping down from his perch, the aged man approached them.

Millie reached into her purse and pulled out two bottles, and handed them to the man. He took both and read the labels. Millie started to sweat more as she watched his eyebrows furrow together.

"Melissa Ann Madison. Long way from home, aren't you? My name's Tom Parker. Glad to meet you," he said as he stuck out his hand for a shake, not waiting for her to answer. Turning his attention to Sadie and Sammy, he asked, "And who are these two fine-looking youngsters?"

Millie quickly responded. "That is Lydia," she said, pointing to Sadie. "And this is Thomas." She touched Sammy on the head.

"Thomas is it? Well boy, we've got the same name. Nobody has called me Thomas since my sweet little mama passed away years ago. I'm just plain old Tom to everybody now." Reaching down, he tousled Sammy's blond head. He took the bottles from Millie and stepped up to his dispensing area.

"Won't take but a minute, Ms. Madison. Why don't you get the youngsters a soda while you wait—my treat." Not waiting for an answer, Tom yelled up to the soda counter. "Becky, give the kids a soda while they wait, will ya?"

Thankful to get away from more possible questions, Millie led the way to the fountain.

Tom Parker took the bottles. Right away he noticed one was a cancer preventive drug. *Poor lady, she sure did look awful young but puny*, and her other prescription was for pain. He went about filling the two bottles with the pills, all the while wondering what her prognosis was, hoping those two young kids wouldn't soon be left without a mother, and also wondering about the Texas address on the pill bottles.

From behind the fountain the clerk Becky asked, "What will it be? Cola or grape?"

Both Sadie and Sammy looked at each other and asked for grape.

"Two grapes coming up. How about you, ma'am? May I get you something?"

"No, thank you, nothing for me." Millie just wanted to get her medicine and leave before she had to answer any more questions.

Sadie watched as the lady mashed down on a lever three times, each push squirting purple syrup into the bottom of a glass.

Then she took a hose and mashed a button on the end, filling the glass with fizzy water. Dropping in two pieces of ice, she stirred the contents and handed it to Sammy. Following the same recipe, she handed the other glass to Sadie.

"What is this?" Sadie whispered, not wanting the woman to hear her.

Leaning down, Millie whispered back. "It's an old-fashioned fountain drink. This is the way they were made before they put them in bottles like you're used to. I remember these sodas being a whole lot better than the ones in bottles though."

With that, Sadie took a sip out of the straw. "Yum. Here, taste. It is good. You're right, it is better than the bottles," Sadie said.

Sammy hadn't said anything but had already drunk half of his and was working on the rest.

Millie took a sip. The sweet fruity flavor that bubbled up her nose made her go back in time. Whenever her daddy had been at the cabin with them, he'd said, "Let's take a ride, Millie," and off they'd go to town, grabbing a soda or ice cream cone right here at this same place. She'd almost forgotten about that. It is amazing how a smell can make you remember . . . .

Her daddy, Jonathan, came up to the cabin many times when she was there with Grandma and Grandpa. She always asked where Lindsay was, and he'd say, 'Home with another one of her headaches.' It all sounded normal then, but now Millie knew her mother's headache had been Luke Turner. The thought almost made her sick. The truth along with the sweet soda was turning Millie's stomach. Remembering all those lost years away from her daddy brought tears to Millie's eyes. She should hate her mother, but what good would it do, hating a dead person? It sure wouldn't right all the wrongs her mother did.

Tom's voice brought Millie back to the present.

"Here you are, Ms. Madison. Got you all ready to go. That one pill is sort of expensive. Sorry I had to charge you so much."

Looking down at the register receipt, Millie saw the two charges, four-fifty for the pain medicine, and fourteen for the cancer drug. The pain pills were almost the same cost as in Texas, but the cancer one was two dollars cheaper.

"That's okay, Mr. Parker. They usually cost more than that. Thank you, and for the sodas too."

Millie pulled out a twenty-dollar bill and handed it to Mr. Parker. He reached into his pants pocket and pulled out a roll of money. He took a dollar bill out of the stack, and then put the paper money back. Next he laid a handful of coins on the counter. He picked up two quarters and handed them along with the dollar to Millie.

"You're welcome, Ms. Madison. I hope everything turns out all right for you."

Millie was touched, knowing he knew that inside her there was a murderous vine growing, hoping to wrap its way around everything and squeeze the very life out of her. She was barely able to get out another faint "thank you" to Mr. Parker as she scooted the kids out the door.

"Are you okay?" Sadie asked. Sadie noticed how nervous her mama had been, how pale and close to tears she was right now.

"I will be, just give me a minute." Leaning back against the storefront, Millie took a few deep breaths. There had been no way to get her medicine filled without Mr. Parker seeing the bottles with her real name on them. It was a wonder he hadn't asked to see her driver's license. He probably would have if she'd been getting a narcotic. She could only pray Brad would never find this town or Mr. Parker. She also hoped Mr. Parker and the other people in town didn't compare notes on the newcomers because she was now known by two different names.

"Come on, kids. Let's get our washing done."

❀ ❦ ❀

Brad Madison leaned back in his recliner, pulled the lever, and threw his feet up. Into his shirt pocket he reached to remove a pack of non-filtered cigarettes. When he tapped the butt on the heel of his hand, one popped out. He pulled it into his mouth and touched the tip with the lighter he always kept on the end table beside his chair. He blew ringlets of the smoke up into the air. His mind wanders.

When he got home on Wednesday from his job at Dallas Delivers, he'd known right away that something was wrong. The car was not sitting in the driveway. Millie was always home when he arrived. She knew how mad it made him when he had to wonder where she was. The house was a total disaster, drawers and cabinet doors left open, clothes and food gone. He was quite furious for a while, throwing things and making an even bigger mess. Then he realized she'd be back. She couldn't make it on her own, dumb, stupid woman. Yeah, she'd be back all right, and then he'd really let her have it. He was way too good for her anyway. But she was his and he wanted her back even if he didn't want her. That had been six days ago, but he still wasn't worried. She'd cool off and come driving up any minute, begging him to forgive her. Nobody in her right mind left a man like Bradley Madison.

~ Chapter Eleven ~

efore they knew it, the cabin dwellers had been at the mountain for two weeks. They stayed so busy that time flew by. It was now the last week in May, and they'd not needed a fire in three days. Millie was glad it had warmed up because they used at least half of the stockpile of wood. She knew they couldn't stay here forever, but she vowed to tarry just as long as possible.

She looked up at the new kitchen curtains. They were white and bordered with roosters like Grandpa's plate; their red heads and brown and yellow wing feathers brightened up the room. She found one of Grandma's tablecloths; it was solid red and matched perfectly. She set a vase of wild black-eyed susans in the middle, their yellow tint standing out against the bright red hue. She could hear her children out back playing with Spook, Smoky, Sonny, and Stripy. She couldn't believe the changes in them all. In just a few short weeks they'd put on some weight. Looking at the food shelf, she knew they would soon need to go back to the grocery store. The sack was also full of dirty laundry. Tomorrow they'd go.

Walking to the bedrooms, she peeked inside. She'd also bought curtains for these rooms—solid green ones for the front because that was Sadie's favorite color, and blue ones for the second because blue was Sammy's most favorite color. She found bright flowery bedspreads at the five and dime, one with lots of green, the other blue. The coziness of the now spotless cabin made her never want to leave, not even for an afternoon of shopping. Tomorrow was Saturday, so she'd go then.

Walking to the door, she called for the kids to come in. "Come on, it's getting about time for the turkeys to roost, and you'll scare them away."

It had become their favorite pastime, watching the birds fly in and roost upon their perches. The turkeys were getting used to the visitors being there. In the mornings when they took flight, several of them would come down and land right behind the house. One especially large tom, his beard dragging the ground, would prance and spread his feathers to show off for the hens. The Madisons watched him every morning for a week. Yesterday they observed as several poults, young turkeys, followed their mama across the pasture.

A week ago the noisy chirps of the baby birds nesting over the front door awakened them. Going out the side door, they walked to the front of the cabin just in time to see the mama wren nudge her final baby from the nest. The little one fluttered his tiny wings, not quite sure what to do with himself, and finally perched on a limb of a nearby dogwood tree. Next they saw the other three young ones, and then the mama wren joined them, chirping loudly, congratulating her young on their bravery and accomplishment.

Millie's thoughts were broken as the screen door opened and kids and cats paraded through.

"What's for supper? I'm starving," Sammy said.

"I was just wondering about that myself. We're running low on supplies, but we've got the makings for hot dogs, or how about tomato soup and grilled cheese?"

"That sounds good."

"Is that okay with you, Sadie?"

"Sure, anything is fine with me."

Millie still couldn't get over how content they all were. They had a television back in Texas, but Brad seldom let them turn it on.

And when he was at work, nothing seemed to be on their three channels that interested the children except on Saturday mornings. Then Sammy would beg to watch cartoons. Sometimes Brad would let him and sometimes he wouldn't. There was no arguing either; they all three knew whatever he said was the law, no matter how mean and unreasonable his decisions were. So they hadn't missed a television much at all. The great outdoors and all God's creatures were better and more entertaining than any character on TV.

Sammy continued to play with the kittens while Sadie moved to the sink to wash her hands.

"I'll help you," Sadie said. Reaching for the last of a loaf of bread Millie had baked on Tuesday, she laid out the six slices on plates.

"There's only five white pieces and the heel."

"That's okay, I like the heel. I'll eat it," Millie said.

Taking the chunk of cheese out of the refrigerator, Sadie sliced off enough pieces to cover the bread. Putting the top on, she handed Millie two of the sandwiches. Millie put them into the skillet of hot butter. In just a minute they were ready to eat.

"Come wash up, Sammy. Your supper's ready." Millie called to him on the back porch.

He came through the door with four little fur balls scampering all around his feet.

"Come on, kitties, out you go. Here, I'll feed you too." Millie shook food from the bag into their bowl, bringing them running to the back porch. Closing the door as she came back in, Millie sat down at the table with her children. They clasped hands and Millie prayed.

"Thank you, God, for my children and this place. Please keep us in your watchful embrace nestled close to your heart. Thank you for our food, and help us always to remember that you will supply our every need. Amen."

"Mama, you didn't thank Him for Spook and Smoky, and Sonny and Stripy, and the turkeys."

"Silly me, I won't forget next time. I promise."

As they ate their simple meal, they talked and laughed, making plans for their days ahead.

"I'm going down to the bog and look for the turtles tomorrow, okay?" Sadie asked.

"Tomorrow we have to go into town for groceries and do laundry, but on Sunday we should be able to start exploring, maybe even do a little fishing."

"I want to catch a fish, a big one. Can I, Mama? We will use your grandpa's fishing pole. It's still behind the bedroom door."

"We sure can, Sammy. I think he'd like that very much."

* 🌿 *

Ann took a tissue from the box and blew her nose for the thousandth time over the past two weeks. Standing in the soggy rain at the cabin watching Blackie, and then getting so hot, had almost given her pneumonia. She only left the house a few times for groceries, medicine, and two trips to the doctor. She was feeling much better but was still awfully weak.

She reached for the stack of mail she'd let pile up. On top were the two electric bills that just arrived.

The first one was for the house. Same as always, it never varied over a couple of dollars each month. She took the silver knife that she opened mail with and pulled it through the top of the second bill, the one for the cabin. Why did she keep paying that three dollars and seventy-seven cents every month?

Ann didn't know why in the world she kept that power hooked up. Look at the money she could have saved over the past eighteen years. Bet it would add up to three or four hundred dollars, and she wouldn't have to listen to the power company fuss about someone having to walk to the cabin from the gate to read the meter. They probably hadn't even read it in years.

It had been the very same every month now for at least ten years. It might not even work; an ice storm could have broken the wire like it did back in 1942. Took them three months to get in there and hook it back up. The bill was another reason she ought to visit the cabin; that and the fact that she couldn't get it off her mind these days. Maybe it was just because she had too much time on her hands while she was sick.

Ann didn't even look at the bill as she pulled it from the envelope. She just laid it in the pile. Maybe she'd feel like running some errands tomorrow. She'd go by and pay then.

Finishing up the mail, she took her empty coffee cup and set it in the sink. Then she went to her bedroom to lie down for a bit. Before she closed her eyes she focused on one of the photos on her bedside table: Millie, about three years old, curled up in her daddy's lap in the bright orange rocking chair at the cabin, brown teddy bear tucked up under her chin, with the three fingers she always sucked on stuck in her mouth.

Peace and pain at the same time overwhelmed Ann. *How could someone's selfish choices ruin so many lives? How could two people just vanish without so much as a trace? How could Lindsay have not let Jonathan know where she took Millie? How on earth could anyone be so cruel? Maybe something had happened to them; maybe Lindsay couldn't let them know.*

Ann tried not to hate. She prayed for strength to forgive every day, and she prayed just like right now for God to lead her to her little Millie. She knew she was out there somewhere. She felt it down deep in the innards of her soul. This was one of the times she wished she were more like her own grandmother, she seemed to always know what was going to happen before it actually did.

Drifting off into a weakened sleep, she dreamed of the cabin. Ann could see two children laughing and playing, one young girl and a small boy. They didn't look familiar. The boy wasn't Jonathan and the girl certainly was not Millie!

Ann woke up remembering her dream: *A little boy with blond hair . . . a girl with almost carrot-colored, wild unruly curls flying in the summer breeze. She had something in her hand. What was it?* The dream invaded her thoughts all day. Trying to remember what the little girl had in her hands tormented Ann. Then late that evening on her back porch as Ann sat watching the birdfeeders sway in the wind, the image came clearly in her head. The girl was holding Teddy, Millie's bear.

Ann stood up quickly which made her head swim. She had to get her strength back and get to the cabin. She knew it was silly and it had just been a dream, but she had to go get Millie's teddy bear. That other little girl couldn't have it.

The next morning, Ann got up and walked the short distance down the road toward the spring. She knew she had to go slow and build up her stamina. Being in bed for over two weeks had weakened her entire body.

She took it easy, then came in and rested, ate lunch, grabbed her purse and the stack of bills. She had four stops she needed to make: the phone, oil and electric company, and grocery store.

By the time Ann got to Drake Electric, she was worn out. She laid the two bills on the counter with a twenty and a five. Sally Marion took the bills and money. After punching a couple buttons on an adding machine, Sally said, "Mrs. Hampton, that will be twenty-eight dollars and thirty-five cents."

Ann was so tired she didn't comprehend what Sally had said.

"Mrs. Hampton, I need three dollars and thirty-five cents more."

A little confused, Ann dug in her billfold for the additional money. Sally took it and stamped "paid" on the bills, handing them back to Ann. She looked down at the stubs. The house bill was twenty-two dollars and fifty-one cents, and the cabin bill that she didn't look at before was five-dollars and eighty-four cents.

That was over two dollars higher than usual. Could it have been a mistake or did the power company just increase the bill because they hadn't in so many years? She could go back in and ask Sally, but she was just too tired to worry with it now. She'd check on it later. Truth was, Ann soon forgot about the electric bill. Her next few weeks were spent building up her strength and taking care of herself.

Bright and early on June twenty-first, Ann got in her truck and headed up the mountain. It had been almost six weeks since her last trip to the gate. She felt almost back to normal, and a steely resolve shone in her eyes. Today she would open that gate, drive over the chain, go to the front door, unlock it, go inside, and get Teddy. He'd been alone way too long up there in that cabin.

When Ann pulled to a stop in front of the gate, she wasn't as resolved as she had been at the foot of the mountain. She turned off the engine and just sat there. It was a bit cooler up here than at home, but Ann didn't reach for the sweater she brought. In fact she felt warm, maybe too warm for the June day. Swiping her fingers across her upper lip, she felt perspiration.

Maybe she wasn't as well as she thought. She sat there for a long while remembering the days of old, like Jonathan as a little boy wading around in the creek, helping his daddy chase cows back into the fence. She often wondered why God hadn't blessed her and Jake with other children. Many times she imagined how wonderful it would be to have another child with her now. It wouldn't be so lonely; she'd have someone with whom to share her losses. But that other child wouldn't be Jonathan. Nothing or no one could replace a lost child. One child had been her lot in life, and deep down she knew other children couldn't have filled the void, the deep, dark black pit in the depth of her being, the emptiness that Jonathan and little Millie had left.

Then, Jake, you had to go and leave me too.

Ann hung her head and softly cried into her hands. With her face covered, she didn't see the black bear as he passed behind her truck. After a short cry, she dried her eyes and noticed she'd cooled off.

"I guess I just needed a good old pity trip, didn't I, Jake?" Ann spoke to herself out loud. Ann didn't talk out loud to herself or her dead husband often, but sometimes she would just to hear the sound of a voice. She never got any answers. Sometimes she just needed to talk to Jake.

Realizing she wasn't yet as strong as she needed to be, she cranked up her truck, backed out to the turn-around place, and headed back down the mountain.

* 🌿 *

Lewis went ahead and gave in to the feeling of floating to places and into other people's lives. Sitting in his office, he closed his eyes. He had never seen things so clearly in his mind before, and not just the sights but the smells and sounds.

The sweet aroma of wild honeysuckle wafts up his nose and tree frogs sound in his ears. And what is that, a creek? Feeling intense heat Lewis needed to fan himself.

> *The older woman is at the gate again.*
>
> *Sadness flows from her . . . she seems to beckon him closer. He needs to touch her, smooth the hair from her eyes, and dry the tears. His chest hurts, exploding with her pain. He can't inhale enough air to take a deep breath. He's never felt so helpless in his life, so helpless that he tastes his own tears. Or are they hers?*

What had it been? Six . . . eight weeks since he saw her? His head had not rumbled and roared but a couple of times this past month. But now a sense of knowing overwhelmed him, and protectiveness for the lady came over him.

~ Chapter Twelve ~

*S*adie watched the black pickup pull up to the chain gate. She was a good distance away perched about halfway up in a young oak tree. It was an easy climb. From its branches she could see Brush Creek flowing down through the bottom, the cabin, and the gate. She had dubbed this her special spot. She roamed the woods every day now for about a month.

Millie wouldn't let her or Sammy out of her sight for the first couple of weeks, but with every passing day, Millie grew more relaxed and unafraid. Sadie relished her new freedom just as those fledglings had the day their mother had nudged them from their nest. Millie felt comfortable with Sadie's adventures as long as she wasn't gone over a couple of hours at a time.

Sadie romped all over the hills, following the creek bed on both sides. She even got up enough courage to cross the aged and half-rotten footbridge Great-Grandpa Jake had built many years before. Time had weakened some of the boards, and enough were missing on one end so one had to jump those last few feet to the bank. The bridge also leaned to the right. Years of floodwaters had pushed against it, the resistance making it set at an angle. Her first trip across was very slow going and more than a little scary, but Sadie was glad she did it because on the other side of the creek was this, her special tree.

She couldn't count how many times since that first time she'd crossed over the bridge. It wasn't anything now since she'd gotten used to it. Mama and Sammy hadn't attempted the passing. It was much too shaky for them, but Sadie was glad because it led to her secret place, which nobody else could get to unless they waded across the creek.

There was also the enormous rock that covered a large part of the land at the lower end of the bottom. It was right on the creek bank in the curve of the flow. Many rocks lay in the water there, so the rippling sound was louder than in most other places in the creek. Sadie would lie back on that warm boulder where the reflecting sun had stored its warmth and listen as the water cascaded over the stones. When she was here or up in her tree, she felt almost like a normal twelve-year-old. She didn't have to worry about keeping her mama and Sammy safe, or about her daddy's punches, followed by his "I'm sorry" and un-welcomed hugs.

All she had to agonize over now was keeping her mama well. Sadie knew more than Millie thought she did. She overheard her daddy hollering and cussing at Millie for being such a weakling. She could hear him screaming in those days after her mama's surgery: "Get your sorry ass up and fix my supper!"

How Mama got up to cook, Sadie didn't know. She looked so weak and frail, especially with the white bandage covering the backside of her shaven head. Millie had told her she was having an operation to get rid of her headaches, and Sadie guessed that was true. The cancerous tumor they removed was the size of a lemon. Sadie knew because she secretly read the report that they sent home. She also comprehended the suggestion that the tumor would come back within five years. And it seemed her mama would probably always have some pain in the location of the tumor because so many nerve endings were exposed. Every time her mama took one of the little pink pills, Sadie knew she was hurting. However, she didn't think she'd seen her take half as many since they came to the cabin.

Fixing her eyes on the truck, Sadie watched as the person in it just sat parked at the gate. She could tell the person was alone, but couldn't make out if it was a man or woman. Whoever it was, they just sat. Many minutes passed until she saw the person sort of slump onto the steering wheel and put his face in his hands. Maybe he was sick, or lost and afraid. What to do? Should she risk it? See if they need help? She'd wait a few more minutes and see what happened.

As Sadie stared at the person, she also caught sight of Blackie. He was sitting back on his rump maybe twenty yards away from the truck, staring at the person as intently as Sadie herself was. He just sat there the whole time, never fidgeting or making a sound. Then very slowly, as the driver still sat with head bent down, Blackie leaned over until he stood on all fours. Then he slowly labored his way toward the truck. He still didn't make a sound, or seem in a hurry or excited. In fact Sadie thought he looked as sad and lost as the person behind the wheel. The person never saw him as he ambled within a foot of the back of the truck. Blackie stopped for a second, turning up his head and flaring his nostrils as if taking in the scent of something. Then just as quickly, he lowered his head and moved forward into the woods.

Sadie sat spellbound. This was the first time she'd seen Blackie since that first morning. She wondered if she dreamt it since she hadn't spotted him again, but now, for certain, he was very real.

Just as Sadie made her mind up to go and check on the person, he raised his head and the truck engine rumbled. Sadie saw the person wipe at his face like he'd been crying. Maybe he just needed a place to go to and be sad. Be sad, just like she had been many times in her twelve years. Sadie watched as the truck left, pulling out of sight, she felt tightness around her heart.

Sadie climbed down from the tree and headed back across the footbridge toward home. Mama would be worried about her since she'd been gone longer than usual. As she got closer to the house, the music sounded louder and louder, Sadie was happy to hear it. Mama bought them a new AM-FM radio at Mr. Taylor's store. It was fun when they turned it on and danced around the kitchen to the sound of The Beatles singing "Hey Jude" or Simon and Garfunkel's "Mrs. Robinson." They listened to all kinds of music, but Mama would always switch it back to that country station down in a town called Stateston. It was over those airwaves that Sadie got to know Merle Haggard and Johnny Cash. Even though Mama said they were not very good role models, she loved to hear them sing. Mama would turn the volume up real loud and sing to Jeannie C. Riley's "Harper Valley PTA," and turn it down low when a lady named Tammy Wynette would sound out the letters D.I.V.O.R.C.E. Sadie's favorite was Loretta Lynn. She sang fearlessly as she belted out the words to "Fist City." Lynn wasn't afraid to tell stories of real life, not sugar-coated fantasies.

Sadie walked in the front door and smelled something cooking. She realized she was outside all morning and was now starving.

"Hey, Mamma, what's for lunch?"

"I'm fixing spaghetti sauce for our supper tonight. I thought we'd just have a sandwich now. What do you want?"

"I'll fix it. Did you get any more of that apple butter when you went into town yesterday?" Sadie hadn't believed her mama had let her stay at the cabin alone, but she had.

"Yes, I thought you guys liked it, the way it was gone so fast."

"Sammy, do you want a toasted apple butter sandwich?" Sadie asked her little brother.

He was sitting at the kitchen table coloring a picture of Donald Duck. He was usually with the kittens, but Millie wouldn't let them in when she was cooking, so they were outside roaming around. Millie also didn't like for Sammy to be out of the house by himself. But he seemed perfectly content coloring and listening to his mama singing to the tunes on the radio. They did listen at home in Texas, but only when Brad wasn't there. Even then the volume was always turned way down just in case he came home in the middle of the day, which he did pretty regularly. Still, nobody ever sang along with the songs; no one ever felt like it.

"Yes, but I want my sandwich *not* toasted," Sammy said.

Sadie grabbed the bread and laid out four pieces. "Do you want me to fix you something, Mama?"

"No, I just finished my second cup of coffee and ate a piece of that fresh apple pie that I made last night. Those apples sure made a tasty dessert. Where did you say that tree was?"

"It's just across the creek between the footbridge and the ford, right along the bank."

"I remember gathering apples but not where the tree is. I wish you'd stay off that rotten bridge. It looks like it could fall at any minute. You're going to break your neck."

"It's not high off the water if it does come down. What could happen? I'd get wet."

"You've become a regular old tomboy, haven't you?"

"Mama, that reminds me . . . " Leaning close to her mama so Sammy wouldn't hear, Sadie whispered, "I saw that black bear again. He walked within a foot of a truck that had pulled up to the gate."

Millie turned toward her daughter. "A truck at the gate? When? What color was it? Did you see anyone get out?"

As Millie questioned her, Sadie watched her mama's face drain of all color. She held Sadie by the shoulders, looking straight into her eyes. Sadie could feel the fear through her shaking hands.

"No one got out! They just sat there for a long while, and it looked like the person was crying. It was a black truck with a Ford emblem on the hood. That was all, Mama. Then Blackie walked by and the person took off. It's all right."

Sadie knew what her mama was thinking—that Daddy had found them—but Sadie knew it wasn't him. Even though she couldn't see the driver's face, it wasn't Daddy or his car. She always felt her daddy's presence when he was around.

Those nights over a year ago when her mama had been in the hospital, Sadie woke up knowing without opening her eyes that he was there standing over her, staring at her. Millie knew it too. That's why she started sleeping with the children—to keep them safe.

Millie made her way to a chair at the kitchen table. Sitting down, she laid her hands on her trembling legs.

Sensing the fear, Sammy started to softly whimper, "Is Daddy coming to get us?"

"No, no honey. It was just someone lost, like Sadie said. It's okay, I promise."

Millie wasn't completely convinced, however. Something just felt strange down in her gut.

❦

Sammy woke them up screaming that night. "No Daddy! Please don't hit me, please don't!"

His loud crying even woke the nesting turkeys. Millie and Sadie could hear their broad wings flapping above the cabin roof. It took Millie a full hour to calm Sammy down and get him back to sleep.

"That's the first nightmare he's had since we left Texas."

"I know it was my fault. I overreacted about the gate visitor; I scared him. I shouldn't have let him see me upset. It won't happen again. Let's try and get some sleep. It's two or three hours before daylight."

They lay down and Sadie snuggled Teddy up to her chest. It was her night to sleep with him. Once she saw the tear-streaked face of Sammy though, she took Teddy and placed him next to her little brother, close to his heart to comfort him and keep him safe. It took Sadie a while, but she finally drifted off to sleep, where visions of Blackie appeared in her dreams the rest of the night.

The same couldn't be said for Millie. She lay awake and watched the new dawn light filter through the crack in the green curtain. She knew this couldn't last forever and she'd have to face Brad again someday, but she really hoped it wouldn't be any day soon.

Blackie? What was it Sadie said about a bear again? Millie hoped all these changes had not made Sadie's imagination go crazy.

Before it became totally light, Millie slipped out of bed and went into the other bedroom. She pulled out the blue metal box from under the clothes in the top dresser drawer. She sat down on the bed and twisted the combination lock. Three to the right, nine to the left, and six back right. Opening it, she lifted the journal. The first thing she saw was the picture of Sammy's bruised face, his eye completely closed from the swelling. Flipping through the box, she saw reminders of the last twelve years. The surface wounds were healed now, except for the scars, but her insides still felt disfigured and maimed. The worst part of it was that she knew her children felt the same way. All the details were there in her journal, every incident, page after page of suffering and misery, and then there were the pictures.

She needed to find a good lawyer, one who believed in a woman's worth. She needed to know what she could do to keep Brad away from them forever. But she already understood the answer. She got brave six months before, drove to a nearby town, and talked to Sam Freeman, Attorney at Law. He pretty much told her that maybe one day it would be more fair, but now, in 1968, the man rules his house, and it would be virtually impossible to keep a father from seeing his children. He even warned her that it wouldn't be out of the question for Brad to get total custody, especially with Millie's health problems.

She closed the box lid and turned the combination lock. Then Millie just sat there and prayed for a miracle again.

~ Chapter Thirteen ~

*B*rad heard the knocking on the front door but didn't get up to answer it. He was tired of people questioning him about Millie and the kids. Nobody had noticed much except the neighbors and that nosy schoolteacher because Sadie missed the last week of school. He explained that there were some family health problems that Millie had to attend to in North Carolina, and the young'uns had to go with her because he had to work and couldn't tend to them. The schoolteacher wasn't too insistent since it was only a week that Sadie missed. Brad didn't see what the big deal was anyway; no one ever really did much schoolwork those final days. Then after several days, the neighbors started snooping around. He finally stopped answering the door.

Where is she anyway? How long had she been gone? It was the seventeenth of July, over two months. Enough was enough. It was time she got her ass back home. Brad was tired of answering questions and washing his own underwear. *It's time to settle the score with that runnin'-around hag. No one, especially a woman, steals my hard-earned money and gets away with it.*

The knocking stopped. Brad got up from his recliner and headed upstairs. *Where did she keep those papers?* Opening up first one drawer of the desk then another, he fumbled through the documents. *There it is, the folder Lindsay gave Millie before she croaked.*

Opening it up, it only took him a minute to find what he was looking for. The newspaper clipping showed the name in bold letters at the top of the obituary: Jonathan McKinley Hampton 1917–1950. Skimming down, Brad found what he was looking for: Survived by father and mother Jake and Ann Hampton, Jonesboro, North Carolina. That's all he needed to know, so he pitched the folder back in the drawer, went into the kitchen, and picked up the phone receiver. Dialing zero, Brad reached an operator.

"May I help you?"

"Yes, I need a number for Jake Hampton in Jonesboro, North Carolina."

"Just one minute, sir, and I'll connect you to a North Carolina operator."

Several seconds passed and a voice on the other end asked.

"What listing please?"

"Jake Hampton, Jonesboro."

"Just one minute, sir, and I'll get that for you."

Brad waited and waited.

"I'm sorry, sir, there isn't a Jake Hampton. Do you have an address or could it be listed another way?"

"I don't know. How many Hamptons have you got?"

"Let's see, there are . . . ten total in Jonesboro."

"Give them all to me."

"Yes, sir," and she started calling out the numbers to him. The first listing was for an A. Hampton at Sunset Drive, Jonesboro.

§ ✤ §

Ann stepped up on her front porch and sat down in the wooden rocker. She just got back from her morning walk. She was back up to her pace from before she'd gotten sick, but it had taken her over two months. She was glad she started her hike early today. It was going to be another hot July afternoon. Ann looked around. The flowerpots, usually full and blooming rich in color with her beloved petunias, were empty. Spider webs were woven all over the windows and doorframe. She went back inside, fetched the broom, went back out, and reached up with the bristles to knock down all the webs.

She never remembered missing a summer's planting of flowers, but she also never remembered being as sick. Making her mind up, Ann decided to head up to Harry's Nursery and see what kind of flowers he had left. She knew it was awfully late to be planting, but she'd give it a try anyway. In a minute she was wheeling her way out of the driveway.

At Harry's, she walked out disappointed. She really hadn't expected him to have the petunias but she was hopeful. Instead she came away with a flat of begonias. They had out grown their small cups and frankly looked half dead, but Ann bought them anyway. Maybe they'd come back to life like she had. Taking in a deep breath, she was glad to feel like her old self again.

Parking the truck in the driveway, Ann got out and carried her seedlings with her. She'd transplant them this afternoon.

* 🦋 *

Marty Johnson pulled up to the chain gate just like he'd done for the last nine or ten years. Getting out, he grabbed his clipboard and the brown paper bag with his lunch. Stepping over the gate, he started the short stroll to the meter head on the side of the cabin. He was anxious to see if anyone was there today. He doubted it though, since the chain was up and it didn't look like there were any car tracks. Last month he noticed someone had cleaned up around the old place and hung different colored curtains. He sat down that day on the oak stump and ate his lunch like he'd done a hundred times. This used to be Old Man Barr's route, and he'd raised so much cane about having to walk so far, they had switched meter readers. Marty didn't mind. He enjoyed the peacefulness and sounds of the creek as he sat eating his sandwich. Now truthfully, he would skip some months during the winter when it was cold and snowy. It didn't really matter; the meter always read the same every month, at least until last month.

As he approached the cabin, he could hear the sound of music coming from inside. There was a vehicle sitting out front; its tag was from Texas. Mrs. Hampton must finally be renting it out to vacationers. These old mountains were becoming awful popular to out of town folks. Poor Mrs. Hampton. How was she doing? Marty didn't really know her but had heard the sad story about her boy dying right here. Folks said she never came back. Maybe she hadn't.

Writing down the numbers off the meter, Marty slipped the pencil back behind his ear and walked back up the trail. Guessed he would eat in the truck today.

Inside, Millie, Sadie, and Sammy never saw the stranger who had silently gotten so close to them.

❦

Ann stood up and stretched out the kinks in her back. Taking off her gardening gloves, she judged her handiwork. The begonias were unquestionably a pitiful sight, and she was sure the pots might have looked better empty.

Honking the horn, Steve the mailman waved as he pulled away from her box. Ann threw her gloves on the porch step and dusted off the knees of her faded jeans. At the box, she opened the lid and took out two envelopes. She recognized the bills from Drake Electric. The cabin bill made her think of the dream she had some weeks back. Time had lessened its intensity, but every day she still felt the overwhelming need to go and get that teddy bear. *Tomorrow. I'll go tomorrow*, she said to herself.

She heard the phone ringing as she closed the mailbox door. Hurriedly she moved up the drive. Stepping up to the porch to open the front door, she made her way to the phone on the kitchen's pale yellow wall. Just as she picked up the receiver and said hello, she heard the click on the other end. *Oh well, they'll call back.* Hardly anyone telephoned though. Her friend Margaret would call to check on her from time to time, but she didn't drive anymore, so Ann rarely saw her. There were some cousins that lived in town, but they weren't close. Ann was not chummy with anyone anymore. She just didn't have it in her to socialize.

Ann pulled the knife through the top of the envelope and took out the cabin bill. When she saw the amount, twelve dollars and three cents, she said out loud, "What the heck?"

She then slit the top of the other one; her house bill was within a few cents of what it was last month and the month before. Something was very wrong here. An almost unstoppable urge came over her to head to the cabin. She suddenly felt a little faint and sat down in the closest kitchen table chair.

She must have overdone it today. She'd go tomorrow. Yes, tomorrow she would go get Teddy, and Monday she'd go by that blame power company and give them a piece of her mind. Ann would tell them to disconnect the line.

* ❦ *

At the first number on Brad's list, A. Hampton, there was no answer. Some little kid answered at the second number, and Brad simply asked if Millie was there.

"Millie, who's Millie? Mommy, a man on the phone wants Millie. Who is Millie?"

Brad hung up and marked through that number with his pen.

He found no one home at the third number either, and there was no one named Millie at the other seven. *No one had acted funny, so it had to be that first number, A. Hampton. Yes, A. for Ann, the old lady's name from the obit.* Looking at the clock, Brad realized he'd been on the phone for over two hours. But he had to try that number one more time. Dialing, he heard the ringing on the other end, one, two, three rings.

"Hello."

"Hello ma'am, this is Chuck Norman from Enterprise Sweepstakes. How are you today?"

Ann said, "Fine."

"I was wondering if Melissa Ann Madison is home this afternoon?" Without pausing he continued. "Melissa has won a large amount of money, but we're having trouble tracking her down."

Ann pulled a chair from underneath the table and sat before her shaking knees collapsed. That was the second time today she'd felt faint.

"Lady, are you there?"

It took Ann a second to find her voice. "I don't know who Melissa Ann Madison is."

"Don't you have a granddaughter named Melissa Ann?"

"Yes I do, but I haven't seen her in over twenty years."

On the other end of the line, all Ann heard then was a click.

Brad found out all he needed to know. The old woman seemed nervous, so Millie was there. *Yeah sure, haven't seen her in twenty years. All women are nothing but liars.*

Turning up the bottle, he finished off the Jim Beam. Then he leaned back and laughed out loud as he devised all the heartless things he would do to his dear loving family. *Nobody leaves Brad Madison. Before this is over they'll wish they'd never been born.* Brad would soon be making himself a little trip to North Carolina.

Turning on the Saturday evening news, Brad saw many riots popping up all over the South. Martin Luther King's assassination had spawned a fury of fear and violence. As Brad watched, he drew strength from the disturbance. He had almost three months of fresh pent-up rage inside him, and knowing he had to drive all the way to North Carolina to unleash it made him even more furious.

He'd tell them on Monday at the delivery company that he needed some days off. By this time next week, he'd have his brood back under his roof. He might even bring the lying old Granny with them to join in on the fun. The more the merrier.

❦

Ann heard the click but was screaming "hello" into the receiver anyway. She needed to know more. Maybe they were disconnected, and he'd call back. Ann hung up the phone and sat down. For almost an hour she stared at it, willing it to ring. *Why didn't he call back?* Realizing the man figured she couldn't help him, she decided he wouldn't call again.

Standing, she reached for her pocketbook and keys. No matter that it was almost eight o'clock, she got in her truck and headed to the police station. This was the first lead she ever had about Millie, Melissa Ann *Madison*. She had a last name now, surely Millie could finally be found. Little did Ann know just how close to locating Millie she was, and how near she was to leading the last person on earth Millie wanted to see right to her doorstep.

» 🦋 «

When Ann told Ben, the night duty officer, the story about the phone call, his graying brow furrowed. He had never seen Ann this excited. Granted, it was much easier to find someone when you had their entire name, but this was a big old world, and sometimes people didn't want to be found. The whole sweepstakes story was more than a bit odd, but he didn't dwell on it. Stranger things had happened. He promised Ann he'd get Millie's name out on the wire service tonight.

As she was leaving, Ann couldn't help but wonder why Ben had told her to be careful. Did he know something she didn't? She felt the same suspicion too.

Ann didn't go to sleep for a long time that night. Hope and excitement pumped adrenalin through her veins. The last thing she remembered as she eased into darkness was the antique Bell and Howard mantel clock striking three o'clock.

Later Ann was trying to open her eyes and rise from the bed. She was dreaming about the young red-haired girl again who was dangling Teddy in front of Ann's face, taunting her. Ann tried to pick up her arm and reach for the bear, but in her deep sleep the arm was like dead weight, unmoving. She had absolutely no control over her body. When she finally did wake up at six-fifteen, her head was foggy and she felt like she'd been fighting a war all of the three hours she was asleep.

It was Sunday morning, so she decided to try and sleep another hour and then get up and go to the mountain. Ann was back asleep in minutes, this time not dreaming, and when she woke back up it was eight forty-five. She stretched and realized she'd never slept this late in her entire life. Feet hitting the floor, she didn't even take time to put on her slippers as she went to the bathroom. She wanted to hurry up and get to the cabin. There was a teddy bear waiting for her.

~ Chapter Fourteen ~

*J*uly had quickly turned into August. Millie sat at the table and sipped her coffee. She couldn't believe how quickly time was passing. She knew at best they could only stay here another two or three months before it would be much too cold and too dangerous trying to get out of the steep, winding driveway for supplies. Sadie also needed to be in school in another couple of weeks.

Millie was also out of her prescription refills. Mr. Parker had reminded her of that when he filled the bottles two weeks ago. Next week she would see if there was a doctor in town who would see her. She felt better than she had in a long time, and could probably do without the pain pill, but she couldn't risk not having the cancer pill. This was the drug that was supposed to keep the tumor from coming back. Worrying wouldn't help matters; she was going to have to risk revealing her identity soon. She knew all along she wouldn't be able to keep her sickness a secret forever.

There had been no sign or indication that Brad was looking for them. He was a smart man and would contact her grandma, but she wouldn't be able to tell him anything.

So many times Millie had longed to call Ann. One day when she was in town, she borrowed Mr. Taylor's phone and called information to get the number. They didn't have an Ann, but they did have an A. Hampton. As soon as the operator said the phone number, Millie knew it was the right one, for she had called her grandma many times as a young girl.

Then again, maybe Brad wouldn't even look for them. It was obvious he hated them. She felt she couldn't risk revealing herself to her grandma, no matter how much her heart longed to.

Millie moved to the couch. Picking up her Bible, she looked for a story for this Sunday morning's devotion.

❧ ✿ ❧

By the time Ann got her clothes on and ate a bite, the phone rang. She hesitated a minute before answering it because she didn't want anything to detain her from her trip. It was Margaret.

"Good morning, Ann. How are you?"

"Fine, Margaret, just fine. Hope you are."

"Yes, doing fairly well for an old woman. What have you got planned today?" Before Ann could answer Margaret continued. "Thought you might come pick me up and we'd go down to the Burger Chef to have some lunch. I sure wish my old eyes hadn't given out on me, so I could drive myself. I miss not being able to go when I want to. I have a hankering for one of those big, sloppy hamburgers."

Ann started to tell her she couldn't, but it was already ten-fifteen, so what if she started an hour or so later? She felt sorry for Margaret. It would be a sad day for her when she couldn't take care of her own self.

"Sure Margaret, but we need to go early. I've got something I have to do this afternoon. I'll pick you up by eleven."

"Sounds good. See you soon."

Ann decided to water her begonias since she had some time. Filling up a quart mason jar, she carried it to the front porch. She poured the entire amount in one pot then went back inside to get another quart for the other pot. As she poured it she was again amazed at how beautiful the flowers had become. In three weeks, under the nurturing care of Ann, they had sprouted new leaves and were full of red and pink blooms. They had come back to life as she had. Too bad she couldn't pour water on the two mounds at the cemetery and bring Jake and Jonathan back too!

After lunch with Margaret, Ann dropped her off at home. Ann held her elbow and guided her to the door. She wasn't completely blind, but close. She could still make out images and outlines of things and people. High blood pressure had ruptured vessels behind her eyes, and there was nothing the doctors could do about it. Her family was good to take her grocery shopping and such, but she, like Ann, was by herself and lonely most of the time.

"Thanks, Ann. You never did tell me where you are off to," Margaret said, stepping into her doorway.

"I'm off to rescue a teddy bear." Ann answered on her way to the truck.

"A what?" Margaret called.

But Ann was already in the truck looking at her watch. Eleven forty-five: it would be after twelve before she got there.

❊ ❦ ❊

"Did Noah even put snakes and spiders on the ark?" Sammy asked. They had just finished their Sunday morning devotion about Noah and the ark.

"Yes, silly. That's what the Bible said, to take everything clean and unclean." Sadie answered impatiently before Millie could.

"May I go out now? I just know I'll see one of the turtles today."

Millie looked at her daughter. How she had come alive these past three months! She could hardly keep her still long enough to eat, always outside coming back to tell this and that animal story. Sadie named all the regulars. There was Roscoe the Raccoon, Rebecca the Rabbit, Shirley the Squirrel, and Thelma the Frog that lived under the front rock step, Tom and Tammy the Turkeys, and Bonnie the Beaver. Dori the Deer had turned out to be a buck—

the sure sign was when he started growing horns—so she now called him Dandy. She even saw two chipmunks, so of course they were Heidi and Hannibul. Millie was hopeful to see if they built in the outhouse like hers used to. And of course Sadie still talked about Blackie, even though she said she hadn't seen him again since the gate visitor.

"May I go now?"

"Let's eat a bite of lunch first, and then you can go."

"I'm not hungry. We just ate breakfast."

It was almost twelve. Millie realized the kids had slept late and ate only a couple of hours before.

"I want to go too. I want to see the turtles!" Sammy yelled.

As he jumped up, Smoky fell out of his lap and landed with a thud. The kittens, too, had grown this summer. The other three were already curled in balls asleep on the floor at his feet.

"Yes, let's all go. Sadie, didn't you say you saw beavers by the creek the other day?"

"Yes, Bonnie has her family down below the first bog. They've started a dam."

"We'll just go on an adventure then, first to see the beaver dam, then to spy on the turtles, and Sadie can be our guide," Millie said.

"Mama, you'll have to cross the footbridge to get to the beavers."

"No, I won't. Sammy, get your oldest sneakers. We're going for a wade in the creek like you've been wanting to do all summer. I can't think of a hotter day than this to do it."

"All right!" Sammy squealed as he ran off to collect his shoes.

"May we take the camera? If we see a turtle I want to take its picture," Sadie said.

Millie hadn't thought about the camera since they'd been there. She hadn't needed to. "Sure we can," she said. "I'll go get it."

Slipping into the second bedroom, she opened the top drawer, and took out the blue metal box. Millie turned the combination lock until it clicked open. The picture of Sammy was still on top.

She reached under her journal and pulled out the 35 millimeter camera and a handful of photos. In the first one, she was eight years old, the age when her mama moved them in with Luke Turner. Millie knew why her mother didn't marry Luke until she was twelve: it was because she couldn't until her real husband, Millie's daddy, had died.

She took the camera and left the picture of her, her mama and Luke on top of the box. Turning back to the kids, she forgot to close and lock the box. Her thoughts were on the past and the father she barely remembered.

❖ ❧ ❖

Ann pulled her truck to a stop at the chained gate and glanced at her watch. It was twelve-thirty. She didn't hesitate this time as she reached into the glove box and felt for the keys. Taking them, she opened the truck door and went straight to the gate. She willed herself to think of only one thing: she would go in, get Teddy, and leave—no looking around, no remembering.

The key slipped right in and the lock popped open as if it were oiled and used regularly. Jumping back in the truck, Ann pulled the gear stick down to drive and eased forward down the hill and around the two sharp curves. Ann hadn't realized it, but she'd been holding her breath. When the cabin roof came into view, she exhaled, forcing the jailed air from her lungs. The next thing she saw was the gray-colored vehicle.

Ann put on her brakes and stopped. *What in the world is going on here? Who could that be and how did they get in here?* Letting off the brake, she coasted to a stop behind the other vehicle, a million thoughts and questions swirling around in her head.

Immediately she noticed the Texas license plate. Someone obviously picked the locks and broke in. *Why would anyone driving that nice a vehicle need a free place to stay? There certainly isn't anything in the cabin worth stealing.*

Ann didn't even think about being scared as she climbed out of the truck and walked toward the cabin door. Red and white petunias were in full bloom on both sides of the steps. She felt like she had slipped back in time because that was exactly what she had always planted there, right in those same spots.

She stepped up on the first step and took hold of the screen door handle. Pulling it open, she touched her fingers to the knob of the brown wooden door. When she turned it to the right, it didn't open. Reaching into her jeans pocket, she took out the two keys. Slipping the door key into the lock, she turned it and it clicked open. A sudden thought flashed through her head that maybe she should knock, but she pushed the idea aside. There was no way she was going to ask permission to enter her own house! Pushing it gently, she half opened it.

"Hello, anybody here? My name is Ann and I own this place. Hello."

There was no response, so Ann stepped up the other two steps and went inside. She stood in the doorway and looked around. It had been many years since she gazed at this place, but what she was looking at wasn't what she left behind. Colorful green and mauve curtains were on the living room windows. New kitchen curtains had bright red roosters printed on them. On the table was her red tablecloth with fresh daisies in a vase in the middle. There were several boxes on the counter beside the sink—cereal, moon pies, and crackers. A bag on the floor behind the table was full of canned goods.

The fireplace, void of any ashes, now sported a plastic array of flowers. Ann didn't know who had done all this, but she was impressed at how cute and homey it all was even while she was angry at the intrusion. Stepping ahead, she walked behind the table. She knew that was where she left Teddy in the wagon, but neither was there. Her heart started pounding at the thought of Teddy being gone. She was more upset at that than she was of the gypsies who had homesteaded in her cottage.

Hurriedly she rushed to the front bedroom. Even though the windows were open and a breeze blew through, Ann was burning up. She dabbed her sweating face with a tissue from her pocket and blocked out the memory of her son lying on that same bed. Then she saw Teddy, propped up between two pillows as if the most loving of hands had placed him there. There he sat on the floral bedspread, another item of the gypsies. She went straight to him and grabbed the stuffed bear, hugging him to her heart tightly. From somewhere a cat's meow broke the silence. Ann looked around and knew someone had been here for a while; they seemed to be quite settled in. Something rubbed against her leg and she jumped. She looked down and saw a black cat with white feet.

"So that's where the noise came from!" Reaching down, she rubbed the half-grown kitty on the head. "What's your name, little fellow?"

She heard another meow and walked around the corner to the second bedroom. There curled up on the bed were three more kitties, two asleep, and one who looked like he just woke up. Looking around at the rest of the room, she took in the bright blue curtains and matching bedspread. There were clothes stacked in the floor everywhere. Ann laid Teddy down on the bed, walked over to one of the piles, and picked up a small, white tee shirt. Well, there was one thing she knew for sure: there was a child here. She picked up a few more pieces of what looked to be small and medium-size women's clothes.

A snap outside drew her over to the window where she noticed a blue box on top of her mama's antique dresser. The box lid was open, and Ann saw the picture. Immediately she knew who it was: Lindsay with Millie and some strange man. She took the box and sat down on the edge of the bed beside Teddy and the kittens. She doubted her legs would hold her shaking body up another minute. Picking the picture up, she gazed into the face of her only grandchild. Ann's hands were shaking so badly that she could barely grip the photo.

What could this mean? Who would have this picture here? One after another, Ann picked up the pictures. Some were shots of Millie and her mother. There was one of Millie with her daddy, the edges worn where it had been handled so much, and then the one with herself and Jake. Ann saw the next one and gasped. Right there in front of her was a grown Millie, belly huge with child, apparently standing in front of a mirror taking a picture of her own image. Her shirt was raised and there were reddish, purple looking welts all over the mound of flesh. *What in the world?* Then she took out the next photo. It was a picture of a small child, his hair short like a little boy's, but his face was so swollen and bruised that she really couldn't tell.

The next one was a picture of a young girl. Ann knew right away this had to be Millie's child; she was the exact image of her own son Jonathan, who would be this child's grandpa. This picture showed large bruises on the child's arms, as if she had been beaten with a ball bat or something else very hard.

Picture after picture revealed more and more evidence that these children and Millie had been severely mistreated. Ann didn't realize until the tear plopped on the picture that she was crying. She picked up what looked like a child's diary and opened it to the first page.

This diary belongs to Melissa Ann Hampton.

Ann was sure her heart was going to pound out of her chest any minute and fall right to the floor. *It was Millie here with her children! But why keep it a secret? Why hadn't she contacted her?*

She flipped to one of the last pages where an entry had been made. The date at the top of the paper read May 5, 1968.

I know now what I have to do. I have to get Sadie and Sammy away from him. Poor little thing, pounded by his own father's heavy fists. I just knew he'd kill him before Sadie and I could pull him off. Tomorrow, we'll leave, tomorrow.

Ann closed the journal. Putting all the pictures back in the box, she shut the lid and set it back up on the dresser. With the journal held tightly in her hand, she rose and made her way to the front door. She needed to know what had been happening these past twenty-three years to Millie. She closed the door behind her and went to the truck, all thoughts of rescuing Teddy forgotten. Millie and her children would need the bear. He wasn't the one after all who required rescuing; it was her grandchildren who must also be saved.

Ann never saw the noisemaker that had drawn her toward the window and to the box. Blackie did what he needed to do.

> ❧

I watch as the black truck rolls across the fallen chain. Down the hill, it pulls up behind another vehicle. The same older woman unlocks and enters the shack.

Lewis had sensed an intense need for this woman to look at the pictures and read the words in the book. Oh God, he felt sick. The words and pictures from the journal had flashed through his head for days. The lady never saw what slapped the underside of the window to the second bedroom; she didn't see the bear lumber away, out of sight. She couldn't know that Lewis now lay at home in his bathroom floor hugging the toilet. Lewis knew though and felt it all. Those words . . . those horrid things that had been done to this family. Lewis threw up again.

Soon the images were gone and the sickness ebbed. Lewis was again puzzled by the intense urge to protect this woman. He didn't know where or in what form it was coming, but he knew now what was on its way . . . evil. The person the words were written about was coming!

As the lady drove her truck out past the now fastened gate. A deafening growl vibrated through Lewis's head . . .

He was sick again.

With eyes closed, he watches the brake lights of the truck flash on and off . . .

It reminded him of a caution light warning of trouble ahead.

There were no sounds this time, no smells, only silence and a foreboding that weighed his body against the floor for what seemed an eternity.

Doom takes its time . . .

＊ ❦ ＊

Driving over the chain gate, Ann put the truck in park, set the emergency brake, got out, reached down and picked up the heavy links. Pulling the chain around the tree, she slipped the lock through two loops and clicked it shut against the tree.

Back in the truck, she was still shaking but had cooled off. Looking at her watch, she saw it was almost two-fifteen. She could be home by three.

She laid her hand on the tattered journal beside her on the seat. In it were sealed all the secrets she had been longing to know all these years, but she felt horrified as visions of the battered little bodies came into focus. She knew sometimes one was better off not knowing things, but nothing would stop her from finding out exactly who the monster was that had been torturing her family. Yes, *her* family. That thought made her straighten up in her seat and grit her teeth. Ann vowed to make sure they were safe. No one would ever hurt them again, whatever she had to do.

As if to seal the treaty, a loud growl sounded in the distance.

~ Chapter Fifteen ~

*L*et me hold your hand while we cross." Stepping her foot in the cool water, Millie took Sammy's hand.

"Why is it so cold?" Sammy asked.

"Because mountain streams are just that way. Stays cooler up here in the hills. The streams don't have enough time to warm up like the ones in hotter climates. See why I didn't let you wade earlier?"

Sadie didn't really think it was that cold. It wasn't the first time she soaked her feet, though her mama didn't know it. Actually she'd been in the creek almost every day for the last month, so she was used to its chilliness. Climbing up the bank on the other side, Sadie led the way.

"Right up there's the apple tree."

Millie saw it and knew it had been growing bigger all these years, but she really didn't recognize the tree from her childhood.

Across the bottom and into the wooded area, they passed by the first bog. Then on a bit farther, they ran into the creek again. It was just a little way up another crook in the creek to where the beavers were building the dam.

Sadie stopped. "Let's watch from here. If we get too close, we'll scare them off."

Sitting down on a tree that had been felled by the beavers, they waited.

"Where are they?" Sammy asked

"Shush, you have to be quiet." In less than five minutes, Sadie pointed. "Look Sammy, there comes one now, down the creek. And look, he's got a tree limb in his mouth."

Sammy's eyes were fixed on the furry animal, watching as he swam up to a pile of brush in the edge of the creek. Then he watched as the beaver disappeared under the water with his limb.

"That's Bonnie. She's working on her nest. It's twice as big as it was the other day."

In a minute Bonnie swam out of her home and behind her came two smaller beavers.

"Look, she's got babies," Sammy said, speaking softly to his sister.

"Boy, they've grown. I saw them about a month ago but haven't seen them since."

The three of them sat for at least a half hour. They saw five beavers including Bonnie's two babies.

Sammy was getting bored and soon asked if they could go find a turtle. Off they went hand in hand back to the creek ford and across. On through the bottom to the other side and into the pine tree grove they walked.

Millie stopped. "Look kids, isn't this beautiful?"

Millie remembered this place. She and Grandma would come here to pick up pinecones, especially in the fall when it was getting cool. Grandma liked to use the cones to start fires. Millie could almost hear them popping and cracking in the fireplace.

Millie saw the ground was blanketed with the soft pine needles. It looked like a brown carpet had been laid. There were nothing but giant pines as far as you could see to the right. One couldn't even see the tops; they were so tall and thick. The blue sky was concealed completely.

"It's dark in here. Where did the sun go?" Sammy asked.

"It's up there. The trees are just so thick they're blocking the light out."

"Let's hurry up and get out of here."

Sadie scolded her brother. "Don't be such a baby. We have to go through here to get to the other bog."

Sadie led the way out of the darkened, mystic maze. When they had cleared the woods, the sunlight showered down on them, bright and warm. Sadie jumped the small branch and Millie lifted Sammy across. Through the pasture to the other side, they came to more woods. Into them a bit farther, they started to sniff the odor of the bog and see the deadened snags of drowned-out trees. A path worn slick by all the animals traveling back and forth ran along the edge of the bog. But they were smart enough to stay out of the bog.

Up ahead Sadie spotted the rock. It stuck up from the bog waters maybe two or three inches with a flat surface about as big as a dollar bill where a dragonfly perched as it took refuge.

Sadie stopped short and put her finger to her lips. A few days earlier, Sadie heard something roll into the water from the rock and saw the water rippling, but she was yet to see a turtle.

Easing closer, they all three squatted and stared, five, ten, fifteen minutes, but no turtle. All around, eyes were upon them. An aged hoot owl looked down from his seat on a limb not far away. Several deer had bedded not too many steps from them in the tall grass. When the bobcat cried out his warning on the hill behind them, Blackie was there, far enough in the distance to be hidden, but close enough to stand guard over his wards.

"What was that sound? Was it a baby crying?" Sammy tried to be quiet as he whispered his question.

"I'm not really sure. It was probably a mountain cat of some kind."

As Millie realized the danger they might be in, she quietly motioned for them to go.

"No, I want to stay," Sadie said. "I know I'll see a turtle. I just know I will."

"I don't see any turtles." Sammy yawned. "I want to go home and play with my kittens and I'm getting hungry."

"Come on." Millie said. "Let's head back. We'll come and look for them again another day."

"I'm going to stay a while longer. You and Sammy go on back."

"No, it might not be safe out here this far from the cabin."

"Mama, do you know how many times I've been out here? I know my way around and can promise you nothing's going to hurt me out here. The animals are my friends."

Just then they heard a plop as something fell into the water. They saw the snake's tail just as it disappeared under the mossy bog growth.

"Yes, and I guess that snake's your long lost buddy, right?" Millie asked as she backed away from the swamp, pulling Sammy with her.

"As a matter of fact, he is. His name is Sole because God made him to crawl on his belly at the soles of man's feet. He doesn't bother anything, just lies around in the sun and then takes a swim to cool off. I've seen him a bunch of times. He never hurts me. He's just a poor old, brown water snake looking for some peace and quiet on a lazy summer day."

Millie could not help but smile at her daughter and didn't argue with her either. What she said was smart and sensible. Tired of fear forming her every decision, Millie gave in and threw caution to the wind.

"Sadie, be back home in an hour, not a minute later, okay?"

"I will. Let me keep the camera, and then you'll get to see the turtles too."

Millie pulled the camera cord from around her neck and handed it to Sadie. Grabbing Sammy's hand, Millie led him back to the cabin.

Sadie plopped down on the moist, composed ground. She felt the coolness of the shaded bog as the breeze blew across her face. Picking up a stick, she dug and dug, until the stick hit something hard, and she couldn't dig any deeper. Looking at the hole she burrowed, she noticed the smooth surface of part of a stone. Excitedly she began to dig it up. From its edges, she loosened the earth. All the while she scanned back and forth from the bog to the hole. It didn't take long to free the granite from its dampened tomb. With the edges loosened, she wedged the stick up under the rock and pried it up and out of the dirt. When it popped out, it flipped over. Picking it up, Sadie recognized that it wasn't just a rock—it was a bowl fashioned out of stone! It was about the same size as the one she ate cereal in at the cabin. Wiping the dirt off, she saw that it was perfectly rounded, hollowed out and smooth.

She almost forgot about watching for turtles, and the vanished snake was forgotten, but when she looked over at the protruding rock, there one sat, close enough to touch. Its wee shell was no bigger than a quarter. It sat unmoving as Sadie lifted the camera and snapped half a dozen pictures. Just as if it knew the photo shoot was over, it sluggishly labored across the rock to the edge and into the water out of view.

Sadie sat for a long time gazing into the murky water trying to see some sign of him. Realizing it had probably been over an hour since her mama had left, she stood, looped the camera around her neck and took her newfound bowl up the well-worn path to home.

✽ ❦ ✽

Ann had to stop at the highway overlook to calm down. The realization that Millie was right there at the cabin had made her stomach flutter—or was it her heart?—and her hands shake. It was almost three-fifteen when Ann pulled the truck into her driveway.

With journal in hand, Ann went inside the house. She laid the frayed book on the kitchen table, pulled out a chair, and just sat there and looked at it in wonder. Finally she rose, fixed herself a cup a coffee, sat back down, and touched the ragged cover. She heard the mantle clock strike four o'clock. She opened the diary to the first entry.

December 25, 1949

I can't believe Mama finally got me a diary. I wanted one with a lock on it, but it really doesn't matter as long as I've got one. I'll hide it under my mattress, so no one can find it. All the other girls in my class have had one for a while. Anyway, now I have my very own journal and I'm going to write in it every day. Since I turned eleven, funny things have started happening to my body. Mama says it's all normal, but I'm not so sure. I'll just write it all down and try to make sense of it all.

Entry after entry, Ann read the innermost thoughts and ideas of the young granddaughter whose youth Ann was denied. Sometimes there would only be a few words, other times a paragraph or whole page. When Ann got to the entry dated January 8, 1950, she heard the mantel clock again. This time it struck seven. She needed to get up and eat, but she had to read this one more day's writing, for this was the same day she and Jake had found Millie's daddy cold and lifeless on the cabin bed.

January 8, 1950

It's real late and Mama's still locked in her room. I can hear her sobbing into her pillow. She got a phone call around 7:30 that really upset her. She wouldn't answer me or even look at me when I asked her what was wrong. She just told me she had to go to bed, so to her room she went locking the door behind her. I called Luke and he came right home from his second shift job. Mama did let him in for a few minutes. I stood at the closed door but couldn't understand their whispers. I did finally hear Mama tell Luke to go and leave her alone. He came out in a minute. His face was wet with tears. Not saying a word he left. It's almost midnight now and he isn't back and Mama's still crying. I'm going to try and go to sleep now.

Ann let the volume slip out of her hand. Lindsay knew. Someone called and told her Jonathan died. Who could it have been? Someone here in town knew all along where she'd been. *Who could it be? Are they still spying on me, telling Lindsay my daily doings? They probably have a big laugh at an old woman who still goes to the police station every week and takes flowers to the graveyard regularly.*

"Damn Lindsay to hell and her accomplice with her," Ann said out loud. She gritted her teeth. She made her supper and went to bed. She had all the information she could digest for one day.

~ Chapter Sixteen ~

*B*rad eased his 1967 Galaxy 500 into the rest stop off I-85 just outside of Spartanburg, South Carolina. It was almost three o'clock on Wednesday morning. He'd been on the road since eight-thirty Monday morning. He'd swung by his workplace and told Bubba his boss that he needed a week or so off because of family sickness. Bubba didn't like not having more notice since he'd have to drive Brad's truck and make deliveries himself until he could rearrange the schedules.

Brad got out and stretched his arms toward the sky trying to loosen the kinks out of his back. He knew he had to sleep a few hours. Tomorrow would be a big day. According to his calculations, he would be at Grandma's house in three-and-a-half to four hours. Walking to the rest area building, he went inside to use the bathroom and wash up a bit. There was no one there even though there had been many vehicles parked in the lot and six or eight semis with their engines running so the air conditioners could keep the sleeping drivers cool. Next car he got you could bet it would have air conditioning. He swiped his forehead with a couple of wet paper towels. The southern August night was hot, sultry, and sticky, not dry like in Texas.

The restroom door opened and another man about his age stepped in. Brad watched him in the mirror as he entered a stall without saying a word. Brad finished up quickly and headed back to his car. He'd heard all kinds of stories about what happens at rest stops late at night. His suspicious mind beginning to work overtime. He looked around to make sure the man wasn't following him out. He'd hate to have to shoot somebody tonight, but he would if he had to. He slipped his hand into his right pants pocket and touched the 22-Magnum.

Brad knew a thing or two about guns. He'd fired more than one round at those Viet-cons, sneaky foreigners . . . popping out of trees with their bodies covered in leaves or rolling out of a swamp ditch, mud covering everything except the whites of their eyes. Being in Vietnam for almost a year had fueled the already smoldering anger of this abused foster child. (Every time he shot, he pretended it was old man Sig Carter, a foster dad.) He shot and laughed. The army finally sent him home. They determined he was either insane or just plain old evil. His papers were stamped "medical discharge, mental issues." No one knew that but Brad, and no one would find out the truth about where he came from. No one ever would.

Brad opened his car door, stepped inside, and locked his door. He wasn't afraid; he just wanted to sleep in peace without being bothered. He waited until the man came out of the restroom and watched him get into his truck and pull away. Then he pulled the seat lever, letting the seat recline as far as it would go. Laying his head backward on the headrest, he closed his eyes and was asleep in minutes.

❂ ❧ ❂

Ann closed the journal. It was almost midnight on Monday night. She had read Millie's last entry again. With shaking hands, she lowered it onto the table. All day long she read and re-read day after day's events. She felt as if someone had literally thrashed her old body, the way her back ached as she straightened in the chair. She was in knots all day. Reading the brutal, frightful stories of her grandchild's last twelve years had not only made her sick to her stomach, it had caused her heart to ache. Her chest felt as if an anvil iron had been laid on it.

Ann stood up and stretched her tight muscles. What in the world was she going to do now? She knew beyond a shadow of a doubt that the phone call she received from the sweepstakes man had been Brad, so therefore it was only a matter of time before he showed up here on her doorstep.

She walked over to the kitchen door and checked the lock, and then went to the front door and did the same thing. She walked across the room to her bedroom, went to the bed, raised the mattress on Jake's side, and took out the Ruger. That was where Jake had always kept the gun, so she just left it there all these years. She knew it was loaded because Jake always kept it that way. She never in thirteen years felt the need for the security of the cold steel in her hand, but now as she looked down at the pistol, she drew strength from it. It had been many years since she and Jake had shot at tin cans, practicing, but she hadn't forgotten how to use it. It was loaded, but she twirled the cylinder anyway. No way was she going to let that monster Brad near those children ever again. She'd kill him first and answer to her Maker later.

Ann walked back to the kitchen with the gun still in her hand. She laid it on the table and picked up the journal. She opened it to one of the places she'd bookmarked with a scrap of paper.

September 17, 1962

I've just put Sadie to bed. Tomorrow is a school day. I'm so glad she likes it. Her first two weeks of first grade have gone well for her, and Brad has been so much calmer these past weeks. Even though he has come home at lunchtime every day, it hasn't been bad at all. He says he likes our time alone with Sadie in school. I don't know what he'll do or say when I tell him I'm pregnant.

September 18, 1962

It's early. I can hear Brad still snoring in the bedroom; his clock will be going off soon. I don't know whether to wake Sadie up and run, or just stay behind the locked door. This was the worst beating he's ever given me. I can barely see to write these words. But my face doesn't look half as bad as my stomach. When I told Brad last night that we had another baby on the way, due sometime in April, he was very quiet for a little while. Then he stood up and went to the pantry and took out the broom. Slowly he walked toward the kitchen table where I was waiting. Calmly he started talking.

"You planned this, didn't you? You know how happy I've been to have you all to myself these past few weeks. You just did it for spite to hurt me, didn't you? Somebody's always trying to wrong me. How many men did you have to lay with before you got knocked-up? How many?"

Then he whacked me across the head and face so many times I lost count. Next he made me stand up. Time after time he struck me across the abdomen with the broom handle. Then he threw it down and pounded my stomach with his fists. The last thing I remember—before I passed out—was him saying he was going to "beat that baby right out of me." A few hours later I woke up in the floor where he left me, crawled to the bathroom and cleaned myself up as best I could. Then went to Sadie's room and locked myself in. Thankfully it looks like she slept all night.

Again, Ann ran her hand over the gun's cold steel. She needed to go to bed, but knew sleep would waft and wane its way from horror to horror in her mind. She flipped to another bookmark.

April 5, 1963

I brought little Sammy home this morning. He is truly a gift from God . . . Lord knows he is one of His miracles. I truly can't believe he survived being in my womb. Not a day went by after I told Brad I was expecting that he didn't give my rounded belly a few whacks, and he only came to the hospital one time since my labor started. He didn't even stay till Sammy was born. He stopped by the next day and told me it was a damned good thing my baby resembled him or he'd have to "kill the little nuisance"! Said he wouldn't have anybody looking at him and thinking he hadn't "been man enough to sire his own son." I'm still afraid—I'll have to have my eye on little Sammy every minute.

Brad picked us up this morning, brought us home, set my things in the door, and left. Said he had things to do. I'm positive that what he's doing is a girlfriend. He's been staying out late these past few months, and when he comes home he's left me alone in bed with Sadie. The phone rings sometimes and no one is there. After that happens he's out the door.

I don't care; I count it a blessing every time he leaves. As soon as the baby is a little older, I'll try and get away from him again. In the meantime I'll fight to keep my kids and myself alive.

Ann read over Millie's last line. Thinking of the pages that covered the next five years, she knew it was only by the grace of God that Millie and those children had survived. Millie had tried a couple of times to leave Brad, but each time he threatened not only her but the innocent children. The last time she tried, Sammy was almost three. Brad found some packed clothes under Sadie's bed one night. The kids were already in bed asleep. He went to the kitchen, opened the silverware drawer, and took out a long, thin paring knife. Millie was at his heels asking him what he was doing. He grabbed her by the hair and pulled her into Sadie and Sammy's bedroom. In a whisper he told her that if she ever tried to leave him again, he'd cut the children's throats and make her watch them bleed to death. To prove he meant it, he went over and laid the blade against Sammy's little neck, bearing down. Millie could see the sharp edge indenting his soft skin. As Sammy stirred, Brad pulled the lancet back, made a stabbing motion toward Millie, and left the room laughing hysterically.

Ann was mentally devastated from reading these secrets. She ran her hand through her hair as the mantel clock struck one o'clock in the morning. She had to at least lie down for a few hours. Again she not only checked both doors but also made sure the window nails were angled so the windows wouldn't open. She went to the bathroom and ran a tub of water; maybe a hot bath would help her relax. Before stepping out of her clothes, she laid the Ruger on the toilet seat. It was within a hand's reach of the tub.

~ Chapter Seventeen ~

Sadie ran back to the cabin just in time to see her mama step out the side door to call her.

"I'm right here. I saw it! I saw the turtle. I even got some pictures of it. Look what else I found," Sadie said, handing the bowl to her mama.

"Wow! You've had a prosperous afternoon, haven't you?" Millie turned the bowl over in her hands and dusted the dried, crusted earth from its smoothness. "Where did you find this? It looks like an Indian artifact!"

"Right beside where I was sitting at the bog. I just started digging for the heck of it and found it six or eight inches under the dirt."

Sammy walked outside just in time to hear the word "Indian." He grabbed Millie's pant leg. "Are we going to get shot with arrows?'

He was so serious Millie couldn't help but smile. "No, there aren't any Indians here now, but there used to be. I remember Grandpa and I would walk around down in the bottoms after it rained to see if we could uncover any arrowheads. We didn't find one often, but every once in awhile we would. He found part of something that looked a lot like this bowl except, it was larger and not as hollowed out in the middle. I don't know what Grandpa did with that piece, but he gave the arrowheads to Grandma. She took them home and laid them in her kitchen window. She always said Cherokee blood ran through her veins. I don't remember how that heritage was passed down to her, but she always cherished every little piece of Indian relic we found."

Sadie stood quietly listening to her mama talk. Then she spoke up. "So that means we are part Indian?"

"Well, I guess so. I can't imagine why Grandma would say such a thing if it weren't so. But that is so many generations ago I wouldn't count on much Indian blood being in us. I believe with your and Sammy's red-streaked hair, the Irish genes have over-powered the Indians."

At that minute a loud crack of thunder sounded and a bolt of lightning struck the ground not far from them. "Where did that come from? There wasn't a cloud in the sky a while ago!" Millie said as she herded her children inside.

The storm raged on through the late afternoon and by bedtime, the rain was still coming down. When Millie got up the next morning, she pulled the kitchen light string—nothing. The power was off. The storm must have blown out a transformer or something.

Out the window in the early morning daylight, Millie could see water puddles everywhere. Sticks and branches lay all over the soaked yard.

They'd have to go into town and call the power company. What would she tell them? That she was Ann? What if the person she talked to knew Ann's voice? She'd have to do it and take the chance. She also had to find herself a doctor.

Millie let the children sleep longer than usual. She helped Sammy get ready as Sadie dressed, explaining that they needed to get into town to report the power outage. They ate a quick bowl of cereal and left their burrow.

Unlocking the gate, Millie drove over the chain. She locked it back, and the kids swished the branches over their tracks. The routine was familiar to them all by now. First stop: the Taylor's store to use the phone.

"Hey, Mrs. Taylor." Sammy burst through the double doors of the storefront. He didn't wait for her to answer as he went straight for the glass jars that held the store's candy stock. On the way he did slow down to stroke Daisy's furry head. Sammy stood at the jars and looked from one to the other.

"What'll it be, Mister Thomas? Peppermint or an orange slice?" Gladys asked. She always gave him and Sadie a piece . . . free of charge.

Sammy looked back and forth a few more times. "I believe I'll have a peppermint. It lasts longer."

"Smart boy," Gladys said as she took the tongs that lay beside the candy jars, using them to fish out Sammy's candy.

"How about you, Lydia? What'll you have?"

"Peppermint is fine with me, too, thank you."

"How about you, Mildred? Will you have a piece today?"

"No, thanks, but I do need to borrow your phone if you don't mind. The storm last night knocked our power out."

"Storm, you had a storm? We didn't get a drop of rain. Far as I know, the stars shined bright all night long."

Millie thought that was quite odd since she only lived a few miles down the road, but who could predict the weather?

"Sure, go on back to the office and help yourself. I believe I've got the power company's number on a list of important ones on the wall behind the telephone.

"Thanks, Mrs. Taylor," Millie said as she made her way to the back of the store, leaving Sadie and Sammy at the counter with Gladys and Daisy.

In the storeroom that doubled as the office, Millie found the number to Drake Electric. She took a deep breath and picked up the receiver. Her hands were shaking as she dialed the number. When a pleasant voice answered on the other end, Millie almost slammed the receiver down.

"Drake Electric. This is Lisa, may I help you?"

Millie hoped she could mimic an elderly voice, and keep it short and simple. "Yes, I need to report a power outage."

"What name is the account set up in and what is the address?"

"Ann Hampton, 113 Skunk Cabbage Bog Road, off Shaw Road."

"Oh, Mrs. Hampton. I didn't recognize your voice."

Millie didn't answer; she figured the less said the better.

"Now, let's see. Is that the location where there is a gate?"

"Yes."

"I can probably have Marty come out after he gets back from running his meter reading route this afternoon. There have not been any more outages reported, so you'll be first on his list. Will the gate be open?"

Millie mumbled a strained "yes" and politely thanked Lisa and hung up.

What would Millie's story be to this Marty guy? Did he know Ann? Maybe not since Ann hadn't been to the cabin in years. She could just tell him she was leasing the cabin from Ann for the summer.

Millie dabbed at the thin line of sweat on her upper lip before she left the small room. Walking back to the counter where Mrs. Taylor was keeping Sadie and Sammy entertained, she noticed Mr. Taylor wasn't there and asked Gladys about him.

"Where's Mr. Taylor today?"

"Oh, he ran over to Doc's office. His gout is giving him a fit. He's got it real bad in the foot. He could barely walk this morning."

"Who is his doctor?"

"Lewis Townsend. His great-grandpa was the medicine man for a tribe of Cherokees that settled a little ways down the mountain years ago. Story has it they ran and escaped from camps over in Macon County before they were herded off like animals to reservations. His mama was half-Cherokee, so I guess that would make Lewis a fourth, or something like that. I lose count. You'd never know it though by his looks. He's as white-skinned as you and me, real smart too. Did his studying down in Chapel Hill, worked there till Doc Stanley retired, and then he moved back home here to Spartan and took over Old Doc's patients. Been practicing here for close to ten years. There's more doctors now since the hospital was built, but I think Doc Townsend's about the best there is."

"Does he see new patients?"

"Sees anybody who walks through the door. Works all the time. Never did marry that I know of, so doctoring is all he ever does. His office is just a block out on Highway 18. Just turn right at the light, big, old two-story house, sign's out front with his name on it. His grandma, Nyoaka she's the old medicine man's daughter, signed the house over to him when he moved back. She's a full-blooded Cherokee who married a white man, Bud Nettles. They only had one young'un, a daughter. Nyoaka named her Morning Glory. Some say it was for the flower that Nyoaka loved so much; others say it was because her name was Glory and she was born in the morning."

Millie listened as the tale went on and on. Sadie was as interested as she was, and even Sammy was being quiet as he heeded Mrs. Taylor's words.

"Does his family still live with him in the big house?" Sadie asked.

"No family left that I know of except Nyoaka, and yes, she lives in the big house with him. Doc tends to her like a baby. She gets around pretty well to be as old as she is, near ninety or a bit passed it."

"What happened to his mama and daddy?" It was Sammy's turn to question this time.

"Oh my, that's a long story, young man. Romy might be better at telling you that one. He's quite the historian. Here he comes right now. I just saw his truck pull up."

Romy flung his truck door open and stepped out on his good foot. Slowly he hobbled his way to the storefront. Once inside he saw his favorite visitors, little Thomas and Lydia. He'd become really fond of them these past couple of months.

"Well, Romy, what did Doc tell you?" Gladys questioned her husband as she patted him on the back.

"Said to stay off this foot and take one of these here little pills every morning," he said, reaching his hand into the front pocket of his overall britches.

Gladys patted the cushion of the old swivel office chair that set behind the cash register. Its brown leather had long past worn through in the seat and the stuffing was gone, but Gladys sewed him another pillow and stuffed it with foam from the five-and-dime store. It still was an awfully comfortable old chair.

Romy shifted around and sat down in the pivoting seat.

"Don't know how Doc thinks I can stay off this foot. I've got a business to run and animals to feed at the house. Work don't get done by itself, or it never has for me anyway."

"Now Romy, a few days of rest will be good for you, and I can take care of things here. Lord knows Jim's boy Josh next door has offered to help you with the animals plenty of times. I hate to tell you, dear, but the world will still turn even if you are sitting on your butt."

Millie, Sadie, and Sammy all smiled as they listened to Mr. and Mrs. Taylor banter back and forth.

"Don't mind him, young'uns. He gets ornery when things ain't going to suit him." Mrs. Taylor said. "Mildred, was one of the kids needing to see the Doc?"

"No, they're fine. I just need to get a refill for a prescription."

"Well, why don't you run on up to Doc's and the young'uns can stay here with us. Romy can answer Thomas's questions about the Doc's family."

"Yes, I want to hear more about the Indians," Sammy said, excitement showing in his voice.

"Are you sure it's okay to just pop in at the doctor's office?" Millie asked.

"Sure am. That's what everybody does. You might have to wait a spell, but he'll get to you," Gladys said.

Millie knew she had to take the plunge and do it. How much of the truth would she have to tell? And yes, it would be good if the kids weren't with her, for then she wouldn't have to explain them to the doctor and lie even more.

"Okay, if you're sure you don't mind. I'll run up there and see if I can get in quickly. We've got to be home though for the power company repairman who's coming right after lunch."

"Mr. Taylor, will you tell us what happened to the doctor's Indian family?" Sammy asked, not worrying one bit about staying with the Taylors.

Sadie on the other hand was a little troubled about them being away from their mama. She was afraid Sammy might slip and tell the Taylors something he shouldn't. Being around people made her nervous even if she did like them.

"I'll be back as quick as possible, okay?"

Reluctant, Sadie shook her head yes, but her eyes pleaded no.

"I'll be back soon, kids. Don't talk Mr. Taylor to death, Thomas. Okay?" Millie said as she patted Sammy's head. She didn't look Sadie in the eye. She knew her daughter would be anxious about her leaving. Millie left the store walking hurriedly, so she could get back to them as quickly as possible.

"So you want to hear about the Indians, do you?" Mr. Taylor said while patting Sammy's head. "Let's all sit down."

"Now, let me see. Way back, nigh on a 130 years ago in the summer of 1838, the government started rounding up all the Indians from Georgia all the way up through Tennessee to Arkansas clear to Oklahoma. Congress called it The Indian Removal Act. Said there was too many of them and they were taking up too much of the white people's land. I never did figure how the government thought it was white folk's land when the Indians had been settled on it since the American Revolution. Anyway, headed up by that traitor Andrew Jackson, the army herded up every man, woman and child who even resembled an Indian. Kept them pinned up like a bunch of wild ponies till late fall. Then they started marching them all the way to Oklahoma. Government said they had special land there to give them. A reservation is what they called it."

"You mean they made the Indians leave their homes and land?" Sadie cut in.

"Just like we did. Right, Sadie?" Sammy hung his head in sadness. He was glad he was away from his daddy, but sometimes he did miss his more modern house with the inside bathroom.

Sadie laid her hand over Sammy's and hoped Mr. Taylor hadn't heard Sammy call her by her real name.

Romy did hear the slip of Sadie's name but didn't question them about it. He just continued with his story. He suspected there was more to their history than he knew, but he liked them anyway.

"When it was all said and done, over seventy thousand Indians had been driven to some worthless piece of land west of the Mississippi. Folks say that the march through the winter of '38 killed one out of every four of those Indians. They were pushed too hard, half frozen, sick, and starved to death."

Sammy was looking sadder by the minute.

"Thomas, why don't you go over to the cooler and get us a pop?" Romy thought he'd better get the boy's mind on something else or he'd be crying any minute.

"Bring me one of them grape sodas and your sister one too."

"Mr. Taylor, did the doctor's family get driven away too?" Sadie asked.

"Yeah, let me tell you how Doc Townsend told it to me. Doc's great-great-grandpa lived up in Macon County in the western mountains near a town called Murphy. He hid out in the woods for as long as he could with his wife and two young'uns. The soldiers finally caught sight of them late one night as they were patrolling, rounding up the strays just like cattle. Tomeka was his name. He was the local tribe's medicine man and he knew that what was happening to his people was very bad medicine.

"Not far into the trip, a fever broke out among his people. The army would not let them stop, so that he could harvest the fever-breaking herbs that he needed to make them well. Soon his wife and young daughter were plagued with the fiery heat. If someone was too sick to walk, they had to be carried or pulled by someone else. If no one would or could, the soldiers would just simply shoot them. They couldn't risk leaving them lying and possibly getting well. They wanted every breathing redskin, as they called them, across that Mississippi River."

"Oh no, what happened to his wife and little girl?" Sadie asked, her eyes wide, the grape pop untouched in her hand, no thoughts of her mother now.

"Tomeka broke two strong branches off a tree and tied a few feed sacks around them to make a stretcher to lay his sick wife and child on. Tomeka pulled them for two days before the little girl died in her mama's arms. Late that same day his wife died too. Tomeka continued to pull the stretcher until they stopped for the night, and then Tomeka and his six-year-old son Wahya stayed up the entire night digging a grave to place them in. The soldiers would have made him leave them on the side of the road that day if they'd known they were dead.

"Legend has it that Tomeka was always saddened that he wasn't able to bury them where their spirit had left them, as was Indian custom. He just couldn't let them lie on the side of the road where any kind of wild animal could get to them. He laid them together, and as each shovel of dirt hit their wrapped bodies, a blood-curdling moan growled and groaned from his inner soul. It was a sight the young son Wahya would never forget. Even at that age he vowed to someday return to the land of his people. His father's spirit died right there on the road along with his wife and child.

"Tomeka did what he could for his people over the years. He worked his medicine and taught Wahya all the ways of the medicine gods, but his heart was always sad. When Tomeka died, Wahya was twenty-five years old. He took his new wife Snowy Dove and simply walked out of the reservation late one dark night. The sentry never saw them; he was sound asleep. You see, Wahya had fixed him his special relaxing tea, as he always did, but this time it had a little more kick to it."

Sadie was glad Sammy had gotten bored with listening and had taken his pop over to the door where Daisy lay. There he sat rubbing her soft fur as Sadie sat wiping the tears from her streaked cheeks.

"Go on, Mr. Taylor. What happened then?"

"Wahya walked for many months through eight states, stopping to do odd jobs and letting Snowy Dove rest. They had both unwillingly taken on the dress of the white man, knowing they'd be herded back to Oklahoma by the army if seen in their Indian clothes. Finally they arrived in the mountains of The Great Smokies. They found their homeland, which was by now populated with modern little towns full of white people.

"Their hearts were heavy as they roamed the hills. It was as if their souls were searching, longing for the promised land. Wahya's dreams told him to keep goin', he'd know when he found his new home. Story has it that he stumbled on a small Indian village late one afternoon down the mountain a bit from here. They were Indians who had either hid from the army years ago, or who had escaped like they had, forming their own little community right there on the banks of Brush Creek.

"Walking into the village, Wahya saw a gray wolf standing on the hill above the village as if it was watching, guarding. Wahya and the wolf stared at each other for a long while before the wolf turned and walked off. Wahya, whose name means wolf, never saw the gray ghost again, but he felt as though the wolf was welcoming him to his new home. Finally he knew this was where he was supposed to be. His spirit was settled.

"When he and Snowy Dove walked into the village, they were greeted warmly by Mountain Lair. He said to Wahya, 'Medicine man finally here. Come quickly, everyone waits at Still Water's house.'

"Not knowing what else to do, Wahya and Snowy Dove followed Mountain Lair. Inside a small wood shanty, Mountain Lair walked through the room full of people to the bedside. Lying there upon the bed were a woman and little girl. Wahya stepped back, and flashes from all those years ago crossed his senses: his mama and little sister, so sick, so still, so dead. Then another set of faces, an unknown woman and young girl and small boy each with red and golden streaked hair. . . . . . then the vision was gone.

"A thin film of sweat broke out on Wahya's brow as he surveyed the scene before him. The color was not good on either woman or child. Stepping to the bed, he reached down and touched the child's forehead, burning hot. This movement caught the attention of a man sitting at the bedside. Raising his head, he looked as near death as the woman and child. When he spoke, it was in Cherokee. I can't speak the words, but Doc Townsend said the words were, 'please heal my family.' How they all knew Wahya was a medicine man, we'll never know.

"Wahya immediately threw the thick woolen blankets off the two sick ones. Then he told everyone to please leave and open the windows. It was hotter than a bed full of coals in that-there place. He then took the pouch from his side and took out two or three different kinds of herbs. Handing them to Snowy Dove, he asked her to brew them in two cups of water for one hour. She went to the wood stove, saw a metal pot and poured the water into it. She added kindling to the already hot coals. Meanwhile Wahya had told the man at the bedside to bring him cold water and rags.

"All that evening and into the night and next day, Wahya applied the cold rags to the woman and child's fevered bodies. All the while he and Snowy Dove held their heads up enough to let every possible drop of the homemade tonic slip down their throats. On the morning of the third day, the little girl opened her eyes and said, 'I'm hungry.' Later that day the woman roused too.

"Wahya had not slept in three moons. He had doctored over the two as if he was desperately trying to bring his own mama and little sister back to life. He worked on those strangers as his own father had worked his medicine on all those immigrants at the reservation in Oklahoma. Not knowing them had meant little to Tomeka; he simply did what the gods had gifted him to do, just as Wahya was now doing. When Wahya finally lay down to rest, a vision of the woman, girl and boy with the red and golden hair came to his mind. He knew the future would unfold their identities. He was seeing what was to come, and he smiled.

"Wahya and Snowy Dove were accepted as part of the community of just over fifty Cherokee men, women, and children in that tiny village. They lived there till they died back in the late 1800s. Legend has it that Wahya died on the edge of a bog close to the village, so that's where they buried him. That's what some Cherokees believe, you know, that you should be buried where your spirit departs your body."

By this time, Sammy was back listening and quickly asked, "But what about Doc Townsend's mama and daddy? Where are they?"

As Sadie continued to listen, all she could think about was the bowl she dug up on the bank of the bog. Could their cabin be in the same place as Wahya's village?

Romy continued his story.

"Wahya and Snowy Dove had only one child. They named her Nyoaka which Wahya said meant independent. Wahya said his daughter would grow to depend on no one. She would never live herded into a reservation like cattle. She would be free of spirit and filled with pride for herself and her ancestors, and he raised her like that.

"Snowy Dove said the name Nyoaka meant the horizon sun, for every time she looked at the child she saw hope for a fresh start, a new time for her people, a promise of better days to come. In Nyoaka she saw peace for the day, saying, 'sometimes that is all we can hope for, just one new horizon at a time.'

"Nyoaka participated in the white man's world, but every day Wahya and Snowy Dove taught her lessons from their people, their ways, and customs, such as how to hear the whisperings of the pines, the silent speaking of the trout in the cool mountain streams, and the mysteries that the hills hold from the valleys to the cresting tops.

"And that Nyoaka, she turned out to be quite a young lady. A real beauty too. Heck, for ninety she's still a looker, but don't tell Gladys I said that, okay kids?"

Gladys had walked away to help some customers and was out of hearing range.

"So Nyoaka is Doc Townsend's grandma who lives with him?" Sadie said.

"Yes, she's lived here in Spartan her entire adult life. Married Bud Nettles, a full-white man from here in town. They only had one young'un, Morning Glory. Most called her Glory. But not Nyoaka, she always called her Morning Glory. Morning Glory could always be found, even as a small child, out early roaming the fields. She'd bring her mama back a big bunch of those morning flowers almost everyday, along with this root or that herb or something for their medicine pouch. Every one of them had the gift—Tomeka, Wahya, Nyoaka, and Morning Glory, and of course Doc Townsend. He's the only one with formal schooling in medicine, but I reckon he'd do just fine without it."

"So where are Doc Townsend's mama and daddy?" Sammy chimed in, getting a little bored with all the storytelling and wondering when his mama was coming back.

Romy still had to finish his tale. "Sad, sad happening: Morning Glory married Dennis Townsend and again, only one child was brought into the union—the doc. Both of them died while Doc was still in Chapel Hill. They were hiking up in the mountains on part of the original trail that Morning Glory's Grandpa Wahya had walked all those years before. Morning Glory tripped, breaking her ankle, and being several miles from anyone, Dennis tried to carry her out. He had a heart attack. Close to a week later someone found them while hiking, her head lying in his lap and his in hers. She maybe could have crawled out, but it didn't even look like she tried. Just laid right down with Dennis and either thirsted to death or died of a broken heart, one or the other."

"Oh, my gosh, how awful," Sadie said.

"The Cherokee call the trail Nunahi-Duna-Dlo-Hilu or Trail Where They Cried. Yeah, that Trail of Tears has claimed way too many of Doc's people. All he and Nyoaka have left are each other."

By this time over an hour had passed. Romy had not only Sadie and Sammy at his feet listening, but three of the locals had pulled up straight-backed chairs to hear the story they'd all heard many times before. Romy was known for his storytelling, and folks knew that most of what he said was true, or as close to the truth as he knew anyway. Now everybody knows that any truly good storyteller has to stretch things a bit, but Romy kept his stories as close to the gospel as possible.

"Tell them about their spirits, Romy," Davis Wheeler spoke up, mouth half full of peanuts and pop.

"When Indians are young, especially the boys, they are taken out into the woods and left alone. They wait for a vision of some sort. In this vision they will see an animal of one kind or another. This animal will be their guardian spirit. The Cherokee believe that this spirit will help them cross to the other side when they die," Romy said.

"Is the other side Heaven, Mr. Taylor?" Sammy asked.

"Well I reckon so, Thomas. Ain't no other good place to go that I know of when we die."

"What about the girls, Mr. Taylor? Do they see this vision too?" Sadie asked.

"I believe that some girls choose to be left in the woods the same as the boys. But some are too scared, so the medicine man gives them some sort of potion that makes them see such visions."

"Mama says we have guardian angels watching over us. She says they are God's angels. Do you think animals can be angels?" Sammy questioned further.

"I don't see why not, sonny. I reckon God can make anyone or anything whatever He wants them to be." Romy answered with a click of his tongue.

The small crowd started breaking up then. Sadie couldn't help but close her eyes as a picture of Blackie crossed her mind. *Was Blackie her vision? Was he her guardian spirit?*

~ Chapter Eighteen ~

*M*illie left the store feeling a little shaky about deserting Sadie and Sammy. She knew it was better this way. There would be fewer questions, and she wouldn't have to cover with so many lies.

She got in the car and headed up Main Street turning right on Highway 18. Not quite two blocks ahead on the right was the house with the small wooden sign dangling over the front door: Doctor Lewis Townsend, M.D.

Millie sat quietly gazing at the historic structure. Whoever built this house must have been really rich. It stood two stories with a very high-pitched roof that could have housed a third floor. On both sides of the roof were cathedral or gazebo structures. Windows were on all sides of the towers. Millie could envision seats all around the circle, places to relax and read or stare out at the majestic mountains and lowly valleys. It was sort of strange, but the house was painted pale lavender, trimmed in snow white. The front door was solid glass. A rock-paved walk led to the large, covered porch and some type of vine had crawled its way up the wrought iron columns that held the porch roof up. The climbing foliage had large leaves and purple blooms, and on closer inspection Millie saw long purple beans on the vine. The rock walk was lined with a tiny purple flower (Millie believed it was called thrift), and white petunias were overflowing the wooden boxes beneath the windows. The house had a loveliness about it that drew a person in; inviting warmth poured from it.

Millie wiped her sweaty palms on her slacks, took her purse with the almost empty medicine bottles, and stepped out on the street and toward the house.

As Millie approached the front door, she again noticed the strange bean vines and saw a white wicker swing at the end of the veranda with several more wicker chairs and rockers scattered about. There was a hand-woven rug placed at the front door, its flower design pattern done in a sweet lavender. Standing on it, Millie knocked on the glass door. She knew it was a doctor's office, but couldn't bring herself to just walk into what looked like someone's home.

In just a second Millie heard a cheerful, "Come on in."

Turning the knob, she stepped inside. A voice beckoned her directly toward the large walnut desk in what appeared to be a formal parlor. A huge fireplace took over the entire back wall, and its mantel was made from the same rich walnut grain as the desk.

Millie's eyes turned to the happy voice behind the desk. She saw a stout, little lady of perhaps sixty with salt-and-pepper hair pulled high in a bun above a face that looked as nice as the voice sounded.

"Good morning! What can we do for you today?" the lady asked.

Millie noticed that not a single person was waiting in the bright paisley patterned chairs.

"Hello. I'm new in town and need to get some prescriptions renewed."

"Of course, that shouldn't be problem. Let me just get you to fill out a bit of information."

Reaching behind her on a shelf filled with papers, the lady pulled out three sheets and a clipboard with an ink pen attached to it by a thin chain. Handing it to Millie, she introduced herself. Board in one hand, she stuck the other hand out to shake Millie's.

"Welcome to town. My name is Lafayette. Just fill out these few pages and Doc Townsend will see you shortly. He's got old Mr. Snyder in there, but he shouldn't be too long."

Millie took the papers and turned to sit in one of the armchairs covered with soft padded material. Millie couldn't help but notice how lovely everything around her was. Nervously she started on the papers. She couldn't use her alias because her real name was on the medicine bottles, and eventually one of the children would come down with something and need to see the doctor anyway, so she need not try to pretend here. Millie was thinking as if they'd be here on the mountain forever.

The first sheet asked for general information, name, address; she put the cabin address. She didn't put anything on the insurance line since she knew it would show up at Brad's workplace and he'd be able to track her here.

The next page was health history questions. Millie hated writing the name of the cancer—carcinoma. Beside "Have you ever had any surgeries?" she checked yes.

The third page wanted to know whom to contact in case of an emergency. Oh my God, what was she to do? Leave it blank or put her Grandma Ann's name down? In the end her children's well-being won over. She wrote in the blank space, Ann Hampton 919-555-0107.

Just as Millie was signing her name, she saw a lady entering the parlor from the double French doors on the other side of the room. The woman stood inside the doors, one hand holding the top of a hand-carved cane. She was dressed in a solid black dress that fell below her knees, black stockings, and high-topped shoes. Through the glass, the lady looked as intently at Millie as Millie looked at her. The woman had to be the doctor's grandmother. Millie could see the thin braid of her grayed hair. The only color on the woman was a bright purple string woven into her braid. Though her skin was not wrinkle-free, it had a dark richness about it; and it was easy to recognize she was very much of Indian descent.

Millie knew she shouldn't stare but couldn't help herself. Then the woman turned the doorknob and walked slowly toward Millie. For a woman who was in her nineties, she moved quite gracefully. As she approached, she never lost eye contact with Millie.

The woman reached out her free hand and took Millie's in hers. "I am Nyoaka."

Millie pressed her hand in Nyoaka's and spoke. "Hello, I'm Millie." She didn't even attempt to lie to this woman about who she was. She knew better for some reason.

"You have much pain and sadness on your face. The eyes are the mirror to the soul and showplace of the heart. Everything you are or feel can be seen in the eyes. Your sorrows have been many, but you must be brave, and not fear the evil ones. Two different demons will come back and you must battle one as hard as the other. I am glad you are finally here. My grandson and I have waited for very many moons for you. It is good that you have finally come. My body has grown weary waiting for the peace, healing, uniting and the final resting you will bring."

With that, the woman called Nyoaka squeezed Millie's hand, turned, and walked back through the double doors shutting them behind her.

Millie's heart pounded in her chest and she sat back down in her chair.

"Well, I'll be dogged," said Lafayette. "Nyoaka hasn't spoken to a patient since Doc's been here practicing. She stands and looks through those doors but never comes out to greet anyone. What was that she was saying about the evil one? We'll have to tell Doc about this. Strange, very strange."

Millie stood back up then and took the clipboard to the desk, handing it to Lafayette.

She glanced at all three pages and then asked, "No insurance or employment information? Being new in town, I guess you haven't gotten that far yet. Heard the pipe plant is hiring if you're looking."

Millie felt the office assistant was worried about payment, so Millie took out her billfold and asked her how much the office visit was because she'd be paying in cash.

"Just wait till the doc's finished. Depends on how much time he spends with you, but knowing him, it will be the minimum."

Millie put her billfold back in her purse, and turned to sit back down. Glancing at the windows of the French doors, Millie saw only a silhouette of the woman Nyoaka.

In about five minutes the door on the other wall opposite the French doors opened and out popped a slight little man all bent over bow-backed.

"Thank you, Doc. Sure hope this tonic helps, can't hardly get out of the bed in the mornings with this rheumatism."

"Mr. Snyder, I think you'll feel much better in a couple of days. Take the aspirin. Rub the tonic on your stiff joints, and remember . . . the tonic's for rubbing not drinking."

"I know, I know. Gave that up years ago, but can't say I don't have a hankering for a snort now and again."

The man who Millie presumed to be Doctor Lewis Townsend threw his head back and laughed a deep-down heartfelt chuckle. Putting his hand on Mr. Snyder's shoulder, Doc followed him to the door.

"Can you put this on my bill? Won't get my check till the third."

"You bet, Mr. Snyder. Let me know if you're not moving better in a couple of days."

"I'll do it, Doc, thanks."

With that, the stooped little man left the office holding the wooden rail as he climbed down the four front steps.

Turning toward the desk, Doc spoke to his assistant.

"Okay, Laf." He knew she hated the condensed version of her name, but he always called her that every day just to pick on her. He loved her like a treasured aunt, and not a day went by when she didn't scold him for calling her Laf. "Who have we got next?"

Looking down at the clipboard Lafayette said, "This is Melissa Ann Madison and she needs to see you about refilling some prescriptions."

Dr. Townsend noticed right away that the woman sitting in the waiting room was very nervous. Her hands were folded tightly in her lap and there was a weary look in her eyes. A flicker of another set of eyes like hers spun in his head. He felt the urge to pat her on the head as a master would sooth a new puppy, one who had been mistreated by his old owner. She was quite pretty, dark brown hair falling to her shoulders, with the sunlight through the windows bouncing off streaks of auburn. She anxiously pushed her hair behind one ear. Lewis didn't usually sum up new patients like this, but something about this young woman pulled at a part of him deep down that he thought he'd never feel- his soul, his spirit, or maybe his heart?

As he approached the chair where Millie sat, she stood up. Offering her hand, she said, "Please call me Millie."

Taking her hand, an odd sensation came over him. His grandmother's words echoed in his head: "You will be able some day to help one who is now walking their own trail of tears. Then your heart will be free."

Lewis knew his grandmother was very wise, but when she talked to him of this vision of hers, he wondered if her age wasn't catching up to her. Nyoaka knew he felt a tremendous amount of guilt about his parents' deaths while they walked a section of their ancestors' Trail of Tears. He should have sent out a search party when he didn't hear from them for four days, but he knew it wasn't unusual for his parents to hike and stay in the wilderness several days at one stretch. Still this time he'd sensed something was wrong. He'd had those visualizations about his Great-Grandfather Tomeka on the trail with his sick child and wife, but as usual Lewis tried to push those kinds of intuitions away, he'd had to learn the hard way the meaning of regret, and the shortcomings of logic alone. Lewis had been thrust into a world of happenings impossible to prove.

When the call came eight days after he last talked to his parent's, he knew his senses had been trying to tell him the truth. Ever since then, he trusted and acted on these gut feelings that his grandmother called visions, whether it involved his own life or the lives of his patients.

Realizing he was still holding the woman's hand, Lewis reluctantly released it.

"So, Millie it is then. Come on back to my office."

Before the doctor realized what he was doing, he reached for Millie's hand again to help her up from the chair.

Not being used to the assistance of anyone, Millie stood, not taking his outstretched hand but following him. As the doctor passed Lafayette's desk, she stopped him. "You're not going to believe this, but your grandmother came out and talked to Melissa. What she said didn't make a whole lot of sense to me, did it to you Melissa?" Lafayette said. "Something about sorrows and evil one, and that she and you had been waiting a long time for her . . ." She nodded toward Melissa. ". . . to get here."

Millie didn't say a word as Laf talked about her as if she wasn't there. What could she say? That the old woman had, to a certain degree, made complete sense to her? It was as if the lady called Nyoaka could read right into her soul, past, present and future.

Knowing she had to respond, Millie simply said, "Your grandmother seems like a very sweet woman. It was interesting meeting her." Millie couldn't bring herself to outright lie to Lewis Townsend, so she danced around the truth.

"Well, you must be pretty special Melissa Ann Madison if Grandmother spoke to you. She only says what has to be said, even to me."

As Lewis Townsend headed toward his office, he didn't question the lady who called herself Millie any more about her conversation with his grandmother. He could only imagine what it had been about. As much as he wanted to believe Nyoaka's declaration—he was trained to trust the facts, but . . . somewhere deep down, he knew the truths. He knew his grandmother was as sane as he was; he just didn't know how to explain it all. But he couldn't altogether revert to or count on the old ways. He was much too modern to completely trust the magic, or was he?

"Come on, Millie. Let's see what I can do for you."

Once inside, Dr. Townsend asked her to sit in the only chair in the room. Then he eased himself down on the stool with wheels on it and took up the clipboard Lafayette handed him containing Millie's information. He looked it over. As he read, the furrows between his eyes deepened and the wrinkles at the corner of his eyes became more deeply indented. After a few minutes, he slipped the reading glasses off his nose and swiveled the stool toward Millie.

"So you need prescriptions refilled?"

"Yes, two of them."

"Do you have your bottles?"

Fishing inside her purse, Millie took out the two pill bottles and handed them to him.

After looking at them, he turned back to her and looked straight into her eyes. "The surgery you listed on this paper was to remove a cancerous tumor, right?"

Millie nodded her head. *Yes.*

"When was the surgery and where was the tumor located?"

Before she could answer, he had another question. "What was your prognosis?"

Millie cleared her throat and wiped her sweaty palms on her black pants. Looking towards the doctor, but not directly into his eyes, she spoke. "The tumor was as large as a lemon and was right here at the base of my brain," Millie said. Reaching her hand behind her head, she felt the ridge where the stitches had been.

"My doctors felt sure they got the entire thing, but warned me that this kind of cancer can pop up again anywhere. That's why they wanted me to take the little green pill. Some studies showed it helps stop recurring tumors. I don't need the other pill for pain very often, but sometimes the exposed nerves rub against some-thing and it hurts pretty badly." Millie rubbed the back of her neck.

Again Dr. Townsend looked down at Millie's papers. "So it has been almost sixteen months since your operation. Have you been closely monitored by your doctors in Texas?" He saw the address on the bottles.

"No, I haven't seen a doctor in almost a year now. That's why I need the refills."

"May I see the location of the removal?"

"Yes, right here," Millie said, turning sideways in her chair and facing away from the doctor.

Lewis felt the area around the incision, examining the location thoroughly and all the surrounding tissue including her neck. Then he sat down and again looked her straight in the eyes.

"I want you to have a full-body exam and x-rays. Your doctors are right. Some tumors come back, and the key is finding them early and removing them. Will you be going back to Texas to see your regular physician?"

This took Millie a little off-guard; again she couldn't lie to him.

"No, I won't. I'm not sure where I'll settle, but hopefully it will be close by here."

"I'm going to give you a two-month refill. In the meantime I want you to either let me schedule some tests for you, or if you have another doctor in mind, let him do it. Either way for your own good, it is imperative that you see a doctor regularly."

Millie already knew what the doctor was telling her was true; she was told this by her regular doctor in Texas the last time she saw him a few weeks after her surgery. But after the fit Brad had thrown when she returned, she knew she couldn't go to the doctors as much as they wanted. Brad constantly told her she was better, the cancer was gone, and to stop hanging onto it expecting any more sympathy from him . . . as if he ever gave her any in the first place. Anyway, every time there was a doctor's visit, there was money to pay, and God knew Brad Madison didn't want to spend a dime on anyone but himself.

"Let me know if you want me to set up the tests. I advise you to have them done sooner than later. You've already been too long without a thorough exam."

When he finished filling out the prescriptions, he handed the paper to her. He once again looked into her eyes, searching deeply. He wanted to ask her many questions but knew he shouldn't. He was a medical doctor not a shrink.

Before he looked away, the words of his grandmother's vision came to him again: You will find the peace you desire when she comes to you. She has survived her own trail of tears, so far, but will need you to lead her the rest of the way through. She will lead you on the path to your own future, the future of true happiness you've waited for your whole life.

True, he was feeling something different about the woman, but he just wasn't sure about his grandmother's words of the future or if this was the woman of whom she spoke. He knew the old stories of visions and had experienced the truth in them, but he just wasn't sure a vision could lead him to the right person, a person who would understand him or the ways of his people, or the guilt he felt from his parents' deaths on that cursed trail, the trail that had been bringing his family pain and suffering for one hundred and thirty years.

A little girl lies on a rickety stretcher beside her mother ...

Lewis shook his head.

"Pardon me . . . now, where were we?"

Taking the paper from the doctor's hand, Millie rose to leave. "I will call you about the exam soon." Still, she needed to ask him one more thing. She locked her eyes into his. "Doctor Townsend, could you please not tell anyone I was here, and ask your secretary to do the same? I know that sounds strange, but it is very important for me not to be found. I promise you I haven't done anything wrong; it isn't the police who are looking for me."

Millie's eyes never wavered from his as she voiced her plea. Lewis had never seen such anguish on anyone's face before. His feelings were right; there was much pain in this woman's heart.

He knew it might not be the right thing to do, but nodded his head yes anyway as he asked, "What should we call you here at the office?"

"Mildred Burke, and thank you so very, very much."

As Millie turned to leave, Lewis had to resist not reaching out and touching her. He watched her as she opened the office door, walked through it and out the front door.

Lewis moved from his stool to the chair where Millie sat. It was still warm from her body heat. He leaned back, rested his head on the chair, and closed his eyes.

Men, women, and children half-clothed walk in the snow, their feet wrapped only in rags, some carried or dragged by another person. Different faces loom. None are the same except for their eyes—they all hold the same pain and hopelessness. They are as sheep being led to the slaughter.

Melissa Madison held a glimpse of that lost look in her eyes too.

When Lewis Townsend was twelve years old, he was ready to be initiated as were his ancestors before him. Going into the woods, he watched for his vision. He awaited the journey to manhood. Late on the third day, the giant black bear appeared to him. As they faced each other, Lewis could see into the bear's eyes, and what he saw was the procession of his people being led to their new home in Oklahoma along the Trail of Tears. But he not only saw each of their faces, he also understood the stirrings of their souls and the desperation in their hearts. He felt his great-great-grandfather Tomeka's agony as he watched his wife and daughter die on that trail. He felt the numbness in his own arms as his grandfather dug their graves that cold, dark night so many, many years before. He sensed the presence of Wahya, his great-grandpa, as a six-year-old child watching his father bury his mommy and baby sister. He could perceive the child's emotion of loss and the years ahead as the child became a man, a man who intended every day to go back to the heritage of his people, home to the mountains, back to the Indian's way not the white man's. Lewis Townsend felt all their pain.

❀ ❦ ❀

When Lewis opened his eyes, the roaring in his head stopped. He slowly rose from the exam room chair. He'd not felt the power of his vision quest this strongly in many years. His hands were shaking and his legs were weak as he stood. When he looked up, his grandmother was standing inside the door.

"Your guardian spirit—the bear—will help you protect her." That was all she said as she slowly with cane in hand walked away from him.

God only knew what was in store for them in the coming days. Lewis knew something profound was happening, and he knew it was going to be life changing. He just wasn't sure how. He did, however, know he had to protect this woman, with or with out the spirits' help.

Walking out to Lafayette's desk, he took the papers containing Millie's history. Handing them to her, he spoke with authority. "Laf, change the name at the top of these records to Mildred Burke and forget the name Melissa Ann Madison. Pretend you never heard it." Stepping back into his office, he closed the door behind him.

Lafayette thought his request was very peculiar, but she knew there must be a good reason for it. Without hesitation, she transferred all the information from the page with the real name on it to another sheet. This time the name at the top was Mildred Burke. Melissa Ann Madison was marked through and thrown in the trash. Lafayette was loyal and trusted Doctor Lewis Townsend completely.

When Millie sat down in the car she didn't attempt to move for a few minutes. Her thoughts were racing as she replayed the encounter with Doctor Townsend. Now someone else knew her real name, not just the pharmacist. This made Millie really nervous, yet something inside told her that her secret was safe there in that house. Taking a deep breath, she cranked the car, and headed back to the store to collect her children. She must get the prescription filled and rush home to let the electric repairman through the gate. It was impossible to shake the strange feeling she had. Too much stress for one day . . . too many things to think about . . .

Eyes closed and thinking of the big black bear back at the cabin, Sadie heard the store door open. She looked up when she heard Sammy holler.

"Mama! You're not going to believe it, but Mr. Taylor said animals can be our guardian spirit, just like your grandpa told *you*." Sammy's eyes were dancing. He was alive with mystery and intrigue from the good storytelling he just heard. Sadie, on the other hand, looked a bit downhearted.

"Are you all right?" Millie asked, walking to stand beside her daughter.

Looking up into her mama's face, she couldn't hide the sorrow. "I'm okay, just sad for those Indian people. I want to meet the doctor. Did you see him and his grandmother? What did they look like? Did they talk like us? When can we go see them?"

Millie was a little taken aback by the seriousness of her daughter. What in the world had Mr. Taylor told them?

"May we go to their home now?"

"No, not today. I have to get my prescription filled, and then get back to let the electric company through the gate. I did meet

Doctor Townsend and his grandmother Nyoaka. They were both very nice, though the grandmother said some strange things to me.

"Do they look like Indians?"

"The grandmother did. She was dressed very old-fashioned in a long black skirt. Her clothes looked similar to ours, but her gray hair was braided Indian style with, I believe, a purple ribbon woven into it. Her skin had an olive tint to it and her cheekbones were high and proud. She spoke to me in English, not Indian."

"What about the doctor?"

"No, he didn't look Indian at all." Flashing back Millie could see the details of his face. "He had brown hair that was graying at the temples. Cut short, no braids or feathers. His skin may have been a touch darker than ours, but not enough to notice. He dressed like a regular doctor, white coat and all, though he did wear moccasin-style shoes with no socks."

Millie was surprised she had noticed so much detail about him. Then his eyes came to mind. "I guess the only thing I really noticed that looked Indian about him were his eyes. They were very dark, almost black. He looked to be in his mid-forties, maybe a little older."

Millie didn't tell Sadie, but all in all Doctor Townsend was a very handsome man. She hadn't really thought of that at the time. She guessed she was too nervous to acknowledge it.

"When can we go see them, Mama?" Sadie asked one more time.

"I'm not sure Sadie. We'll just have to wait and see." Millie couldn't just take Sadie over to the doctor's office and say, my kids want to see you Indians. How rude would that be?

"Let's go kids—we've got to get home." As they left Millie thanked Romy and Gladys for watching Sadie and Sammy.

"Our pleasure, let them come back real soon and stay again," Romy said.

"Yeah, he loves it when he's got an audience for his story-telling," Gladys said.

Millie, Sadie, and Sammy all three left smiling. It was so much fun watching and listening to those two playfully fuss back and forth. They could all see how much in love The Taylor's still were. They were good examples to Sadie and Sammy of how a real husband and wife should treat each other. God knew they never saw a good marriage at home in Texas.

§ ❧ §

When Ann stepped out of the tub, she did feel a bit better. The hot water had eased her tense muscles. She rubbed lotion all over her body just like she did every day for as long as she could remember, and again just like every time, she could recall little Millie say, Grandma, that smells so good. Pulling the fuzzy white robe closed over her pajamas, she once again checked both doors, and then lay down on top of the bedcovers. The Ruger was on the nightstand within easy reach.

~ Chapter Nineteen ~

*B*rad woke to the sound of a horn honking close by. Opening his eyes, he saw the first signs of day as the sky lightened in the east. He sat up, reached down between his feet, and pulled the lever to bring the seat back to an upright position. He stretched and grabbed for the door handle. He stepped out. The horn was still sounding a few car spaces away; he could now see the source of the noise. Some damn kid, three or four years old, was standing in the driver seat punching away on the steering wheel of a dark blue sedan. In the passenger seat sat a woman not paying one bit of attention to the kid.

Brad was just about to visit the car to tell the stupid woman to keep the brat quiet when out from the rest area came a man about six feet tall heading toward it. Brad turned away and said nothing to the man.

He could beat on women and children, but did he have the guts to stand up to someone his own size? He knew the truth but no one else ever would.

Walking toward the bathroom instead of the honking horn, he glanced at his watch: six forty-five. *I'll be at Granny's house long before lunch,* he figured.

＊ ✻ ＊

Ann didn't know when she finally drifted off to sleep; she was still lying on top of the covers in her robe.

She woke up with a start. She was dreaming. A man was pointing a gun at Millie's head. She was trying to get up to help her, but her body would not listen to her brain. The weight of her arms and legs was so heavy she couldn't move them at all. Ann felt totally helpless, sort of the same way she felt now even though she was awake and could move.

Ann went into the kitchen and put the coffee pot on. Then she went to the bathroom, but not before stopping back in the bedroom to pick up her gun. She slipped it into her fleece pocket. She had an uneasy feeling from the dream she just had.

By the time Ann drank her coffee, ate a bowl of oatmeal and got dressed, it was almost eight-thirty. She decided to take her morning walk; it might clear her head. She wanted so badly to go to the cabin and see Millie and her grandchildren, but she knew she couldn't. Brad could be watching her, and she would not lead him to her precious family. She had finally found Millie and would never risk losing her again, no matter what she had to do.

As Ann walked, she prayed. She asked for guidance, wisdom, and the strength to do whatever came to her.

＊ ✻ ＊

Brad sat hunkered down in the front seat of his Galaxy. He had parked in a driveway a few houses down from 219 Sunset Drive. He'd made better time than expected; it was only nine-thirty. He wasn't sure what he'd tell someone if they came home to find him in their drive. He wasn't really worried about that, he just wanted to watch Ann's house and catch Millie coming or going. Their car wasn't there, just a Ford pickup in the driveway. That didn't mean anything. Millie could have the vehicle parked somewhere else or traded it for something, though he knew that would have been hard for her to do. The title was in his name just like everything else. That's why he gave their bank hell for giving her his money.

He sat there only a minute or two before he saw someone walking up the road. As she got closer, he saw the old woman turn up the sidewalk to the house numbered 219. Brad's pulse quickened and it took all the willpower he had to not go after the old broad and pound on her head until she told him where his clan was.

He watched the woman unlock the door and go inside. He had to be patient. Sooner or later Millie or one of the brats would have to show their faces.

By one o'clock he was fuming. There was no sign of anyone going or coming to the house. The old woman hadn't even stuck her head back out the door. He was starving and needed a bath. Cranking the car, Brad backed out. Turning toward the highway, he headed into town to find some food, a hotel, and a bar. He needed a drink.

Neither was easy to find in that rinky-dink town, but he finally did. Fed and showered, Brad sat at Willie's Tavern tossing back his third drink, straight Jim Beam. He didn't speak to anyone. The locals shot glances at him, wondering who the newcomer was. But they didn't approach him; he didn't look like the socializing kind.

One more drink and Brad got up to leave. He wasn't drunk, just had enough in him to want to fight. His watch read seven thirty-three, so it would be an hour before dark. He'd go back and watch Ann's house.

This time there was a car in the driveway he used that morning, so he drove past Granny's house. Not too far down, he found a place to back into the woods. He didn't have as clear a view of the house, but he was more hidden and could still watch the driveway.

❦

As soon as Ann walked in sight of her house, she saw the strange vehicle parked in Bert Holcomb's driveway. They all lived together in the same community forever. One neighbor could always tell when something was different at another one's place.

Ann acted as if she didn't notice the car. Just went up her steps and into the house, making sure to lock the door behind her. She immediately went to the cabinet beside her back door and took out the pair of binoculars she and Jake used to watch the deer grazing out back. Taking them to the side window of the living room, she stood back a ways, so whoever was in the car couldn't tell what she was doing. She could see the black car really well, some kind of Ford, and there was a man slouched down with a baseball cap pulled down over his eyes. Ann hardly took her eyes off that car for the next three hours. Finally around one o'clock, it pulled out of Bert's drive.

Ann had been tempted all morning to call Sheriff Cook, but what would she tell him? That after all these years Millie's husband was right there across from her house? She didn't really know for sure. She didn't want to air Millie's dirty laundry by telling anyone about Millie's diary and how dangerous Brad could be. She'd just try to be patient and see what happened the next day or two. Ann had been handling her own affairs for a long time; she wasn't inclined any other way.

All afternoon Ann watched the road in front of her house, but nothing else happened. She was just stepping into the bathtub, hoping the hot water would do the trick again on her tensed, aching body, when at seven-forty the black car backed into the overgrown logging road down the street.

⁂

Brad sat staring ahead of him. There still had been no sign of Millie's car in Granny's drive, just the same Ford pickup. He sat there till almost midnight. He saw absolutely no movement outside, and inside it looked like all the lights went out around ten o'clock.

Brad steered out of his concealed spot. Returning to the hotel, he told himself he'd get closer to Granny tomorrow.

Ann lay in bed, sleep eluding her. There had never been this much dilemma in her life. Knowing her granddaughter was right up the mountain and realizing she couldn't risk going to her was tormenting Ann into a deep agony. Right as she looked at the alarm clock beside her bed, the mantel clock in the living room started striking twelve. Then she heard a vehicle crank up in the distance. Jumping up, she felt her way to the living room window that faced the street. As she pulled the curtain back a small way she saw the dark-color car creeping by. Ann knew it was the same car that had been parked at Bert's house all morning, and now she knew beyond all doubt it was Brad Madison behind the wheel.

~ Chapter Twenty ~

*L*eaving the hardware store, Millie made a U-turn in the street and headed back toward Abernathy's Drug Store. They all three got out, and Millie told Sadie and Sammy to stop at the fountain if they wanted a soda.

"Hey kids, will it be the usual grape today?" Becky asked, smiling at the cute kids who came in with their mother once a month when she got her prescriptions filled.

"That's what I want, Becky." Turning toward his mama, Sammy asked, "May we have lunch too? Those hot dogs sure smell good."

"I guess since it's almost noon, but you guys hurry up and eat. We've got to get home."

They both ordered hot dogs with only catsup as Millie made her way back to the pharmacy.

"Good morning, Mrs. Madison. How are you today?"

Millie cringed every time she came in there, always afraid Mr. Parker would say her real name in front of someone. She couldn't very well lie to him when her real name had been right there on the bottle.

"I'm fine, Mr. Parker. Hope you are too."

"Yes, yes. Every day's a gift when you get my age. If my grandson ever gets through school, he's going to take over for me, and I'm going to quit and go fishing."

"That sounds nice. How much longer does he have?"

"Supposed to finish up around Christmas time, and then he'll have to take his state exams to get his license. I should be on the river when the bass start spawning."

Millie handed the prescription to Mr. Parker as they talked. He saw it was for the same two drugs she got the past few months, even though she didn't fill the pain medicine every time.

"Well, looks like you met Doc Townsend. What a fine young man he is." Mr. Parker was at the age where he thought anyone under sixty was still young. "He takes such good care of that grandmother of his, and from what I hear, she can be a handful at times. A dang good doctor he is too. I've been seeing him ever since he moved back to town several years back. He's been doctoring my high blood pressure, and I guess it's working 'cause I'm still here."

Mr. Parker worked as he talked, and in a minute he was handing Millie the small white bag with the two full bottles in it. He charged her the same thing he did the first time she came in.

"How did you like the Doc, Ms. Madison?"

Millie thought for a minute then answered. "Well, I've only met him that once, but he seemed very nice. I spoke with his grandmother, too, and I must admit she was a bit mysterious. Said some strange things to me."

"You mean to tell me Nyoaka Nettles spoke to you? As far as I know, she hasn't said a word to anyone but the Doc in years or ventured out of that house. Whatever she said to you, you better take it to heart because if there ever was a person clairvoyant, it's surely her. I believe the Indians call it visions. She's been like that since she was a young girl, they say."

Millie took her billfold out of her pocketbook and handed Mr. Parker the money for her medicines. All the while echoes of Nyoaka's words ran through her head: pain, sadness, eyes are mirrors . . . you'll face two different demons . . . she and grandson are glad I've finally come . . . .

Millie didn't understand any of it except for the demons. She knew Brad was one of them, and if what Nyoaka said were true, she'd have to face him again. A shiver ran up her spine at the thought. Pulling away from the drug counter, Millie bid Mr. Parker goodbye.

"Are you finished, kids?" Millie asked as she wiped a big glob of catsup off Sammy's chin.

"Almost. Just one more swallow," Sadie said.

After jumping down from the stools, they headed for the door while Millie paid for their lunch. She'd grab something at home. She wasn't at all hungry, especially after her conversation with Mr. Parker. Visions—were there really such things? She remembered talk that her great-grandmother was strange and endowed that way, so maybe there was some truth to it.

۞ ❧ ۞

When she pulled up to the chain gate, Millie saw the electric truck parked in front of it. Stopping the car, she jumped out. At the driver's door, she started apologizing.

"I'm so sorry you had to wait. I hope you haven't been here long. I had to see the doctor in town this morning, and it took a bit longer than I'd planned."

"Oh no, just got here. Did you see Doc Townsend?"

"Yes, I did."

"He's a good friend but not much of a fisherman. We've been buddies ever since he delivered my last young'un the first night he came to town. That was over ten years ago. Little Allie decided she wanted to come into this world a little early. It hit Ellen quick. We called over to the Doc's house and asked him what to do. He was over at my house in five minutes. Allie was born within the hour, little ole bitty gal not more than five pounds. Boy you wouldn't know it now, she's 'bout as big as her mama . . . Just listen to me ramble."

Marty opened the door and stepped out. Sticking his hand out to her he said, "Name's Marty, Marty Johnson."

Millie took the hand of the smiling man and shook it stoutly.

"I'm Mildred Burke, and that's Lydia and Thomas, my children."

"Glad to meet you folks. Are you any kin to Miss Ann who owns this place?"

Millie's heart lunged in her chest. "No, just renting the cabin for the summer."

"Never met the lady myself, just heard a lot about her. She had a pretty rough spell several years ago, losing her family and all."

Millie turned away from Marty quickly so he wouldn't see the hurt on her face. She took the key from her pocket and unlocked the chain. With a wave, Marty drove off toward the cabin.

Millie got back in the car and followed him in, leaving the chain down. She'd lock it back when he left.

Marty parked his truck underneath the power pole. Putting on rubber gloves and special boots with spikes in them, he then proceeded to climb up the pole.

Sadie and Sammy stood at a distance as he geared up, but the higher he got, the closer they came. "Hey mister, isn't that hard to do?" Sammy hollered up at Marty.

"Not too bad. It was at first, but you get used to it."

The kids watched from the ground beneath as Marty worked on the transformer above. Millie went in the cabin and observed out the window, still unable to shake the words of the Indian woman Nyoaka . . . evil . . . demons. She shivered as a feeling of dread came over her.

* ✻ *

Ann stood at her living room window until the car's taillights were out of sight; then she stayed a little longer just to make sure the man didn't come back. Knowing she wouldn't be able to sleep now, she went to the kitchen, switched on the light, and fixed herself a cup of hot chocolate. It was too late to be drinking coffee. She picked up Millie's journal that lay on the table. In the morning, she'd go into town and talk to Sheriff Cook whose help she knew she was going to need. Anyway, she needed to pay the electric bills again.

❄ 🍃 ❄

Sadie and Sammy were still watching when Marty made his way down the pole, but now they were sitting on the ground with the four kittens playing around them.

"Look at the kitties. What're their names?" Marty asked, walking toward them.

Both children spoke, so the kittens' names jumbled up in different order: "Stripy, Sonny, Spook, and Smoky." "Spook, Stripy, Smoky, Sonny."

"They are cute as they can be. You want to give one or two of them away? My least girl Allie would love to have one."

"No!" Sammy said, gathering all four kittens in his arms.

"We can't separate them even if we wanted to. They have the same blood. They play together and are friends. They love each other," Sadie said.

Marty looked at the young girl. She wasn't as tall as his Allie, but from the look in her eyes, he sensed she was probably older. He saw more stuff there than should be for a girl her age. He always read people well, and her mother watching out the window had the same look in her eyes too. His heart went out to them. He felt something was amiss.

Looking at Sadie, Marty said, "You're right, little lady. Families should stay together."

"Not if they hurt each other," little Sammy said.

Quickly jumping up, the girl took the boy's hand.

"Come on, Sammy. We've got to get inside," Sadie said, half dragging her brother to the door.

Millie noticed them rushing and opened the screen door for them. "What's wrong?"

"Oh nothing, Mama. Sammy was just talking too much."

Marty walked behind the house then to the power meter. He felt he was right. Something very wrong had happened to this family.

He then flipped a switch. The buzzing sound of electricity flowed back into the cabin. He headed to the front door to tell Ms. Burke everything was all fixed. But he didn't see the metal rod that Ann used to hang plants on sticking out from the corner of the cabin wall. The sharp edge caught him right under his eye above his cheekbone. Reaching up to where he felt the searing pain, Marty right away felt the sticky blood dripping off his fingers.

"Doggone it. How did that happen?" he said out loud to himself. Then he tossed his tool satchel down and put his other hand over the injury too. Heading to the front door, Marty called for Millie.

"Ms. Burke . . . Ms. Burke. Could I get you to help me, please?"

Millie heard Marty and headed to the door. When she saw all the blood, she almost swooned, but took a deep breath and told Sadie to take Sammy into the bedroom for a minute and close the door.

Sadie knew by the tone of Millie's voice not to question her. She rounded up Sammy and the kittens and shut the door.

Inside the house, Millie took Marty's arm and led him to a chair at the kitchen table. She reached behind her and opened a drawer pulling out a clean dishtowel. Folding it double, she placed it on the blood-squirting wound. Marty's hands, arms, and the front of his shirt were covered in the stained liquid. While Millie stood applying pressure, Marty started to talk.

"Do you believe I did that? Walked right into that metal rod. Boy, do I feel stupid. I'm sorry for all the mess," he said, looking around at the blood splattered on the floor. "But your power is back on."

"You must have a pretty deep cut for it to be bleeding this badly. Sadie," she called, "you and Sammy can come out now because I need your help. Mr. Johnson has cut himself. There is a lot of blood, but don't be scared. He's all right."

Sadie opened the bedroom door and saw the drops of blood on the linoleum floor. There was a trail from the door to the chair where Mr. Johnson sat.

"Mama, is he going to die?" Sammy asked softly, more than a little scared.

"No, no, it's just a cut. You go outside and play with your kittens and Sadie and I will fix him up. Stay right there in front of the door where I can see you."

Millie's protectiveness didn't go unnoticed by Marty, nor did the fact that she wasn't calling them by the same name she'd introduced them as. Again confirming that this family had seen some trouble and seemed to be worried there might be more on the way.

"Sadie, get another clean towel and wet it in the wash pan," Millie said. She was so upset by Marty's injury that she wasn't even noticing she was calling the children by their real names.

After wringing out the towel, Sadie handed it to her mama. Millie slowly pulled the towel she was applying pressure with away from the wound. As she did, another squirt of blood spurted forward. Millie saw enough of the cut to know he was going to need stitches. Putting pressure back on the wound, she handed the wet towel to Marty.

"Here, maybe you can clean up a little. Then we'll get you into town for some stitches," Millie said to Marty.

"Oh no, surely not! It'll stop bleeding soon. Let's just give it a minute. I've never had a stitch in my life."

Thirty minutes later, the injury was still spouting blood, so Marty relented and agreed for Millie to take him to Doc Townsend's office.

"Sadie, get Sammy into the car and I'll help Mr. Johnson."

Sammy still looked a little frightened from the sight of all the blood, but was soon okay when he saw that Mr. Johnson was joking about what a klutz he was as he got into Millie's car. Millie went back in the house. After instructing Marty to continue applying pressure, she grabbed her pocketbook, hipped the side door shut, and clicked the button on the front door before she slammed it. She turned the car around in the yard and sped them out the drive, stopping as always past the gate. She and Sadie climbed out as usual, locking the chain around the tree. This time though they were in too much of a hurry to swish away their tracks.

❧ ❦ ❧

Nyoaka Nettles watched out the upstairs window as Millie's car pulled in front of the lavender house. She knew they'd be coming. She saw the blood.

Millie got out and went around to help out Marty.

"Sadie, you and Sammy come on inside. Hold your brother's hand and don't let him step into the street."

Again Marty noticed the pressing need this woman had to protect her offspring.

Going up the walk with Sammy's hand in hers, Sadie couldn't take her eyes off the beautiful old house before her, painted in lilac colors. Beautiful flowers were everywhere. Her eyes followed a vine up the trellis where Sadie spotted the lady standing in the window.

Up the steps and through the door, Millie led Marty. Looking up from her paperwork, Lafayette saw all the blood.

"Yikes, Marty! What in the world happened to you? Come on in here and I'll get the doc." Lafayette led them into a smaller version of the exam room Millie had been in that morning. It was probably once used for a small study or sitting room. Lafayette hurriedly left the room in search of Doc Townsend.

Sadie and Sammy waited very quietly. When the door opened, they expected the doctor, but it wasn't. It was Nyoaka. She looked at Marty and spoke, "The blood has stopped now, but you will need the fiber sewn into it to hold it together. Very deep cut, you should be more careful." Nyoaka smiled.

Marty stood in front of a mirrored cabinet and removed the towel, the blood had slowed to an ooze, but she was correct, you could see right to the bone. He put the towel back over the cut so as not to scare the children.

Doc Townsend walked up as his grandmother was speaking. He couldn't believe his ears. She had spoken to almost no one but him in many years—except for Millie that morning. And here she was today talking to everyone.

She then turned to her grandson and said, "He will need the needle. We'll be in the kitchen when you've finished." With that, Nyoaka turned to first Millie and then each child. She looked them all three squarely in the eye for a long minute and then said, "Come."

The three didn't hesitate but obediently followed her to the kitchen.

Millie looked around as Nyoaka pulled one high stool after the other out from the tall overlap of the bar in the center of the kitchen. Motioning for them to sit, Nyoaka went to the white-fronted refrigerator. Opening the door, she took out a bottle of milk, brought it to the bar, and set it down.

"Millie, would you get four glasses from the cabinet above your head?"

Sadie noticed right away the Indian woman had called her mama by her real name. Tugging on Millie's pant leg, Sadie leaned into her mama and whispered, "She called you by your real name."

Leaning down, Millie whispered, "I know, it's okay. I'll tell you about it later."

Then she and Sadie realized they'd been calling each other by their real names in front of Marty. Whispering, Millie again spoke to Sadie. "It will be all right—nothing we can do about it now."

Millie got glasses and took them to the side of the bar where the milk was. As she was pouring, she noticed all the strung-up bunches of grasses and roots hanging all around the kitchen.

Sammy chimed in, "What is this weed stuff hanging in your kitchen?"

Nyoaka rose from getting something out of the oven. She took the dish in one hand while steadying herself with her cane in the other. "The plates are beside the glasses," she said, looking at Millie.

Without further instruction, Millie got the plates, cut each one of them a piece of rhubarb pie with the knife Nyoaka laid out, and then put the milk and pie at each of their spots.

Nyoaka was still standing. "Eat, enjoy."

As Millie and Sadie took their first bites, Sammy just stared at his.

"What kind of pie is this, Mama? It's green inside."

Nyoaka spoke. "It is rhubarb, a sour bitter vegetable, but when mixed with sugar and butter and a few other things, it is wonderfully delicious."

Sammy licked a little of the juice from his fork. "Yum, that is good." Still staring at Nyoaka, he asked again, "Is one of those weeds rhubarb?"

"Those weeds are for healing, young man, and no, there isn't any rhubarb up there. The healing powers of these plants were taught to me from many ancestors past."

As she spoke she walked to the first bunch. Reaching up, she pinched off a bit, brought it to her nose and sniffed it. Turning to Sammy, she held it to his nose. As the scent touched his senses, he wrinkled his nose.

"What is that?"

"That is catnip. If you boil this into a tea and drink it, your worries will lesson and you will rest better. I will be sending some of this home for you all to try. It will also cure a baby's colic."

Nyoaka proceeded to the next bunch of herbs. "This bag holds oak bark. If you boil it, skim the top layer off, and apply it to a burn, it will take the heat out of your skin."

Touching the next bag Nyoaka said, "This wild cherry bark boiled will make a tea that is good for the cough and cold. It also will stop loose bowel. But don't let your cows eat the wilted leaves off the tree; it will kill them dead."

The next bag held some sort of dried roots. "Mix this sarsaparilla root with sweet flagroot and it will also stop a cough."

On and on Nyoaka would touch a bag of bark, roots or leaves.

"Dandelion tea for heartburn. The dogwood, Hat-ta-wa-no-min-schi, in tea will reduce fevers. Willow tea for chills, pennyroyal tea for headaches, green hellebore for pain. Witch hazel leaves boiled will relieve swelling. Trumpet honeysuckle, wild onion and garlic, stiff goldenrod, saltbush and broom snake-weed are good for insect bites and stings. If you get a snake bite, make a poultice out of these young dried leaves and ground up inner bark of the elm tree—pulls the poison out. Bark off a persimmon tree boiled makes a good mouthwash. A milkweed poultice will get rid of a wart every time. Now, this skunk cabbage root can be crushed up and smoked for asthma, or the sweet syrup from the boiled root cures a child's cough."

"Mama, she's talking about the skunk cabbage at our cabin this spring!" Sammy stared, eyes wide from all the details Nyoaka had been telling them.

Nyoaka stopped her lesson in healing and went to the boy. "So you've seen this skunk cabbage?"

"Yes, it grows in the spring creek where we live."

Then she turned to Sadie, "Have you seen it too?"

"Yes. Mama was going to cook us some. I wanted to try it because my great-grandpa had liked it, but she never got around to it." Leaning toward the Indian woman like she was an old friend Sadie whispered, "I think she didn't cook it because she said it tastes awful. She tried it when she was young."

Nyoaka threw her head back and laughed out loud, her eyes dancing with liveliness. "I'll have to agree with your mama. Skunk cabbage was made by God to be used for medicine, not to eat."

Sitting down now, Nyoaka took a bite of her pie, and they all sat together and ate until they were finished.

Millie loved the bright kitchen. The outside wall was nothing but ceiling-to-floor windows that faced the east, so the afternoon sun wasn't pouring in. She could only imagine how sunny it would be in the mornings. Everything looked modern except for the herbs hanging and the antique cast iron cook stove.

As if reading her mind Nyoaka looked at the stove. "That cook stove was my father's. His name was Wahya, meaning wolf. He, too, like his father Tomeka, was a medicine man for our people. My father lived down the mountain a ways, near the water called Brush Creek. As a young girl I, too, would see the skunk cabbage growing in the spring creeks. Many hours I would spend with my father digging up the roots. We would be covered with the soppy black earth from where the roots came.

"My father's unmarked grave is down that way. As was our custom, we buried him at the place where his spirit departed him. I can see the spot now. You must walk down by the creek through a pine tree grove to the low lands where the bogs start. Deep into the marsh he would go in search of the plants he would use for his healings. There, beside one of the bogs, they found him with his root-grinding bowl in his hand. We buried the bowl with him, which only seemed right since he always carried it."

The hairs on the back of Sadie's neck stood on end. What were the chances that the bowl she found was Nyoaka's father's? Would the old Indian woman be mad because Sadie dug in her father's grave? But she didn't know. How could she? Sadie would just take the bowl back where she found it—that would solve her dilemma.

"It has been many springtimes since I have visited this place of my youth and gathered the skunk cabbage root. I will go back one more time, and soon, very soon." Nyoaka's voice trailed off to a whisper as she spoke to herself.

Standing up, Nyoaka faced Sadie, took her smooth, young hands in her frail, weakened ones and spoke. "You will keep the bowl. It is as it was meant to be; you will be the next to use it."

Just then, before anyone could say anything else, Marty and Doc Townsend walked in.

"Well, I'm good as new," Marty said.

But he didn't look it. He was cleaned up, his face, hands and arms were no longer blood-soaked, but his shirt still held the stains, and his eye above the stitched-up cut was swollen shut.

"Marty, I wouldn't quite say you're good as new. That is really a nasty cut. I'm glad you are up-to-date on your tetanus shot, but I want you to get this antibiotic cream prescription filled and put it on those stitches for at least a week," Doc said.

"Will do, Doc. Now I'd better be going. Mrs. Burke, can I bother you to take me back to my truck?"

"I don't think that would be a good idea, you driving with only one eye. I'm about ready to close up shop here for today," Doc said. "I'll take you by Tom's so you can get that antibiotic, and then I'll run you home. I'll take you to get your truck in a couple of days when that eye opens up. Where'd you say your place is, Ms. Burke?" Lewis was careful to call her by her pretend name, like it really mattered now.

Before Millie could answer, Nyoaka spoke. "She dwells in the cabin above the bottoms where I grew up. I will go there with you when you take Marty."

Turning, Nyoaka this time addressed Millie softly, so no one else could hear. "Be very vigilant, for the evil one is close at hand, very near."

~ Chapter Twenty-one ~

After dozing off and on for a couple of hours, Ann got out of bed. The first thing she did as she made her way to the living room window was open the metal blinds just like always. Looking up and down the road she saw Bert's truck was still home. She didn't see anything out of the ordinary—no black car. It was just turning daylight on that late August day. The orange glow on the horizon promised another hot, sunny day.

The same hall floorboard squeaked as Ann stepped on it. Jake always said he was going to fix it, but never got around to it. At times, the squeak annoyed her, but it didn't seem to matter much now to Ann. She had much bigger things to worry about.

Pulling on her jeans and v-neck tee shirt, she sat down in the oak rocking chair with the green afghan thrown over the back. Her own mother had made the afghan for her as a wedding gift so many years before. It was faded and worn from many hours of tugging around. First she and Jake would sit close together on the couch and cover their legs up with it while they ate popcorn and listened to their favorite radio program, "The Wild and Wooly West." Then Jonathan came along, and Ann would throw the homespun cover over him wherever he fell asleep. And Millie, well, she thought it made a great blanket to cover up her dolly or Teddy as she pulled them around in her wagon. She even had that one tomcat that would let her ride him, and she would cover him up with it too. That throw had been back and forth from the house to the cabin so many times, it was a wonder it held together at all. Ann touched the ratty edges as loving memories filled her thoughts with happiness.

There would be more memories to make with that throw, memories of her with Millie's children. With that last thought, she pulled on her cloth sneakers, touched the afghan one more time, picked up the Ruger from the nightstand, and headed for the kitchen. After a quick cup of coffee, she was on her way to Sheriff Cook's office, but not before grabbing the two power bills and Millie's journal from the table.

＊ 🌸 ＊

Brad squinted as the morning sun filtered through the thin, grimy curtain of his rented hotel room. He threw his arm over his eyes to try and block the rays and to help the throbbing at his temples.

After he left his stakeout the night before, he went back to the tavern for one more drink. But as usual that one shot turned into several, and the bartender finally had to ask him to leave when they closed at two o'clock, just when he'd been making progress with that young lady . . . yeah, right . . . *lady*. She would still be with him, but he had thought better of it. He needed to keep his identity a secret, especially till he found his wife and weakling young'uns. Then he might just lock the family up somewhere and see if he could find his young friend again.

Sitting on the edge of the bed his head spun. He swallowed the bile as it rose in his throat. He knew better than to mix beer and whiskey. Slowly he made his way to the shower. The hot water plummeting against his skin slowly brought his senses back to life. He twisted the rusting lever to shut the water off. *Damn, what a dump.*

It was Thursday. He was going to have to hurry and find them. He was tired of this game and he knew he needed to be back to work on Monday.

He'd go to Granny's house this morning. They might not be there, but she'd know where they were. Sliding his jeans on, he felt the weight of the 22-Magnum in his pocket.

Out the door to his car, he headed for the diner down the road. The shower made him feel a lot better, but he still needed a couple cups of coffee to clear his head.

＊ ❦ ＊

It was half-past eight o'clock when Ann pulled to a stop in front of the county sheriff's department. She took Millie's journal, locked the door and got out, leaving the bills laying over the Ruger in the seat.

At the sound of the door opening, Amos Cook looked up to see Ann stepping in. She was a familiar sight, for she'd been coming through that door at least once a week for over twenty years. It was always the same question, "Amos, any news, any new leads?" And he always had the same answer: "No leads on your granddaughter." He'd long since stopped trying to tell her to forget it. If the girl was still alive, she obviously didn't want to be found. But Ann would hear nothing of it. She believed little Millie was out there somewhere and needed her. Little Millie, what a cute kid she had been. Darn shame bad things like that had to happen to nice families.

"Morning, Ann, how are you?"

"I need you, Amos. I've found Millie and she's in danger."

Amos could tell by the look on Ann's face that she was very serious; she looked pale and wore a worried frown, with bags and dark circles under her eyes.

Amos walked to the other side of his desk. He took Ann's arm and led her to the straight-backed chair across from his desk.

"You've what, Ann? Are you serious?"

"Yes, Amos. I've not seen her, but I found this up at the mountain at our cabin."

Amos took the cover-worn book and flipped to the first page: *This diary belongs to Melissa Ann Hampton.* Thumbing through the first several pages he recognized the scribbling of a young girl's dreams; then halfway through it, he stopped at an entry dated June 11, 1965, only three years earlier.

June 11, 1965

Oh, God, please help me. I beg you, God, don't let little Sammy cry and be sick again tonight. Last night was a horror. Sammy with the croup not being able to breathe, coughing, gagging. Sadie scared to death that her brother wasn't going to be able to get his breath . . . and Brad hollering.

"Can't you shut that little maggot up? A working man's got to have his sleep."

I tried everything. I took Sammy and Sadie into the bathroom, shut the door, put a towel under it to conceal the noise, and turned the hot water on full blast. In a while, the steam had opened up Sammy's airways and he wasn't as hysterical, but then Brad stormed in.

"What are you doing in here wasting hot water, running my well dry?" As Brad walked past me where I was sitting beside the shower on the toilet, he backhanded me across the side of the head, knocking it against the tile wall. He turned the water off and told us to get to bed. I can still feel the ache from the knot on my head. Then he told me to put the brats to bed and come to him. Thankfully little Sammy had drifted off. Even though it was a fitful sleep, I put him to bed. I snuggled Sadie up for a minute until she was resting, then I went to him. I knew if I didn't, he'd come in the children's room. As soon as I walked through the door, he slapped me, sending me

reeling into the bedpost. Then he shut and locked the door, said he didn't want them "brats" bothering us. No hope now for any help from Sadie, but that's better, she'll be safe from his fists. I can't write down the ways he tortured me, it's too awful to put down on paper. When he'd finally tormented me to the point of insanity he yelled, "Get out of here! I'm sick of looking at you, go back to your sniveling whelps. I'm done with you . . . for now."

I crawled to the bathroom thankful I didn't hear any coughing or wheezing, just sleeping sounds coming from the children's room. All that had kept me sane was praying that Sammy wouldn't have another attack and need me.

I've given Sammy medicine all day and he seems a little better, please God don't let him be sick again tonight, please God, please.

＊❦＊

But Sadie hadn't been asleep. As soon as she was sure Sammy was breathing steadily she'd gone to test the door… locked. She'd known there was nothing she could do but go back to Sammy and try to keep him safe, and pray that God would be behind that bedroom door protecting her mama.

Sadie added that night to the list of many that she'd laid awake. Knowing the noises she was hearing were not happy sounds, but pleas for mercy. She released a deep breath when she'd finally heard the door being unlocked, and the sound of her mama making her way to the bathroom. Only Sadie knew the creaking was not being made by footsteps… but hands and knees touching the floorboards.

She would go to her mama but Millie would send her away. No good mother would want her child to see them that way… and no good daddy would ever do to his family what Brad Madison did to his... Sadie felt the dark grip of hate squeezing her heart...

﹡ ❦ ﹡

Amos Cook closed the journal. He took his glasses off and rubbed his eyes. When he had composed his thoughts, he spoke to Ann.

"Ann, what in the world kind of man would treat someone like that? What has Millie gotten herself into?"

"You should read it all, and you'll see hell is where Millie's been the past ten or more years. Living in hell with the devil himself."

"So I'm assuming this man is her husband?"

"Yes, Brad Madison."

"Is he up at the cabin with Millie?"

"No, she ran away from him. Came all the way from Texas, so the journal says. You know that strange phone call I got the other day from the sweepstakes people wanting Millie? It was Brad. He found me and now he's here, probably thinks Millie came to me. He sat in Bert's driveway all afternoon yesterday in a black Ford car, and then parked down in the old logging road till midnight last night. I heard him crank up and saw the same dark car again. I didn't get a good view of the license plate, but I'd bet my life they're from Texas."

"So how do you know Millie's at the cabin?"

Amos had been up the mountain many times with Jake and Ann, fishing, cooking hot dogs over the open fire. All that ended when Jonathan died. What life that was left in Jake and Ann went right out of them. Jake was sick with his heart, and Ann was sick, too, heartbroken sick.

"I drove to the cabin on Monday. Deep feelings have been pulling me up there, but I've been sick all summer. I never got past the gate though. Just didn't want to face all those memories. And one time the bear kept me out."

A little part of Amos was beginning to wonder if Ann was getting senile, but she did have the journal, so he continued to listen.

"When I finally drove down through the gate, there was a vehicle with a Texas license plate. Flowers were planted out front, red and white petunias just like I always planted. I went straight into the cabin, but no one was inside. There were new curtains, bedspreads, food on the counter, and a woman's clothes as well as a small boy's and young girl's. I figured a family of gypsies had settled in until I stumbled on the journal. Oh yes, and there were four half-grown kittens in there too. After I read a little of the journal and saw Millie's name in the front, I took it and left. I don't know why I didn't stay and confront them. A part to me wanted to read the journal first, so I could see what she had been doing all these years and what kind of person she grew up to be. I hope she'll forgive me. I wanted to get to know her before I talked to her. I know that probably doesn't make sense to you, but it does to me. Maybe I was wrong to take it, but at least now I know what we're up against."

Amos leaned back in his chair, listening intently. "So does the journal say she's got the boy and girl whose clothes you saw?"

"Yes, the girl is called Sadie and she is twelve. And the little boy she calls Sammy, he is five."

"Is this husband of hers mean to the kids too?"

"Oh Lord, Amos, you wouldn't believe the awful person he is and how he's beaten and banged on them all, physically and mentally. Millie's tried to leave him many times, but he always catches her and threatens the children. Even put a knife to Sammy's throat one night."

"How long do you think they've been at the cabin?"

"The diary says they got there on May eighth, so over three months now."

"Why do you think her husband has just now come looking for them?"

"I don't know, Amos. I just don't know. All I do know is that Millie and her children have come home. I can only guess why she hasn't contacted me. Maybe she's afraid I will lead Brad to her. I want to go to them now, but I know he's watching me, hoping I'll guide him to them. Maybe he's been lurking around for longer than I think. I just don't know, Amos. Can you help me?"

God, how Amos hated to see anybody suffer, especially a good-hearted woman like Ann. They'd known each other for close to forty years. She and Jake had been two of the first people in town to welcome him as a young deputy. They were good neighbors and friends to him and Lottie. So of course, he'd do everything in his power to help Ann and her grandchildren. Lord knew she could sure use a streak of good luck.

Little did Amos know that you have to have a whole lot more on your side than luck when you are getting ready to go up against the Devil.

♦ ❦ ♦

Brad snuck his car down the deserted logging path, way past where anyone could see it from the street. He opened his door, still feeling a little shaky from his night with Jim Beam and Blue Ribbon. In his pocket he felt the hardness of the 22-Magnum. Then he crept through the woods heading for Granny's house. *How sweet this was going to be! That stupid Thanksgiving song sprang to mind . . . over the river and through the woods to grandmother's house we go . . .*

He never had a grandma, as far as he knew.

Brad smothered a laugh at the thought of the things he'd do to the old granny if she didn't tell him what he wanted to know. Things wouldn't be so sweet then.

Brad made a wide sweep through the woods. He crossed the road below the house where no other homes were, so he wouldn't be seen, and then he went to the back door. He knew Granny wasn't home 'cause her truck was gone. He stepped on an old river rock and then a cement step. Grabbing the metal handle of the screened door, he opened it. Then he tried the copper-colored knob on the wooden door, locked. He then walked to the double windows on the left. He could see the kitchen sink through the glass. Pulling on each of them, he also saw the ten-penny nails twisted over the wood so they wouldn't open. He walked to the other window and didn't even try it, for the nails were there too. The curtain was closed, so he didn't know what that room was.

Walking back to the door, he opened the screen again reached in his jean pocket and pulled out his Case XX knife. Inserting the blade he toyed with the lock—nothing—so he put the blade between the door and the frame, trying to push the metal bolt back into the door. Finally, flustered and more than a little impatient, he balled his fist up and knocked out the bottom pane of glass closest to the knob. Reaching in, he turned the inside doorknob and the door clicked.

Inside, he saw drops of his blood hitting the broken glass. Kicking the fragments aside, Brad went to the sink and turned the water on to let it run over the cut. Nothing more than a cat scratch; he dabbed at it with Ann's dishtowel.

Looking around, he saw a neat, cozy, little kitchen. Everything was clean as a hospital room but worn and outdated. The range had one of those pots that set right down into the stove. Used to have to heat water on the stove before the day of hot water heaters, he figured. The walls were painted a faded-out shade of yellow and the curtains were so bleached out, you could see right through them. On top of the refrigerator sat an old tube radio with a yellowed doily under it. The linoleum under his feet was worn through in places, but again he noticed it, too, was clean.

There were a few envelopes laying on the kitchen table. Picking them up, he saw one was from Uncle Sam. It was Ann's retirement check for seventy-three dollars. No wonder everything she had was worn out—she didn't have any money to replace things. Who could live on seventy-three dollars a month? The other two envelopes looked like junk mail, so he didn't even bother to open them.

Before he left the kitchen, he pulled his knife out of his pocket and cut the telephone cord. The rotary-dial phone was now dead.

In the living room, he saw more of the same, wearied, old couch and chair. But there were a couple of wood items, a secretary and what-not cabinet, that was probably worth some money. That wind-up clock on the wall might also be valuable.

Brad walked to the secretary and opened every drawer, flipping through papers and odds and ends. Nothing related to his wife. Then he went down the short hall, oblivious to the loud squeak in the floorboards. The first door on the right was the bathroom. Opening the medicine cabinet over the sink, he noticed the usual stuff. Aspirin, cough medicine, toothbrush, only one, and toothpaste. There was one prescription bottle with a name on it, Ann Hampton, nothing suspicious in there either. As he left the bathroom, he noticed the bottle of lotion on the back of the toilet. He picked it up, unscrewed the cap, put it to his nose, and sniffed. Wrinkling his nose, he put the lid back on. He hated that almond smelling stuff. Millie used it every day and every day she stunk just like it. Was she here and left it, or did Granny use it too? Probably where Millie picked up the habit.

Leaving the bathroom, Brad stepped out into the hall. The creaky floorboard underneath the hand-woven rug protested again loudly. Riffling through every drawer in both bedrooms, all he saw were granny clothes. He did find a box of pictures in the closet. Just about every one of them had a little girl in it. He guessed it must have been Millie before her ma took her away. On the night table in the bigger bedroom were two pictures—one was the same little girl sitting in a nice-looking young man's lap, probably Millie's daddy, the other an older man with eyebrows that met in the middle and tough weather-beaten skin. His eyes looked like Sammy and his ears were a little oversized like Sammy's too. That must be the old, dead grandpa.

There was not a trace of them there. Didn't look like anybody had been in that house but the old woman in years.

"Where could they be if they aren't here?" Brad said out loud.

Then as he threw the shoebox of pictures back on the closet floor, he noticed the young Millie standing beside a cabin of some sort. *Well now, wonder where that was taken?*

He hoped Granny got home soon. They had a lot of catching up to do. They had much to talk about. Brad was growing anxious, wanting to get to know Granny better.

He laughed a high-pitched cackle as he thought about that.

When Brad had cleaned up the broken glass, he pulled the window curtain closed. He didn't want Granny to know he was here till the time was right.

❦

"Of course I'll help you, Ann. I've got to think about all this and come up with a plan. First thing we need to do is keep you safe," Amos said.

"Me! I don't give a hoot about me. I've lived my life and now I want them young'uns to have their chance."

"Calm down, Ann. I've got to think about all this. May I keep the journal? I'll have to talk to the sheriff up in Allegain County. You know I don't have any say up there, so we'll have to work together. If I read this or at least skim it, I'll have a better idea of what we're dealing with."

"Certainly you can read it, but no one else can. That is Millie's life and no one but Millie's business unless she chooses otherwise. Don't lose it either."

"I won't. I'll get it right back to you no later than tomorrow. I'll start looking it over right away, and in the meantime, I'll have Hank ride by your house every few hours. I'll get Ben to do the same tonight. If you see any sign of that car again, call me right away. I'm only a phone call and few minutes from you."

Ann rose to leave. "When you talk to the Allegain sheriff, tell him not to go to the cabin. I want to be the one to tell Millie that Brad is looking for her. If someone goes to the cabin, it will scare her. Maybe he could just send his deputies by the gate to make sure it's still up and locked? If Brad finds them, he'll have to park his car on the outside of the chain, so just have them on the look-out for a black Ford with Texas license."

Amos almost laughed. Ann always had been a bossy little woman. He thought it was funny, her telling him how to do his job.

"Will do, Ann. I'll talk to him this afternoon when I've skimmed the journal. In the meantime, you watch your back. I think we've got a real snake on our hands with this guy."

"Yes, I'm sure of that," Ann said as she made her way to the door.

"Call me if you think anything is out of the ordinary."

"I will, Amos. I will."

~ Chapter Twenty-two ~

*L*ewis heard the words from his grandmother's mouth but could hardly believe them. Nyoaka wanted to go with him to take Marty to get his truck. She hadn't been to the bogs since shortly after he returned to practice, ten years before. He'd always remember that day. They had driven to an overlook off the Blue Ridge Parkway. Nyoaka knew her way well. She led him through the woods down by the creek. She walked a path up by the rushing water at least half a mile. Her age didn't slow her down at all. She trudged forward, intent upon making sure her only grandson knew where his great-grandfather was buried and where the village she was raised had been.

Lewis could smell the murky bog as they made their way deep into it. Hanging muscadine vines brushed his face and the fragrance of mountain laurel drifted up his nose. Through the pine grove they'd gone. Nyoaka stopped by a huge rock that halfway jutted into the wet waters of the bog. Beyond that a smaller rock stuck above the bog a few inches.

"Here is the resting place of your great-grandfather Wahya. His guardian spirit led him away many years ago. A person should know where they come from. It will help them get to where they need to be."

Lewis had often heard the stories of his great-grandfather, as well as the horrors of his life during and after he walked the Trail of Tears until he found his way back here, close to the mountains of his ancestors.

"The wolf still watches over this place, as will the bear watch over you and the ones who will be close to your heart. I know; I have seen them both."

Nyoaka talked to her grandson as she closed her eyes, envisioning the scene in her mind, visions she glimpsed many times in all her years.

Then she opened her eyes. Taking his hand, she led him out of the bog to the bottomland by the creek.

"Here is where our village stood when I was a young girl."

He knew that through the years, the old had died out and the young, being around the white man so much, had adopted their ways, moving closer to towns, living in houses. The village became no more.

As Lewis remembered that visit ten years before, he could picture the cabin up on the rise of the hill. Looking up toward the shack his grandmother spoke.

"The dwelling above holds much sorrow, but it wasn't always that way." Then she looked him square in the eyes and said, "You and the woman will bring safety, peace, and togetherness to those walls again. There your past will meet the future. There your heart will find freedom from the guilt. There you will smile."

Ten years ago Lewis could not fathom what she was saying, but now Nyoaka's words not only echoed in his head, he could feel them in his heart as he looked to the woman with the brown hair streaked with auburn, the woman sitting between the boy and girl.

"Oh Doc, there ain't nothing wrong with me," Marty said. "I've always joked I could drive that old work truck of mine with one eye closed and an arm tied behind my back."

"Stop arguing with me, Marty. You know if I let you drive in this shape, Ellen will have my head."

Marty knew the doc was right, so he gave up the argument and looked over at Millie again.

"Guess I'll have to leave my truck at your place, Ms. Burke, for a day or two if that's okay. I sure am glad I got that power going for you before this happened."

"Me, too," Millie said. "And you can leave your truck there as long as you need to. I am so sorry this happened to you. I'm going to knock that flower hanger off the wall as soon as I get back. Can I do anything for you before we head home? I'd be glad to drop you off at your house on my way out."

"No, Doc said he's about done and will run me home. Ellen will want to question him to see if I'm going to live anyway. He really just wants to see if she'll invite him for supper. Have to admit, she is a heck of a fine cook."

Millie could tell by the way the two men spoke of Ellen that she must be a lovely woman. She felt a little pang of sorrow for the friends she herself never had. Brad wouldn't allow her to be buddies with anyone. If someone happened by, he'd say or do something awful to scare them off. Maybe that would change now. Surely if Brad hadn't found them by now, he'd given up trying.

"If you're sure I can't do anything for you, I guess we'll go. Come on kids, thank Mrs. Nettles for our treat," Millie said.

Nyoaka looked at Millie and spoke to her before Sadie and Sammy could thank her. "You will call me Nyoaka." Then looking to Sadie then Sammy, she said, "And you will, too and you."

Then turning back to Millie, Nyoaka said to her, "And you will be called Camarin—One Who Protects."

"And you," turning to Sadie, "will be known as Wakanda. You will not fully understand its meaning for many years, but someday you will remember back and hear the words of my tongue. Your name means Possessor of Magic Powers."

Sadie was more than a little disturbed. What was this old lady talking about? Magic powers?

Sadie looked Nyoaka directly in the eyes, "What do you mean, magic powers?"

"You will find your answers in the screech of the owl and the liwanu of the bear. You will use your gift when the time is right. As the wolf howls and the crow squawks, you will know. The gift can only be used for good."

Not really satisfied, Sadie sat quietly pondering the ramblings of the old woman.

"What's my name going to be? Tell me mine," Sammy said.

Nyoaka turned to Sammy. "You will be given the name which means Little Wolf. Honiahaka. You are to be called after my father Wahya, meaning wolf, for as of this day, you all, having Cherokee blood running through your veins, are brought back to your home. The grandmother called Ann made your route possible many years ago by loving Camarin, your mother, so much. Camarin didn't forget that love. It brought her back here to these mountains, back where you all have belonged since your beginnings. Your great-grandmother Ann is your Hania, your spirit warrior. Numerous years and many tears she has lived and yearned to see you again. Her time has come."

Lewis and Marty both stood in silence as Nyoaka spoke to the unsettled family. Marty didn't get any of it. He guessed the old woman was just being nice to them, but she'd never given him an Indian name before.

"Hey, Doc, what's your Indian name?" Marty asked, turning to face him.

All eyes were on him as he answered, "Nita, which means bear."

A slight shiver ran down Sadie's spine. *What was up with all this bear stuff and magical powers?*

Millie, feeling in awe of Nyoaka, wanted to ask her how she knew about Grandma Ann. Then she remembered the papers she had filled out right there at that office. She'd probably seen the name there, but how could she know about her tears? She guessed she could have made that up, or then again, some things just were not meant to be explained.

"Come on, kids. We need to get home. It's going to be dark soon," Millie said. "Marty, do you want me to come get you in a couple of days so you can get your truck?"

"No, that's all right, I'll get Ellen to run me down there when I can see out of this eye."

"I guess I could leave the gate down till you get your truck."

"No," Nyoaka simply stated.

All eyes turned to her.

She said, looking at Millie, "The Matchitehew will come for you soon, so you must not make it easy for him."

Millie didn't know what that word meant and she wasn't sure she wanted to. But Lewis knew it well: "He Who Has An Evil Heart." Nita knew the meaning, for in his visions he'd seen its presence and had felt its power.

"Well, maybe I will leave the gate locked. Why don't you just let me come get you? I'll check with you tomorrow afternoon and see how you're feeling," Millie said to Marty.

"Okay, just come by the house. I'll be there. Do you know where the high school is?"

"Yes."

"Turn up the next street, Fir Street. I'm the fourth house on the right, house number 108. Surely I'll be able to see by then."

Slipping off the kitchen stool, Millie said goodbye to everyone. She, Sadie and Sammy went back out through Doctor Townsend's office to the front door. Nyoaka followed them.

"Remember to watch out for the Matchitehew. I feel his nearness. Be careful, Wakanda and Haniahaka. Watch out for your mother as she has stood vigil over you night and day for all your years."

Sammy took hold of Millie's hand. "She's scaring me. What are we supposed to be watching out for, those bog monsters you told us about when we first came to the cabin?"

"No. I told you there aren't any monsters. Everything is fine. You don't have to worry."

But as Millie made her way to the car she couldn't shake her mounting anxiety.

What a strange day it had been. Sadie wasn't sure what was happening. Another chill crept up her spine. Her daddy's face flashed in her mind. Sammy, too, had bad thoughts as he imagined his cats clawing and hissing at the monster Matchitehew. He couldn't help but whine.

Millie pulled Sammy close to her on the car seat. "It's okay. Let's play a counting game on the way home. You count the cows on my side of the road and, Sadie, you count the ones on your side." Anything to get the children's minds on something other than monsters . . . and their daddy.

With the children occupied Millie thought of all the things Nyoaka had said. She understood so little of her words. Millie couldn't help but believe Nyoaka knew her entire life just as if she'd been right there with her.

"Mama how did that woman say my new name?"

Millie smiled as she pronounced "Honiahaka" for Sammy. She felt a little silly yet possessive of her own name Camarin. Protector? She didn't feel much like a protector. Most of the time, she just felt scared and helpless. She supposed, though, that we don't see qualities in ourselves that others do. She guessed she had protected Sadie Girl and Sammy as best she could. They were, after all, finally away from Brad, happy and doing well, but for how long? Nyoaka's words played over in her mind and the familiar dread overwhelmed her again.

Arriving back on their trail, Millie stopped in front of the gate. Sadie jumped out and undid the lock with the gate key her mama handed her. She stood to the side as Millie drove the car through. Then both made sure the gate was tightly locked.

~ Chapter Twenty-three ~

*P*ulling out of the sheriff's office parking lot, Ann reached beside her. She felt the envelopes that held the power bills—she'd almost forgot about them. Then the coolness of the chrome gun cylinder touched her fingers. Making a turn she headed back toward Drake Electric.

After paying the bills, she again laid the receipts over the Ruger beside her. Ann's mind wandered . . . *what were Millie and the children doing right now?* Oh, how she longed to go to them, to hold them, to get to know them. What would it be like to see her little Millie who was now a grown woman with children of her own? Would the children like her? There were so many questions and too many worries. Before Ann started to pull into her driveway, she first rode up the street a bit to check down the sawmill road. Nothing, she didn't see anything. No black Ford set on the street or in anyone's driveway. She felt a little better but still uneasy.

After Ann maneuvered into her driveway, she turned the engine off. Looking up to her house, she noticed how the paint was chipped and peeling. She should have spent some of the money she and Jake had saved all those years ago while running the store. But she hadn't cared about new things or fancy fine clothes. She just kept what she had. Everything was so full of memories too; how could she replace those? Now that she held hope that she'd see Millie again, she wished she had spruced the house and herself up a bit. Maybe it wouldn't matter. Hopefully Millie would look at her inside and not her outer things.

She gathered her belongings out of the truck. Grabbing the two receipts, she slid them inside her black vinyl pocketbook, another item she'd used for years. She put the Ruger in her jeans pocket. When everything was settled with Millie, she'd call Carl Haynes and get him to paint inside and out.

God knew Ann had bargained with the Devil so many times over the years, swearing to give her last penny to him if he'd just bring Millie back. Was he now collecting? A picture of Brad she saw in Millie's box floated through her mind.

Ann stepped up her two cement steps to the front porch. She needed to water her begonias; they were beginning to droop. She unlocked the door and went inside. Ann threw her keys inside her pocketbook and slid it on top of the refrigerator like she always did as she walked into the kitchen. Out the back door Ann went to get her watering can that set out back beside the well house spigot. She noticed the door window curtain was pulled shut. But she always opened all the curtains and blinds first thing every morning. She guessed she just forgot this morning.

When she pulled the door open, she saw the missing window-pane. A sickening feeling boiled up from the pit of her stomach. Leaving the door open, she walked across the kitchen to the wall phone. As soon as she lifted the receiver, she saw the cut cord. Her heart pounded. Just as she turned to the back door, she heard the loud squeak of the hall floorboard.

"Where are you rushing off to Granny? Aren't you going to welcome your company?"

Ann looked toward the arched doorway that separated the kitchen from the living room, and there he stood, shoulder leaned against one of the frames, one hand on his hip, the other holding a shiny pistol.

"Who are you, and what are you doing in my house?" Ann sounded out to him in a high nervous voice she almost didn't recognize. She didn't want him to know she knew anything about Millie or who he was.

"Oh Granny, that's right. We've never been introduced. Old mother-in-law Lindsay said you wrote off her and Millie when she left that boy of yours. Never did tell anything different till she lay dying. Didn't hear the whole story, 'cause frankly I didn't and still don't give a damn. Anyway, I'm your long lost granddaughter's beloved husband Brad."

As he talked to her, Ann took in his appearance. He was a fairly tall man, maybe six feet, slender build, sun-bleached blond hair stuck out around the baseball cap. He had close-set eyes and a cleft chin. His eyes were dark, a sharp contrast to the lightness of his other features. Normally she would have to say he was a right nice-looking man. His clothes were simple and clean enough—jeans, light blue button-up shirt and loafers without socks. He looked a little citified; clearly he wasn't from the mountains or the country.

"Come on over here, Granny. Let's sit down and get to know each other," Brad said, motioning Ann to a chair at the kitchen table. Ann walked slowly to the seat. Brad shut the back door before joining her.

"Now, well, let's see—how've you been? How's life treating you? And where the hell is my 'wonderful' wife and them brats of hers?"

Ann watched Brad's face turn a glowing red as the evil shone all over his face. The gun he held was only inches from her face. The gun in her jeans pocket felt a thousand miles away.

Trying to compose herself, Ann answered, "I don't know what you're talking about. I haven't seen or heard from Millie since she was seven years old. *You* tell *me* where she is," Ann snapped right back at him.

Brad despised being stood up to, so he reared up, leaned across the table, and back-handed Ann across the mouth. It wasn't a very forceful blow, just enough to bruise her lip a bit and show her who was boss.

"I'm going to ask you again. Where is she?" This time he was towering over her, his voice filled with rage.

"I told you, I don't know. Why would she come here? Did she leave you for some reason?" Ann touched her throbbing lip.

Brad went back to the chair across from Ann and sat down, trying to calm his rising temper.

"Now that I think about it, you might not know where she is. She probably ran off with a man like her tramp mama did. She could be anywhere. What was I thinking, wasting my time coming here?" He stood up again, this time sliding his gun into his pants pocket.

"I'm sorry Granny. Why don't you fix me up some lunch and we'll really get acquainted. You can tell me all about when Millie was a little girl. And pictures—I'll bet you've got lots of them. She is your only grandchild, isn't she? Yes, pictures, go get pictures. I'll look at them while you cook."

Ann didn't move.

"Now, get me pictures. Move."

Ann still didn't budge even when Brad kicked her leg under the table.

"I won't tell you again. The more you go against me, the harder I'm going to be on them when I find them. Now get me the damn pictures!" He hollered, kicking her shin again.

Ann didn't want to get the box of photos. Most of them with Millie were taken at the cabin. What if he noticed? Oh God, what was she going to do?

Brad walked over to her, took his gun back out of his pocket, and grabbed her by the back collar of her shirt, lifting her tiny frame off the chair.

"I said get me the pictures, now!"

Ann still didn't move.

"You're a stubborn old broad. I guess that's where my dear wife gets it. Most of the time I beat on her just to hear her cry.

Sometimes I have to almost kill her to get them tears flowing, tough . . . too tough for my liking. Thought that cancer might get her, but looks like she stood up to that, too. Didn't want them brats left for me to raise, she hovers over them like a bannie hen does her chicks. Won't even sleep with me like a real wife. She wads up in that bed with them. I hate them damned little pests. Everything was pretty good till they came along."

Ann's back was to him, so she couldn't see his face, but she could tell he wanted to hit her or something. Her mind raced. Could she get the gun out of her pocket without him noticing? Could she really aim the gun at him and shoot him? As Millie's words that were printed in her journal floated through Ann's head, she knew she could shoot this man at her back without so much as a second thought. She knew it wasn't her place to judge and punish, but right now she really didn't care. She'd kill anyone who stood between her and getting her Millie back. Yes, she could do it. She carefully reached into her pocket. About the time the tips of her fingers felt the cold metal, her head felt the searing pain as the butt of Brad's gun cracked into her skull.

❧ ❧ ❧

Ann slowly opened her eyes, she didn't know how long she'd been knocked out. She was lying right there on the kitchen floor where he knocked her down. Without moving, she scanned the parts of the room she could see. He was sitting above her at the table. A loaf of bread lay opened in front of him. The mayonnaise jar lid was off. She must have been out for a while because he had obviously eaten, and oh God, he had her box of pictures. She slowly moved her hand down to her pants pocket. The movement caught his eye.

"Well, if Sleeping Beauty isn't back to the land of the living. Did you have a good nap? Get up and join me. You've got some real nice pictures here. Millie was a cute little girl. I don't know what happened to her."

Ann tried to sit up, but her head took a spin and she thought she was going to be sick. Touching the back of her head, she could feel the egg-shaped knot, but there didn't seem to be any blood, just a slight concussion, she hoped.

"I said get up. Tell me about these pictures."

Ann tried again to stand, fighting off the nausea. Taking hold of the kitchen chair, she pulled herself up to her knees and then on up.

"Sit down."

As Ann sat she saw Brad had the pictures sorted into two piles. Picking one up, Brad held it to her face.

"Where was this taken?"

Ann took the picture from him. She saw Millie sitting on the front step of the cabin with Red her dog sitting at her feet. She knew she'd have to be careful and answer as calmly as she could. Ann wasn't used to lying, but lie was what she'd do.

"That was at a friend of ours summer home."

"A friend? You must have been up there all the time. It looks like all these pictures were taken at or around there," Brad said, pointing to the bigger of the two piles. "Where's this summer house?" Brad leaned in toward Ann so close she could smell his breath, hot and sour.

"Up toward the Virginia line, over thirty miles from here."

Millie was leading him away from the cabin as best she could. She was having a hard time thinking with her head pounding.

"How exactly do I get there?"

"There's a lot of turns, and it's been a few decades since I've been there. I'm not sure I remember. It may not even still be there. It was pretty old and rotten twenty years ago."

"Well, maybe you better try to remember. Here, write the directions down, and they better be right too." Pushing a pencil and notepad that served for Ann's grocery list toward her, he repeated himself, "Get it right."

Ann took the pencil. As best she could, she wrote down the directions to a place close to New River where some of their friends used to keep an old RV. She and Jake visited them in the summer. They fished and played in the river. Jonathan was just a small boy then, and oh, how he loved to splash around in the crystal clear water, catching crawfish and putting them in a coffee can.

Finished, she handed the notepad back to Brad. He read over the instructions.

"This better be right," he snarled. "Let's go. You're coming with me. I don't trust any of you old hussies. You're all lairs."

Oh no, what would she do now? She couldn't go with him. She had to get to the cabin and warn Millie.

"I've got to go to the bathroom first," Ann said.

"Hurry it up. And no funny business, or I'll have to kill you."

Looking down at the picture in his hand he asked one more question.

"This sign beside the road says Skunk Cabbage Bog. What the hell kind of road name is that? And it's not on your directions."

Caught off guard Ann didn't know what to say.

"I believe that was some kind of joke our friends had going. Becky hand-printed that sign herself. It wasn't really the name of a road."

Her explanation seemed to satisfy him and he ordered her again. "Hurry the hell up. It's going to be dark in a couple of hours, and I really want to see this summer house. Looks real nice, real nice indeed."

Ann stood up and went down the hall. Brad was right behind her. As she stepped into the bathroom, she pushed the door closed behind her.

"You got three minutes. Then I'm coming in."

Ann looked in the mirror. Her hair was a mess and her clothes were rumpled. Looking at the time on the wall clock, she saw she'd been knocked out well over an hour. She raked her fingers through her hair, smoothing it down, flinching as they trailed over the knot. She knew what had to be done. There was no question about it. She turned the faucet on and splashed some water on her face. Ann was as nervous as she had ever been in her entire life. She reached over and flushed the toilet for effect. Then she grabbed the green hand towel from beside the sink and dried her hands. She took the small gun out of her pants pocket and wrapped the towel around it. Her finger was on the trigger.

Brad was standing only a foot away from her. Ann pretended she was drying her hands as she walked past him. He must have put his 22 back in his pocket because it wasn't in his hand. An old woman like her wasn't much of a threat to him.

Ann walked to the refrigerator, her back to Brad. With her free hand she reached for her pocketbook. As she turned around, she let it drop along with the towel. She faced Brad with the gun pointed straight at him. Only the kitchen table separated them.

"What the hell do you think you're doing, old woman? Give me that gun!"

He lunged around the table. Ann saw Brad put his hand in his pocket—and that's when she pulled the trigger.

She wasn't sure who was more shocked, her or him. Ann couldn't believe she had actually shot a person, but he had the red stain on his light blue shirt just above his right hip as proof.

Brad felt the bullet rip through him. With his left hand he reached down and felt the sticky red liquid. When he saw his hand was covered in blood, he promptly passed out.

Ann's hands shook. She lowered the gun and sat down in the chair before her legs buckled. She did it! She actually shot him. Looking at the small pool of blood on the floor beside him, she wondered if he was dead or dying.

After taking a deep breath, she leaned over and picked up her keys. They had fallen out of her pocketbook when she dropped it before pulling the trigger. She didn't bother to pick up the tube of lipstick that fell and she didn't see the edge of the power bill receipt sticking out from under the stove.

Legs shaking, she headed for the front door. She didn't look back and she didn't check to see if Brad was breathing. She really hoped he wasn't. Either way, she had to call Amos. He could come and deal with Brad, alive or dead.

On her way to the mountain Ann stopped at the Shell station. She put her dime in the pay phone's coin slot and dialed the familiar number.

"Sheriff's office, Amos Cook speaking. May I help you?"

"Amos, I've shot Brad Madison, Millie's husband. He's lying in my kitchen floor bleeding. I'm going to the cabin."

Then Amos heard the click. What the heck did she say? He talked to Ann so many times on the phone that he knew exactly who it was, but what did she say? She shot somebody!

Grabbing his hat and keys off the desk, he hollered for Ben who handled the night shift. "Come on, Ben. We've got some big trouble on our hands. Lock up behind you." Amos was already out the door.

~ Chapter Twenty-four ~

Sadie took the branch and swished their tracks away as Millie drove past the bend in the road. She ran to catch up and jumped back in the passenger seat. Sammy was sound asleep in the back.

After parking in her spot in front of the cabin, Millie opened the back door and shook Sammy's shoulder.

"Wake up, we're home."

His eyes opened wide. He said, "My name is Honiahaka." With that, he slid off the back seat and out the door, chasing after the four kittens that were almost full-grown.

"Well, Sadie, we didn't get a whole lot accomplished this afternoon, did we?"

Millie unlocked the front door and went inside. Before Sadie could enter, Millie was back out the door with a hammer in her hand. She took it to the sidewall of the cabin. Reaching up, she pounded on the piece of metal sticking out until it was mashed flat against the wall.

"There, that should do. We don't need any more accidents."

With her arm around Sadie, they walked together back around to the front of the cabin. Sammy was lying on the ground covered with the four balls of fur, giggling.

Everything appeared to be calm, but Millie couldn't get Nyoaka's words or ominous predictions out of her head. Could their wonderful three months be ending? Could Nyoaka know that Brad was the evil one, and was he getting close to them?

The sound of Sammy's voice broke Millie's thoughts. "Mama, my kitties need Indian names too. Do you know any?"

"No, but we could give them nicknames and pretend they're Indian names."

"Okay, what will we nickname them?"

As Millie thought, she was thankful some things were so simple. Then a recollection came to her.

"When I was five or six years old, my Grandpa Jake had four rabbit hunting dogs, cutest little beagles you ever saw. He turned them loose every once and a while during the day to let them get some exercise. When he got ready to put them back up in their chicken wire fence home, he hollered out their names. Let's see what were they . . . here boys, come on in boys . . . here Mutt . . . here Whitie . . . here Tobb . . . come on in Yogi."

The children watched their mama as she pretended to call the imaginary dogs. Both had to stifle a giggle.

She went through it again. "Here Mutt . . . here Whitie . . . come on in Tobb and Yogi. Yes, that's it. Those were the dog's names, and they sound a little Indian, don't you think?"

Sammy thought his mama was being silly, but he loved it when she smiled and laughed. He liked the way their family was now, just the three of them.

Sadie was watching her mama, too, happy that things were going so well for them. Again she prayed she'd never have to leave this place. This was her home, even though she couldn't shake the feeling that something bad was about to happen. Nyoaka's words again echoed in her head . . . Wakanda, one who possesses magic power . . .

"Okay, that can be their Indian nicknames. What were they again?" he asked as he picked each cat up, one at a time. He looked them in the eye just like Nyoaka had done them as he repeated each name after his mama.

"Spook, you'll be Mutt. Smoky, you're Whitie 'cause you're the closest one to being white." After sitting him down, he picked up Sonny. "Sonny, you're Tobb." And lastly picking up Stripy, he dubbed him "Yogi." Then he looked at Sadie. "Are these names okay for your cats?"

"Yes, they're fine," Sadie said as she picked up Spook and Smoky, or was it Mutt and Whitie?

The cats were getting almost too big to pick up two at the same time. Sadie stroked their heads for a few minutes. Then she looked up at the darkening evening sky until the late day sun completely slid behind the oak trees. She noticed two squirrels scampering around the base of one of the trees, and then the chipmunks ran up the wall of the outhouse. The wind picked up and blew hot waves of air over Sadie, cutting right through her entire body, making a filmy coat of sweat cover her. About that time the turkeys started flying in to roost. The birds usually waited until the people were inside the house, but not tonight, and it looked like there were twice as many as usual. Then up behind the outhouse, the movement caught her eye. Big and black could only mean one thing.

* ❧ *

As Doc Townsend closed up his office, he began to hear a loud noise.

> *Closing his eyes, he sees hundreds of turkey wings fanning the evening sky. Then he sees the woman from the gate. She is frantically moving the key back and forth over the lock, desperate to get it to open. When she faces the cabin, sparks suddenly arc off the lock and land on her skin. Lewis feels the sizzle on his arm. Then he sees the blood. It is everywhere; the ground is covered. It pools around the lady's feet and spills over and down the roadbed toward the cabin.*

The girl and boy named Sadie and Sammy stand in the yard. There are cats everywhere, and they begin to turn red, as blood splatters their paws.

Melissa Madison suddenly appears at the cabin window, watching as the red substance gradually tints the feet of her children. She is out the door in an instant, a white towel in hand, flapping the air as if in surrender. Dropping to her knees, she swabs at their feet.

Lewis feels her thoughts: We came this far. No surrendering now. She struggles to remove the stains from Sadie and Sammy.

Then suddenly, one of the turkeys swoops down and snatches the red-blotched towel. The blood immediately disappears. Lewis can see the three people shiver, their pale skin glowing even whiter minus the red.

The woman at the gate stands frozen looking into the forest, her eyes wild and frightened.

Lewis shudders to think of the evil that is about to happen!

* ❦ *

"Come on, kids, the turkeys are turning in early tonight. We should get inside and fix supper," Millie said.

Then Sadie heard the loud squawking of a crow, and in the great distance, she heard something howling.

Nyoaka's words once again came to her. "You'll understand how your powers will be able to help when you hear the crow squawk and the wolf howl." A chill rippled through Sadie's body.

As Sammy stepped up into the house, Sadie grabbed her mama's arm. "Look up on the hill. Do you see him?"

Millie stared up through the darkening woods. "See what, Sadie? What am I looking for?"

Looking up the hill, Sadie saw him plain as day. He even stood up on his hind legs, motioning with one of his front paws as if waving hello . . . or giving her a warning. Again Sadie still didn't feel scared, just bothered.

"Nothing, Mama, I guess it was just a deer or something running through the woods."

But as she kept looking at Blackie, he dropped back down on all fours and walked toward the rutted roadbed that led to the cabin. There was no way her mama could not have seen him. Was he visible only to her?

As Sadie turned and followed her mama into the cabin, Doc Townsend's words came to her: "I saw the bear in my vision. He is my guardian spirit." Sadie was now beginning to believe the bear was her guardian angel too. Was this the magic Nyoaka meant?

The first thing Sadie saw as she ventured into the cabin was the bowl propped on the counter beside the enamel sink. She walked over to it and turned it over in her hands. Could this really be Nyoaka's father's, the bowl of a true Indian medicine man? Sadie felt strong and brave as she rubbed her thumb over its smoothness. She could just imagine the man, kneeling as she had, at the same place, looking into the bog in hopes of glimpsing one of the turtles. But no, he'd probably been digging for one of the root herbs Nyoaka had talked about. And that's where his spirit had left him. Where did it go? To Indian heaven? Was there really any difference between where white people and Indians go? No, not from what she learned from the Bible. Didn't it say something about one heaven and one earth? So God must think we're all the same if He puts us together when we die. Something about that made her feel real good inside.

Sadie took the bowl and dipped it down in the dishpan of water that was left from the morning dishes. She carefully washed the black earth from the inside, outside, and bottom. When it was clean, she took the hand towel and patted it dry. Nyoaka said she should keep it, that she would use it next. For what would she use it? She didn't know right now, but knew she would some day because she believed the Indian woman. For now she'd put it in a safe place.

Walking to the refrigerator, Sadie asked her mama, "Will you put this up high so it won't get broken?"

Taking the clean bowl, Millie set it safely on top of the icebox.

"What's for supper?" Sammy asked, breaking the somber moment. Millie was remembering all the words Nyoaka had spoken too.

❧ 𝕲 ❦

Ann's hands were shaking as she got back in the driver's seat after phoning the sheriff. In fact she was shaking all over. She had to get hold of herself. In less than an hour, she would be face to face with her long lost Millie.

Pulling the stick to the drive position, she gunned the gas. Gravel flew from beneath her truck tires. She was on her way to the mountain.

❧ 𝕲 ❦

In less than fifteen minutes after Ann's call, Amos and Ben were pulling into the driveway at 219 Sunset Drive. It was seven thirty-two on Thursday evening. It wasn't often they were called to a shooting.

Amos stepped out of the patrol car with Ben right behind him. The front of the house was dark. Except for what little sunlight there was filtering in, he could tell there was a light on in one of the back rooms, either the kitchen or the bedroom. He'd been in the house many times over the years and knew the layout.

Amos reached to his right side and unsnapped the leather strap, releasing his 38 Special. Up the front steps he went slowly, taking notice of the paint peeling off the sagging front porch plank boards. He opened the screen door, wrapped his fingers around the doorknob, and turned it. Ann hadn't bothered to lock it this time, for what she had been trying to keep out was already inside.

Amos could feel Ben's breath on his neck. He was actually so close Amos could smell his aftershave lotion.

Nothing looked out of the ordinary in the living room; everything appeared in place. A throw was spread over the back of the orange and yellow floral couch. A *Lady's Home Journal* was folded in the middle marking the spot where Ann must have gotten to; it was on an oval table beside a worn, brown recliner. Looking ahead, Amos saw the light shining from the kitchen through the archway. Stepping into the kitchen, he saw the blood. You could see the trail the dark liquid made as it formed a small puddle between the table legs, probably due to a dip in the floorboards. Then his eyes followed the blood smeared in front of the refrigerator and back toward the door. There the smudges turned into part of a bloody footprint with that footprint heading out the door.

The officers followed the blood trail to the edge of the yard. When they could see no more traces, Amos asked Ben to go to the patrol car and get a flashlight. The trail in the dim beam of light led them to the now empty logging road. They could see the rut where a vehicle had recently sped off.

"Just like tracking a wounded deer. Always did hate it when the animal gets away," Amos said. He frowned deeply, for he'd finished reading Millie's journal and felt justified calling Brad Madison an animal.

❊ ❦ ❊

By eight-fifteen, Millie's family had eaten supper, the dishes were done, and Millie was just lifting Sammy out of the bath water. The turkeys roosting early had run the family inside sooner than usual, and in the dense forest it was already dark.

❊ ❦ ❊

Ann pulled into the lane named Skunk Cabbage Bog right as something, a dog or coyote, darted across in front of her. She didn't want to scare Millie and the children, but didn't know any other way to get to them than to drive right down. Her next idea was to leave her truck in front of the locked gate, double security, and walk in. Before she rounded the last curve before the gate, she switched off her headlights. Something else darted in front of her, maybe a deer. Coasting to a stop at the locked chain, Ann instinctively switched off the ignition. She reached over and took the cabin and gate keys from the glove compartment. She stepped out of the truck, slipped the keys to the cabin and gate in one pocket, and put the key to the truck in her pocketbook. Finally she reached into the cab, took the Ruger from the seat, and slipped it in her other pocket. With pocketbook in one hand, she eased the door shut. She rubbed the huge lump on the back of her head that had begun to throb again while her eyes adjusted to the twilight.

* 🌿 *

Sadie asked, "What was that?"

Right in the middle of toweling Sammy, Millie stopped. She heard it too. She walked to the front door and made sure it was locked, and then she went to the side door, and shut it, throwing her hip against it. It had been propped open, so they could carry in water from the barrel for their baths. Then she went to the living room window and looked out. It was so dark now that all she could see were the dancing shadows of the night.

"What's wrong?" Sammy asked.

"Nothing, baby. Let's get your pajamas on."

When Sammy stepped his second leg into his pajama bottoms, they heard the turkeys taking flight. The noise seemed even louder than usual. The birds never left their roost until morning, that is, not till now.

"What's happening?" Sadie said.

"I'm not sure. Some animal probably just ran through the yard and scared the turkeys."

"But what was that bang?" Sadie asked.

Not answering, Millie walked to the fireplace and picked up the poker.

⚜

It was totally dark except for the soft glow of her small flashlight beam. Ann slowly made her way down the washed out trail. Up ahead she could see the outline of the cabin, and then she heard a noise to her right. She froze. Not twenty feet beside her stood the black bear, Blackie, and even though it was dark she could see him plainly. *God, please don't let me have a heart attack now, not when I'm this close to my granddaughter.* Ann's heart was pounding in her ears. She looked the bear in the eye and felt something familiar, something she remembered from the past. Surely it couldn't be the same bear from all those years ago?

Turning her head toward the cabin, Ann could see the light through the windows. She took a step toward the glow, then another, and another. The bear stood on all fours, not moving. Then she heard the thundering noise and almost blacked out from fear. Directly ahead was the thrashing of at least a hundred flapping wings—the turkeys, Jake's guardian angels. Finally she made it to the edge of the yard. The bear was still sitting where he'd been. Ann only had a dozen or so steps to the door.

⚜

Walking back to the window, poker in hand, Millie saw the movement and light at the edge of the yard. Then she heard a woman call her name.

"Millie?" Then again, "Millie, it's me."

Floating back in time, Millie closed her eyes. She could hear her Grandma Ann calling her name: *Millie, come to supper . . . Millie where are you hiding? Come on out now.* How many times had Millie heard her grandma call her name? A hundred? A thousand? No matter how many years had passed—more than twenty—now she was here calling it again. It was Grandma! Millie knew it!

Millie dropped the poker to the floor. Her weakened knees carried her to the door. Her fingers clutched the knob and turned it. The door opened. Her foot was on the first, then second step. Then she was running toward her, to her grandma, to the one person other than her children that she knew loved her, to the one who would accept her no matter what . . . to Grandma . . . to Grandma . . .

Ann couldn't move. As she watched the door fly open and the young woman run out, her heart leaped. Her legs threatened to fold and her eyes filled with tears. All she could do was stretch out her arms as Millie ran into them. All either one could do was cry and hold each other.

Sadie and Sammy stood at the door watching their mama and the woman she had called Grandma. Sadie put her arm across Sammy's shoulder and hugged him to her. She knew her mama had longed for his moment ever since they headed to the mountain three months ago. Every time she mentioned the word "grandma" she got tears in her eyes.

Up ahead, Sadie saw Blackie cross the road, but she didn't worry about Sammy seeing him. She knew now that he couldn't. The deer, rabbits, squirrels, chipmunks, crows, skunks, coyotes, wolves, and the bear all watched them. The turkeys had roosted again nearby. Sadie knew they were all as close to the cabin as they could get, watching over them.

Finally the women pulled away from each other. With her hands on Millie's shoulders Ann looked her in the eyes. "I know everything, Millie, and I shot him. I don't know how badly I hurt him or if he is dead, but I know I hit him. There was blood."

Not knowing what to say, and not certain she knew what her grandma was talking about, Millie asked, "You shot someone, Grandma? Who did you shoot?"

"Brad."

The blood rushed from Millie's head to her feet. It took all her willpower not to pass out.

Sadie heard what the grandma said, so she knew Sammy had heard it too. "Let's go in and sit down and let them talk, Sammy. It's been a long time since they've seen each other."

"Daddy's shot? Was it his blood? Did he die? Is he dead? I don't want him to be dead, do I? I've wished he was. Is it my fault he's dead? I wished he was when he was hitting me. I wished he was."

Sadie pulled her sobbing little brother over to the couch, and they sat down. Looking him square in the eye, she took him by the shoulders and jostled him a little.

"Listen. If Daddy is dead, you had nothing to do with it, and if Mama's Grandma Ann shot him, it was because he was hurting her like he did you, me, and Mama. Now calm down. Everything is going to be okay."

Sammy sat with Sadie on the couch for a long time while his mama and her grandma stood outside talking. Sadie sat with him, her arm protectively linked with his. They listened to the murmurings from outside the door. Right now Sadie felt really old.

"Grandma, is he dead? How did you know I was here? How do you know everything?"

As quickly as she could, she told Millie about coming to the cabin a few days earlier, about finding her journal and reading it.

"I'm so sorry for intruding on your privacy, but I just had to take the book when I saw it was yours. It's a good thing I did. If I hadn't read it and found out what a monster Brad is, I wouldn't have been prepared to defend myself. I would have been the one lying on the floor in a puddle of blood. Your diary saved my life."

"Grandma, do you think he's dead?"

"I don't know, Millie. I called the sheriff and I'm sure he's been to the house to see, but for now let's get inside, just in case."

They went in, closing and locking the door behind them.

"I'm scared," Sammy said, jumping up and throwing his arms around his mama's legs. "I don't want Daddy to be dead, but I don't want him to be alive either."

Squatting down, Millie pulled her little boy to her. "Sammy, it's all right. Everything is going to be okay. Come on now I want you to meet my grandma."

Shying behind his mama, Sammy hid his face.

"This is Grandma Ann, the one I talk about all the time. Grandma, this is Sammy."

Peeping out from behind his mama, Sammy asked, "Did you kill my daddy?"

Ann knelt down on one knee so she'd be face to face with the little boy.

"I don't know if he's dead. I did shoot him. I know how mean he was to you, your mama, and your sister. He wanted to find you so he could be even meaner to you. He hit me over the head, and when I woke up I had a chance to save us all from him. I've never hurt anyone in my life, but I just couldn't let your daddy be mean to any of you again. Some people are not nice. They are sick in their heads and it turns their hearts bad. I hope you will understand one day."

Sammy looked at Ann as she talked. When she stopped, he stepped from behind his mama and threw his arms around his great-grandma.

"Do you promise he won't hurt us ever again? Do you promise?"

"I promise with all the power I have in my old body," she said as she hugged the small boy tightly, feeling as if it were her very own son Jonathan's arms around her again.

Sadie sat watching and listening. She'd already made her mind up about the long lost great-grandma. She thought she'd like her just from her mama's stories, and now she was positive. Part of her still missed her Grandma Lindsay, even though Sadie had overheard Millie tell Brad about her Grandma Lindsay taking her away from her daddy Jonathan and grandparents Ann and Jake when she was little. Sadie wasn't sure how she felt about Grandma Lindsay now.

Sammy finally let go of Ann, and she stood up. She walked over to Sadie who was still on the couch and sat down beside her.

Before Ann could speak, Sadie said, "He's not dead. He'll be here. I'm not sure when, but he'll come."

Ann respected the young girl's intuition. She saw the strength and the pain in her young eyes . . . she saw the much younger version of herself.

"Let's get ready," she said to Sadie. Introductions were not necessary.

※ ❧ ※

Amos dropped Ben off at the station, telling him to put out an all-points-bulletin on any black Ford sedans with a single male driver within a fifty-mile radius. Amos would call the sheriff in Allegain and inform him of what was going on. Then as an off-duty sheriff and a friend, Amos decided to drive up the mountain to the old cabin to make sure Ann got there all right. No telling where that good-for-nothing husband of Millie's might be. Could be on the side of the road bleeding to death, or he could be on his way up the mountain right now.

※ ❧ ※

Brad's face twisted in pain as he stood before the motel's bathroom mirror trying to clean his wound. *Damned old woman, she'd pay for this! Just wait until I get my hands on her. She'll be sorry she ever crossed Bradley Madison. Nobody gets the upper hand on me and lives to brag about it. Nobody!*

~ Chapter Twenty-five ~

Sadie kept Sammy occupied playing with the kittens on the rug in front of the fireplace. Ann and Millie checked each door to make sure it was locked. When Ann saw that the windows couldn't be opened from the outside, she felt okay about them.

Next the women went from room to room closing the curtains. When all was secure, Millie put some water on the stove for coffee. Seeing the tub of bath water she'd had Sammy in, Millie looked at Sadie who was still in her day clothes.

"Oh, Sadie, do you want me to warm up the tub? You've not had your bath yet."

"I'll just take a pan bath in the bedroom if that's okay."

"Yes, that will be fine."

She knew Sadie didn't want to get in the tub in front of a stranger, but Grandma was no newcomer to Millie. She was her oldest, dearest and maybe only friend, thanks to Brad.

The pot boiled, and the granddaughter and grandma sat at the table and talked while Sammy continued to play with the kitties. Sadie took her pan of water into the bedroom, bathed, and put on her gown.

At nine o'clock, they heard the turkeys taking flight again. Ann put her hand in her pocket laying it on the Ruger, and Millie again picked up the poker.

Peeping out the window, Ann saw the darting glow of a flashlight coming down the path. Amos had to walk in since her car blocked the entrance, and the gate was locked.

"It's okay. I'm pretty sure it's Amos, the sheriff from home. He's always walked favoring his left side. Says one of his legs is shorter than the other one."

Still the two women stood guard until he came closer and called out Ann's name.

"Ann, it's me, Amos." He knew she was there because he saw her truck parked at the gate.

Opening the door, Ann said, "Come on in, Amos."

Amos opened the screen, swung the door wide open, and stepped up the two steps to the inside of the cabin.

"Ann, are you all right? What in the world happened at your house? All that blood."

Ann's heart sank. He didn't mention a body. She had been afraid Sadie was right. "Did you find him? Was he still there?"

But Ann knew the answer before Amos spoke. "Nobody was there, Ann, just the blood. Ben and I tracked the drops to the old logging road. We saw where a vehicle had pulled out from way down the path, spun around a lot like he was in a big hurry, Ben's putting out the usual alerts for him now. With all the blood the man lost . . . I'll check the hospital at home when I get back to see if they've treated anyone that resembles him. Do you have a picture?"

Millie walked into the second bedroom and took the photo box from the dresser drawer.

Just like her grandma said, she saw the diary was missing. Leafing through the photos, Millie took one out that had been taken that past Christmas. Brad always wanted to have his face snapped. He liked looking at himself. Most would say he was a great-looking man, and she had thought so, too, all those years ago when she met him at a friend's party. Dressed in his army uniform, he swept her off her feet. Looking now at the picture, she saw nothing handsome there. All she could see was what was on the inside, and it was dark and ugly.

Taking the picture, she walked back to the living room and handed the photo to the sheriff.

"I'll get this out over the wire service, but first, Ann, you need to tell me exactly what happened. By the way, Millie, it's good to see you again. Wish the circumstances were different though. You sure have grown up, and with babies of your own. My how time flies. Now what's the story, Ann?"

Millie looked over at her children standing on the woven rug in front of the fireplace. Their hands were tightly clinched together and they looked terrified, the look they always had when they knew their daddy was in one of his moods.

"Grandma, can you fill the sheriff in outside? I need to talk to the children. I think they've heard enough."

Ann walked with Amos out the front door. Millie took her children's hands and sat them one on each side of her on the green vinyl couch.

"Is Daddy dead? Will he ever come back?" Sammy's face was tear-streaked and his eyes were full again as he spoke.

"I don't know where your daddy is, but I don't think he's dead. He is trying to find us, and you know we can't be with him anymore. He hurts us. You remember, don't you, Sammy?"

Sammy shook his head up and down. Moving his hand, he touched his eye where his daddy had hit him, and then he reached up and touched his mama's cheek.

"Daddy is a bad, bad man, isn't he, Mama?" In his little boy's mind, he was feeling guilty about the way he really felt about his daddy.

"Your daddy is a bad man. I don't know why, but no one is supposed to be mean to someone else, especially family. There should never be any hitting or screaming in a home. Every family will have disagreements, but people who love each other talk their problems through. Remember the day you accidentally broke Daddy's favorite coffee cup, and how you tried to pick up the pieces and hide them? You might have gotten away with it except for the cut you got on your finger.

"You were terrified of what Daddy would do, but you shouldn't have had to be afraid like that. You should have felt safe. You shouldn't have had to worry that he would hit you. You should have been able to tell the truth and not be scared. That's the way God wants families to be.

"That's what I want for us. I want you and Sadie, and me and now Grandma Ann, to be the kind of family that isn't scared. I don't want any of us to ever worry that someone will hit us, or scream at us, ever again. I will do whatever I have to, to make that happen for us. I will do anything to keep you safe, and Grandma Ann has proven she will too.

"Your daddy will come here soon. When he does, I want you both to run as fast as you can away from him. He will try to threaten you into coming to him, but *do not* listen. He is a sick, unstable man, and now he is the angriest he's ever been.

"When the time comes, you two stay together and run to the spot where you saw the bog turtle, okay Sadie? Your daddy can't follow you into the bog. Only you know all the paths. You'll watch out for your brother and keep him safe, won't you, Sadie Girl?"

"You know I will." Sadie should have been terrified but for some reason she wasn't. She just knew what had to be done and she was going to do her part, whatever that was.

Millie studied the strong, young girl in front of her. She wanted to get her babies as far away from Brad as possible, and she didn't want them to see what might happen at the cabin. "Are we a team on this?" Millie asked both her children.

"Yes, Mama. I'll take care of Sammy, don't you worry. We'll be just fine," Sadie said.

"Sammy, you listen to everything Sadie tells you and don't leave her side, no matter what you hear or see, okay?"

Sammy didn't answer he again nodded.

Looking at the clock on the back of the cooking stove, Millie saw that it was ten minutes after ten o'clock. "Let's get you guys a snack and into bed," she said.

Sammy spoke then. "Are you coming to bed too?"

"Not right now. I want to visit with Grandma some more first, but we'll be very quiet so you two can get some sleep. What will it be, peanut butter and jelly?"

Neither child was very hungry but agreed the sandwich would be fine. After only a few bites and swallows of milk, they were finished.

"Let me get you two tucked in." Millie couldn't stand to see the troubled looks on their faces. "How about we let the kitties in for the night, just this one time?"

That brought grins to both. Millie walked over to the side door and opened it, calling for the kittens. Sleepily they all four trotted in and straight to Sadie and Sammy they went.

"Come on. I'll read you and the kitties one of the stories out of your favorite book," Sadie said.

She took hold of Sammy's hand and led him into the bedroom along with the sleepy cats.

Millie didn't even think about telling them to brush their teeth before she tucked all six in.

❀ ❦ ❀

Ann sat outside on the tailgate of Marty's electric company truck. Millie had explained why it was there. Ann told Amos everything that had happened with Brad at the house, and he jotted down several things in the small notepad he kept in his shirt pocket.

"You say he hit you twice? One time knocking you plum out, right?"

"Yes."

"Well, I know we can at least have him brought in on assault charges as well as breaking and entering. As far as all that stuff in

Millie's journal, she'll have to press charges for that back in Texas. By the way, I locked her book in my desk drawer."

After settling the children down for the night, Millie walked out the front door and joined her grandma and the sheriff.

"I'm never going back to Texas, not ever!" Millie said, obviously more upset than she looked.

"Millie, we'll cross that bridge when we come to it. Let's not worry about that now." Ann's voice was calm as she spoke to her.

"Ann, are you sure you'll be all right back here tonight?" Amos said.

"Yes, I don't think Brad has any idea where this place is. I hope I led him on a wild goose chase that will keep him busy for a couple of days up in Virginia.

"From all the blood I saw, you may not have to worry about him at all," Amos said. "I'm going to head back down the mountain and check the hospital. I'll call the Allegain sheriff in the morning, so he can keep an eye on things up here. Are you sure you all won't come down the mountain with me?"

While they were outside Amos had tried to convince Ann to go home and take Millie and the kids with her, but she'd have nothing to do with that idea.

"No, Amos. Brad knows how to find me down there, but I'm not convinced he can find us here. In the meantime, maybe you'll get your hands on him."

Millie chimed in. "Besides we've got Grandpa's guardian angels watching over us."

Ann looked at Millie and smiled. She had remembered the turkeys.

Amos shook his head, "Be careful, you two. I'll be in touch through the other sheriff. I don't want to be coming and going much up here in case that hoodlum follows me. But when we get our hands on him, I'll be back up to let you know."

"Okay, Amos. Thanks for everything. And you be careful, he's a mean one."

Ann and Millie watched the flashlight until it was out of sight around the bend. Then they quietly went inside, closed, and locked the door.

They walked together to the first bedroom. Peering in, they saw Sadie and Sammy snuggled up to one another. Sadie's arm was wrapped around Sammy, and Millie's old brown bear Teddy was poking out from under the covers between them. The storybook lay open beside Sadie, and the kittens were sleeping all around them.

Ann's eyes filled with tears. She'd not seen a sight that precious to her since she last saw Millie lying there in that same bed with her arms all wrapped around Teddy.

Millie walked over and pulled the sheet up under her children's chins, and then she leaned down and kissed each one on the forehead. She laid the storybook on the dresser and flipped off the lamp. She probably should put the cats out, but she didn't. Leaving the bedroom, she pulled the door closed behind her.

There would be no going to bed for Millie and Grandma Ann tonight.

* ❦ *

At one o'clock in the morning, Amos pulled into the driveway of his home. He'd been to the hospital where there had been no sign of Brad. He went back to the office to put Brad's picture out on the wire. He also requested a background check on Brad Madison from the feds. He wanted to find out everything he could about this guy.

The light was still on. Lottie was waiting up for him. He sure was a lucky man, wasn't a better woman in the world than Lottie Cook. He thought of the two women and children up on the mountain and hoped and prayed they'd be okay. He would do everything he could to find the man who had been and still was making their lives a living hell. He and Lottie would get on their knees tonight and pray for them. He knew God would listen to his Lottie.

Sadie heard her mama come in and felt her tuck them in and turn off the light. Sadie lay awake for what seemed like hours, listening to the whispers coming from outside the door and the soft purring of the kittens lying beside them. She didn't know what all they were saying, but she knew they were both crying a lot. She didn't think they were all sad tears though.

When Sadie woke up, the sky outside was just beginning to lighten. She uncovered and pulled the quilt back up under Sammy's chin. The kittens were gone. Stepping out of the bedroom, she silently went to the door and opened it. Her mama's Grandma Ann was sitting at the kitchen table, both hands wrapped around a steaming cup of coffee. Her mama lay with her knees pulled up under her chin on the couch and the homemade throw spread over her, fast asleep.

Ann heard the door open and looked up. Sadie saw her pick up the gun she had laid on the tabletop and slip it back in her jeans pocket. It didn't scare Sadie.

Ann motioned for Sadie to come over and sit down. "Good morning. How did you sleep?"

"Fine, I guess. You didn't lay down at all, did you?"

"No. I finally got your mama to settle down around three. She was plain tuckered out."

Sadie liked the way her mama's grandma talked. She sounded like Mr. and Mrs. Taylor at the hardware store and Becky at the soda fountain. They talked so slowly and said funny words like tuckered out. People in Texas talked totally differently.

"The deer are out this morning," Ann said, looking toward the window that faced the bottoms.

Sadie went to the window. There in the dim morning light was the doe with her two babies. "How did you know about them?" Sadie asked.

"They're there most mornings down in the bottoms feeding on the tender moist grass, or so they used to be."

Ann was tired. She had an emotional night telling Millie how her daddy had searched and searched for her, grieving himself into an early grave, and how she and Jake had found Jonathan that fateful morning right here in this very cabin. After Millie had lain down, Ann watched the shadows on the cabin walls. It was as if spirits were dancing, bouncing around everywhere. She was past tired.

Millie had cried and cried for the time lost with them all, and Ann had cried, too, from all the stories of what Millie had been through with Brad. Her eyes felt very heavy and swollen like she had been rubbing them with sandpaper.

Ann got up to stand by Sadie at the window. She knew the child didn't know her and didn't know whether to trust her or not. The girl probably didn't rely on anyone after all she'd been through in her short twelve years. Ann knew it would take time to earn the young girl's confidence.

Without really knowing why, Ann asked. "Have you seen the bear?"

Sadie was a little shaken at the question. She was sure no one else could see him. "Yes, I've seen Blackie several times since I've been here."

"He was here this morning. Caught sight of him first light. He walked the roadbed from the bottom and went up the hill behind the outhouse. See if you can get a glimpse of him out the edge of the window."

Sadie moved over and stood in front of her mama's grandma. Looking up the hill, she saw his black form. He was just sitting there on his back haunches doing nothing.

"Can you see him, Sadie?"

"Yes, that's what he did the first time I saw him. He came up that path from the bottom and went up the hill. He didn't stop there that morning though. He just kept going."

"Have your mama and brother seen him?"

"No, not even when I pointed him out to her last evening. I was wondering if he was just in my imagination."

"I never saw him either during all those years of us coming up here. We saw the signs, scat in the woods and limbs broken out of the wild cherry trees in the fall. But then that day, the morning Millie's daddy . . . your Grandpa Jonathan passed away, I saw him out this very window, just sitting there, looking in at me. He had the saddest eyes."

Sadie looked at her mama's grandma. She had a faraway, torn look on her face, and then she spoke again. "I never saw Blackie again . . ."

Blackie! That's what I call him! A funny little chill went through Sadie.

"Not until the days when I started coming to the gate since you've been here," Ann finished.

"I think I saw you one day. You were parked at the gate for a long time. It looked like you were crying and you drove a black Ford truck."

"Yes, that was me. I couldn't bring myself to come down to the cabin. Until the other day, I haven't been here in over eighteen years."

"Blackie walked behind your truck that day, close enough to touch the bumper . . . I saw him."

Ann noticed, too, how her great-granddaughter called the bear Blackie, and she smiled. "You know Sadie, I guess we've got something very special in common besides being grandma and granddaughter. I believe we've both got a little touch of the magic. It'll be our secret, okay? Blackie can be our private friend. He was even here by the road when I walked in last night. I swear he had those same sad eyes I saw in the other bear all those years ago, the same eyes my son Jonathan had after Millie went missing."

Again Ann wondered if it could be the same bear.

Sadie wasn't sure about keeping a secret from her mama, but she didn't really see how it could hurt since no one could see Blackie but Grandma Ann and her. She didn't realize it, but she had thought of Ann as her own grandma for the first time, and not just her mama's grandma.

"I believe he must be our guardian spirit," Sadie said.

"Guardian spirit? I'm not sure about that. Maybe. But one thing I am sure of is that guardian angels are all around us."

"Don't you believe that all of us have a guardian spirit? I thought all of us who have Indian blood have one."

"Indian blood? Where did you hear that?"

"Mama said you had Indian blood running through your veins."

"Well, as a matter of fact I do, but it is so far back I don't believe it counts. It is something about my great-great-grand-mother falling in love with a young brave all those years ago. They had a child, but the girl's parents took it from her, saying no redskin would raise a grandchild of theirs. The old story says the daughter mourned herself to death over the loss of her baby girl. A surge of energy passed through Ann's body as she thought of her own son mourning himself to death when he lost his little girl.

"Well, I believe it. Nyoaka gave us all Indian names and she said we had the blood. My name is Wakanda."

"Who is Nyoaka?"

"She's Doc Townsend's grandma and she's a full-blooded Cherokee Indian."

"It seems like I have heard stories about her, but I've never chanced to meet her. I just might have to introduce myself to her one of these days. We might have some stories to swap. What does your Indian name mean?"

Sadie hesitated for a minute. She didn't want to sound conceited. "Nyoaka says it means 'one who possesses magic power."

Ann noticed that the words Sadie spoke were not proud or arrogant. She said them in the most humble of ways, hanging her head as she spoke. Ann thought the name had been given to her rightly, for Ann already felt her capability. Folks said her great-grandma also had the gift. Ann knew she herself had a touch, but not enough to even notice most of the time. Now Sadie—she might be a different story.

"I think this lady Nyoaka is a very wise woman. I believe your name suits you perfectly. Wakanda, how beautiful, just like you."

Sadie blushed; no one gave her compliments but her mama. Her daddy always called her "worthless" and "ugly," and Grandma Ann hadn't laughed at what her Indian name meant.

As Sadie raised her head she saw Blackie walking through the woods toward the road . . . Ann saw him too.

"He is my guardian spirit, I know he is," Sadie said in a small, whispered voice, talking to herself as much as anyone.

As Ann listened to the child the words from Psalm 91:11 came to mind: "For He shall give His angels charge over thee, to keep thee in all thy ways."

Call it what you want, guardian spirit or guardian angel. Ann didn't really care as long as they were watching over them. She knew they were going to need all the help they could get. In fact, she prayed daily for guidance since Lindsay had taken Millie away. But now Ann had Millie back and two other great-grandchildren. Now she knew the only aid she would take was from above. No more bargaining with the Devil; she had always known there was no help there, and now here stood this little girl, Sadie, all goodness. There was her proof.

The loud flapping of the turkeys' wings broke Ann's deliberation and also woke Millie. She jumped up with a start: Brad was coming. She was on the verge of hysteria until she saw her grandma standing with Sadie at her side by the window.

"Where's Sammy?" Millie asked, walking hurriedly to the bedroom door.

As soon as she saw him, a wave of relief washed over her, and her heart slowed down a beat or two.

"It's all right. We're all fine."

Ann went to Millie and hugged her tightly. It felt so good to be embraced in this loving way. Millie had forgotten how it was to be loved by someone other than her children. She breathed in the smell of her grandma as she felt her soothing her by slowly and gently stroking her hair.

"I'm so glad you're here, Grandma. I've missed you so much." Millie felt like a little girl again.

"And I've missed you, too, little one." Only Ann knew how much. No one was going to take Millie away again, no one!

"Teddy and I are hungry, and I've got to pee." Sammy broke the spell between the two women and they let go of each other.

"Come on, kids. What have you got to cook? I'll fix you all breakfast," Ann said, suddenly not feeling so tired. She had a family again.

Millie finally got tired of arguing with Sammy about why she wanted him to use the chamber pot, and anyway, the kittens needed letting out.

"Grandma, I'm going up to the outhouse with Sammy. Sadie, you might as well come, too, so we won't have to make two trips."

Sadie didn't argue. She was feeling a little anxious, but then she remembered Blackie was there and she was fine.

"Grandma, will you watch us?"

By that Ann knew Millie wanted her to cover them with her gun. "Yes, Millie. I'll be right here on the front step."

Watching them trod up the path to the outhouse, Ann looked around, all up through the woods, around the corner of the cabin down toward the creek and onto the bottoms. Nothing seemed out of the ordinary. How good everything looked to her, especially the red and white petunias planted beside the steps.

Shortly they were all coming back down the path. Ann took her hand out of the pocket holding her Ruger. The gun held six rounds. Jake always left the first round in the cylinder empty, and she had used one bullet on Brad. Four were left.

As they went back inside, Millie closed and locked the door behind them. Ann went to flip the bacon. She sure had missed cooking on this old stove.

After they ate, and the kids dressed, Ann and Millie finished the dishes. The barrel of water on the back porch was less than half full. Before they had baths tonight it would have to be filled.

"That barrel is a wonderful idea, Millie. I wish I had thought of it years ago. It would have saved me many a trip down the spring path in the dark."

Sadie and Sammy let the kittens in to play, but they were getting so big now that they wanted to sleep more than entertain. It only took a few minutes for them to have spent their energy and fall asleep on the rug.

"I want to go outside. I'm bored," Sammy said, when the kittens stopped playing.

Millie looked at the clock. It was only ten-fifteen. "How about we read a Bible story?" It was Friday, and they had usually already had one devotion during the week and one on Sunday.

"Okay. May I pick? I want to hear about that man killing the giant—you know David and the slingshot."

"I know. Let's see if I can find that story."

They sat on the couch, all four of them, while Millie thumbed to the book of 1 Samuel 17. She read the whole account, right down to David cutting the head of Goliath off with the giant's own sword.

"That part scares me," Sammy said as he snuggled up to his mama.

"May I have a slingshot? I can go down to the creek and get myself five smooth stones just like David, and when Daddy comes to get us, I'll shoot him with my rocks. I won't kill him though. We're not supposed to kill anyone; I'll just scare him and run him off."

Tears sprang to Millie and Ann's eyes, and the Lord's words rang through their heads. Exodus 20:13. *"Thou shalt not kill."*

Sadie broke the silence. "Read to us about angels, Mama."

"Angels, let me think," Millie said, rubbing her chin.

"What about Gabriel?" Ann said.

"Yes, the place where he tells Mary about baby Jesus going to be born," Sadie said.

Millie turned to Luke 1:26 and started reading, *"And in the sixth month the angel Gabriel was sent from God . . . "*

When she finished with that, they wanted to hear more, so Millie turned back a few verses and started reading from verse 11, *"And there appeared unto him an angel of the Lord standing on the right side of the alter of incense. And when Zacharias saw him, he was troubled, and fear fell upon him. But the angel said unto him, Fear not, Zacharias: for thy prayer is heard."*

Sadie's mind drifted as her mama continued to read. Are God's angels just like the Indians' guardian spirits?

When Millie finished, Sammy was fast asleep, snuggled up to his great-grandmother. Grandma Ann had laid her head back on the couch and drifted off too.

Sadie, however, was wide awake. "What are angels?"

"Well, Sadie, I believe they are lots of things. I think they are God's messengers and His helpers. I believe He sends them to earth to assist those of us who are His believing children. Let me see, there is a scripture somewhere."

It took Millie a few minutes but then she found it. "Here it is, in Hebrews 1:14. *Are they not all ministering spirits, sent forth to minister for them who shall be heirs of salvation?"*

Sadie smiled. Nyoaka had to be right about the guardian spirits because that's what the Bible called them, too, spirits.

Slipping down from the couch, Sadie went to the kitchen window. It took her a minute to find him, but there he was, high on the hill close to the curve, there just beyond the locked gate chain, her guardian spirit, God's angel, Blackie.

~ Chapter Twenty-six ~

At five-thirty Friday afternoon, Lewis was following his last patient out the door of the examining room.

"Won't be long now, Amy. Before the weekend's out, you might be rocking your new baby. Just go straight to the hospital if those pains get regular. Call me and I'll meet you there."

"Thank you, Doc Townsend. I hope I'll see you real soon."

Holding her back, the young woman waddled out the front door. Her husband Jim was waiting out front in his truck. When he saw her coming he got out and held her arm as she maneuvered down the front steps. He helped her up into the truck.

"That baby is going to be a whopper. I don't know how she even walks," Lafayette said as she watched Amy leave.

"I know, Laf. I'd almost bet she'll have twins, but for the life of me I can't hear but one heartbeat. Either way, she's in for a hard time, this being her first child."

"Better her than me," Lafayette said before she answered the ringing phone. "Yes, he's standing right here. Doc, it's Marty."

Taking the phone, he said, "Hello Marty. How's the eye?"

"Hey, Doc. Pretty good. The cut is a little red around the stitches and it's all purple and black, but I can open it and see out of it."

"That's great."

"Have you heard from Mrs. Burke? She was supposed to pick me up this afternoon, so I could get my truck."

"No, I haven't heard anything. Do you want me to run you down there? I'm just about ready to finish up here."

"Well, I don't know, Doc. She said she'd come, and it's not like she can forget me with my truck sitting in her yard. Maybe she'll get here yet or Ellen can run me down there."

"No, no. I'll be glad to."

Marty thought the doc sounded a little anxious to go, but who wouldn't be? That Mrs. Burke was a fine looking woman, and Tom at the pharmacy said she told him her husband was dead. Maybe old Doc was finally getting the fever. It was about time.

"Well, if she doesn't come today, can you take me in the morning?"

"Sure, as long as I'm not at the hospital delivering Amy Wilson's baby."

"Okay. I'll call you in the morning if I need a ride."

"Sounds good, Marty." Hanging up, Lewis felt a little giddy at the prospect of seeing Millie again so soon.

When he had finished cleaning up, he locked up his examining room door where he kept the drugs. Bidding Laf goodbye, he went into the kitchen. His grandmother was there. Two steeping cups of wild black cherry root tea sat on the bar in front of her.

Lewis sat on one of the high stools, the same one Millie sat in the day before. Just the smell of the sweet tea had a soothing effect on him. It seemed his grandmother always knew what he needed before he even knew it himself.

Nyoaka sat beside him and picked up her cup. After one sip she spoke. "Tomorrow morning I will go with you down the hill. I will visit my grandfather Wahya's grave and the stomping grounds of my people. I must be there before noon."

"I've got to drop Marty off to get his truck at that cabin on the hill above there, that is unless Millie picks him up this evening. Either way I'll take you if you're sure you're up to it Grandmother."

"It will be as I have already seen it. You will find the answer to that tomorrow." Standing, she took her tea and left the kitchen.

Lewis always marveled at his grandmother's words. Much of the time she sounded like a crazy woman, but she never said anything that didn't come true. *"I'll know the answer tomorrow."* *Now what did she mean by that?*

Images of smoke filled his senses and dulled his view. The smell was so powerful Lewis coughed and his eyes watered. It would be a long time until tomorrow. He wiped his watering eyes with his handkerchief. The visions had never been this powerful . . .

❃ ❧ ❃

A few minutes before four in the morning, the phone beside Doc Townsend's bed rang. Sleepily he answered, "Hello."

"Doc, it's Jim. Amy's in a bad way; just hit her all of a sudden. The bed got wet. Woke both of us up. And now she can't move, she's in so much pain. Said it feels like the baby's head is poking out."

"Keep her calm and don't let her push. I'll be there in ten minutes."

Jerking on his clothes, Doc flew down the steps, unlocked and opened his examining room door. Going to the medicine cabinet, he took out several bottles. One was a painkiller that Amy might need before the night was over. He gathered the items and put them into his black satchel. Doc slammed the front door and ran to his Chevy which was old, but still reliable. It started on the first try. Gunning it, he caused the tires to squeal on the pavement. He didn't worry about telling his grandmother what was going on. She probably already knew, and she was used to him coming and going to calls all during the night.

Jim and Amy's house was just a street over, so in less than ten minutes, Doc was flying through the front door of their one-story frame house. He could hear Amy's scream as soon as the door opened.

After a quick exam, Lewis saw that Amy was right. The baby's head was crowning, and oh my Lord, what a head. He'd delivered over five hundred babies in his years of doctoring, but he'd never seen anything like this.

Trying to calm the young couple, Doc talked softly to them, wanting Amy to relax all she could. It was going to be hard enough to get that big baby through the birth canal, and if she were tensed up, it would make it worse.

"Amy, look at me." Doc said. She had her eyes clamped tightly shut, and when she opened them, he could see the fear.

"Amy you're right. The baby is crowning. It's got a head full of carrot red curls."

Amy looked at her husband Jim's own red top and smiled.

Lewis could see a little of the tension easing from her body.

"Amy, it's going to be a big baby just like we thought, so it may be a long few hours for you. We need to take this slow and easy, letting your body stretch a little at a time. The baby's heartbeat is strong and steady, so everything is all right. Now don't push, no matter how much you need and want to. Can you do that for me? Can you?"

"I'll try," Amy said so softly, he could barely hear her. She held Jim's hand so tightly that Doc could see Jim's fingers turning purple.

Doc Townsend pulled a chair up to the foot of the bed. For the next three hours, he sat massaging the opening of Amy's birth canal. Amy had been working hard trying not to push. Doc almost had the baby's head completely out, and so far there was only a small tear. If she could hold on a few more minutes, he'd have the shoulders out.

But at seven-fifteen, almost four hours after Doc arrived, Amy had had enough. With one hideous growl, she bore down and pushed as hard as she could. Lewis knew it was coming, so he stood up to catch the baby. The carrot-topped little boy wailed his way into the world, and his mama wailed right along with him.

Lewis worked fast. He cleaned out the boy's mouth and clamped off the cord. He was a whopper, at least twelve pounds with wads of fat bunched on his arms and legs. When Lewis had the baby under control, he laid him wrapped in a sheet in his daddy's arms. Jim was as white as the linen cloth his baby was swaddled in.

Lewis wasn't surprised to see the red stain forming under Amy's bottom. After quickly accessing, he told Jim to lay the baby beside his mama and call an ambulance. They needed to get Amy to the hospital; she was going to need a few stitches and maybe a pint of blood.

❀ ❦ ❀

By the time Doc Townsend wrapped things up at the hospital, it was ten o'clock on Saturday morning. Amy was looking better after the unit of blood, and the baby was hungrily nursing at her breast. He felt sure they'd be fine, but he doubted she'd have enough milk to keep that big boy satisfied, not for a few days at least. On the way out, Lewis told the nurse to have a bottle ready. They were probably going to need it.

The nurse smiled, knowing exactly what the doctor was talking about. He was always concerned for his patients. He sure was a handsome man, too, and he was so nice. She couldn't believe some lucky woman hadn't grabbed him up.

❀ ❦ ❀

The phone was ringing when Lewis came through the front door. It was ten-thirty.

"Hello."

"Hey again, Doc. Where have you been?"

"Long night, Marty."

"Do you still feel like running me to get my truck? Mrs. Burke never showed up last night."

"Sure, Grandmother wants to go anyway."

Nyoaka was already standing by the door with her shawl around her shoulders.

"We'll be right there, Marty."

"We must hurry. They need us . . . now," Nyoaka said to her grandson as she stepped out the front door, her hand-carved cane clicking on the wooden planks. Stopping for a minute, she looked over her shoulder at him. "Bring your medicine bag. You may need it. And don't forget the Oak Bark Salve; I smell smoke."

He felt smoke in his eyes as soon as Nyoaka mentioned the salve. He squinted and rubbed them as he made his way into the examining room to get supplies. Lewis shook his head, again wiping his teary eyes.

When he got inside, a warning signal went off inside his head. The door was unlocked, but he never left it that way. He didn't want to tempt anyone with his drug cabinet. Nothing looked out of place except that the drug cabinet was unlocked too. He was tired from his long night. Maybe he just forgot to lock it back? On his way out he made sure the key clicked to the left, locking both the medicine cabinet and the examining room door.

֍ ⚜ ֎

Ann slept till after two o'clock while Sadie and Millie sat and talked, ate lunch, and did a few inside chores. They changed the beds as quietly as possible and swept the floor.

When Ann roused, her left arm was asleep from where Sammy lay on it. She eased herself out from under him and looked around the cabin as she stood up. She could hear noise out on the back porch. Peeking through the cracked door, she saw Millie and Sadie sitting there talking with the kittens climbing all over them.

She heard Sammy ask, "Is it time to get up, Grandma?"

Walking back to him, she knelt down and covered him up with the orange and green spread.

"No, not if you don't want to. Just lie there and snuggle up till you feel like getting up."

She rubbed his temple with her thumb until his eyes eased shut again. She used to rub Jonathan and Millie like that when they were babies. It always calmed them down too.

Walking again to the back door, Ann opened it. "Anything strange been going on?"

"No. Everything seems fine."

Ann wasn't reassured. For the rest of the afternoon, they all stayed in playing a long game of Monopoly. By dusk, they all four were yawning and sleepy, especially Sadie and Millie since they hadn't napped that day.

"We really should have tub baths tonight, kids, but let's just wash off, okay? It's not like we've been outside rolling in the dirt."

Sadie knew she didn't want to make the trip back and forth from the spring to fill the tub. They barely stuck their heads outside all day other than a couple of quick runs to the outhouse. They decided on the pan baths.

Sadie and Sammy were washed, pajamas on, and settled in by nine-thirty. This time Sadie didn't lie awake. She was so tired from not sleeping the night before that she went right out.

Millie found her grandma some clean clothes and underwear. Ann went into the second bedroom like Sadie had to bathe and change clothes; then Millie did the same thing.

They sat and talked for a while. When Millie yawned, Ann told her to go snuggle up with the children.

"You stayed up last night, Grandma. I'll stay up tonight."

"No, I had a nap. I'll be fine. Go catch yourself a few hours, and if you wake up and all's well, I'll sleep for a few hours."

"Are you sure?"

"Yes, now go on. It's almost ten-thirty."

Millie stepped over to her grandma and kissed her on the cheek. "I love you, Grandma."

"I love you, too, Millie. Now get some sleep."

As Ann watched Millie climb in beside Sammy, she couldn't control the urge to step into the room and tuck them all three in, pulling the sheet up under their chins. Teddy was wrapped up in Sadie's arms tonight.

When Millie woke, she rose straight out of the bed. The clock on the windowsill said three thirty-five. She'd slept over five hours. All was quiet in the little cabin. She stretched and walked to where Grandma Ann was standing at the window peeking out at the road from the edge of the window where the curtain didn't close completely.

"Is everything all right?"

Ann said, "Yes, everything appears to be in perfect order. The turkeys are asleep above us, and before you woke up, all my family was asleep in the next room. Right now, everything is wonderful."

But she and Millie both knew this wouldn't last. They felt the battle brewing and the final round was about to begin. Millie walked over and hugged her grandma.

"Go lie down. You've got to be exhausted. Even if you did take a nap yesterday, you didn't sleep at all last night."

"Maybe I will just lie down here on the couch for an hour or so."

Reaching into her pocket, she took the Ruger out and handed it to Millie.

"Oh no, Grandma, I wouldn't know what to do with it. Remember when you and grandpa used to shoot? I'd cover my ears and run away. I couldn't stand the noise. I never did shoot, no matter how hard daddy and grandpa tried to get me to."

"Well, just put it in your pocket while I lie down. I don't want to leave it out with the children here."

Understanding exactly what she meant, Millie took the gun and slipped it into her pant's pocket. The coldness of the stainless steel numbed her fingers.

"Wake me if you hear anything, anything at all."

"I will. Now go to sleep."

Lying down on the couch, Ann pulled the spread over her shoulders. Exhaustion overtook her and she was asleep in seconds. Millie stood vigil at the window. It was a long three-and- a-half hours before the turkeys fluffed up their wings and took flight. It was a minute past seven when Millie saw her grandma open her eyes.

"Good morning," Millie said softly to her grandma. "The turkeys woke you, didn't they?"

Rising to a sitting position, Ann yawned. "Yes they did. I forgot how loud they could be."

"You get used to it. I hardly even notice them anymore," Millie said.

"How about some coffee? I believe I'm going to need a jump-start this morning." The last two days were catching up with Ann. She felt tired and very old . . . happy but very scared.

Millie handed the Ruger back to Grandma Ann first thing. By nine o'clock everyone in the cabin had been to the outhouse and eaten breakfast. Millie stood out front of the cabin and watched each of them as they came and went.

"I've got to fill the water barrel. The children have to have a real bath tonight."

"I'll help you. We'll take turns covering each other," Ann said.

"Okay, but don't give me the gun again. It makes me too nervous."

It didn't make Ann nervous. The Ruger made her feel safer and somewhat in control. She shot Brad once; she could shoot him again. The words that Sammy had talked about from the Bible crossed through her mind again. *Thou shalt not kill . . . I know, I know, God. Vengeance is mine sayeth The Lord. But Lord, we're talking about the Devil here. I know you want me to fight him, and of course you don't need any help, but . . .* Ann rationalized. *Didn't Jesus fight against the Devil himself in the wilderness? I know, I know. You were there handling that, too, weren't you?*

By ten o'clock the water barrel was filled. They all four sat in the living room waiting, not knowing when Brad would come, but knowing he would.

At ten-fifteen Sammy stood up from his spot on the floor, trying to coax the lazy kittens to play with him. "I smell something. What is it?"

Sniffing the cabin air, Ann and Millie smelled it, too. They both stood and peeped out the slit in the drawn curtain.

"It's gas. He's here," Sadie said.

~ Chapter Twenty-seven ~

Brad Madison nursed his wound at the Super 8 Motel out on Highway 77 not ten miles from Granny's house. He backed in his Galaxy, so the Texas tag wouldn't show. Before securing a room, he slipped on his light blue jacket, the one he always kept in the trunk. Zipping it up to cover his blood-stained shirt, he paid for two nights just in case he wasn't able to get out tomorrow to pay for another one. He wasn't too worried about the attendant. He couldn't speak a word of English and just wanted his money.

After inspecting his wound and nearly passing out a few times, Brad decided it wasn't as bad as it looked. The bleeding had stopped. The bullet just grazed the outer flesh of his stomach. He always was a heavy bleeder; even a razor cut appeared life threatening to him. He cut the top sheet from the bed into strips and wrapped it around his middle. One of his makeshift moms had told him to drink a lot of water back when his foster dad beat the hell out of him and his nose bled for hours. She was some kind of butt-wiping nurse and said it would help build his blood back up faster. So all during the night every time he rolled over and felt the wound, he got up and drank a glass of water.

When Brad woke up on Friday, it was nearing noon. It was a good thing he paid for two nights because checkout was eleven o'clock, and his watch said eleven forty-three. As he shifted to ease off the bed, the searing pain of ripped flesh tore through him.

Damn woman! How could I have let her shoot me? He was too smart for this to have happened. He wouldn't give her another chance, not if he got the first shot in next time.

After he rolled off the bed, he stretched as best as he could. He undid the sheet binding, cleaned his wound again, and then wrapped himself in more of the white cloth. He drank another glass of water and packed his stuff. He was off to find his beloved family, dear Granny and all.

By that evening at six-thirty, Brad realized the old lady had pulled one on him. The directions she gave him to the summer home had led to a broken-down camper on the side of a river, and it was obvious no one had stayed in it in many years.

When he stepped back into his car, he leaned over and picked up the piece of white paper in his floorboard. It was stained with his bloody footprint. It must have stuck to his foot. Just before tossing it out the window, he saw the name Ann Hampton. It was a power bill for a residence at 113 Skunk Cabbage Bog Road, Roaring Valley, North Carolina. Well now, that sure wasn't Granny's home address. Must be her summer place, the one where she and the brats were hiding.

Roaring Valley? Hadn't he passed through a town called that while following Granny's directions to Virginia? It was right before he went through that one-horse town called Spartan. It wouldn't take him more than an hour to get back there. How hard could it be to find a road called Skunk Cabbage Bog?

By the time Brad drove into the town called Spartan, he was starving and needed a drink. The dull ache in his side had turned into a throbbing pain. He pulled into a drive-in diner on the edge of town. The menu was painted on a cinderblock wall in front of him.

When the girl came to his window, he ordered a cheeseburger with the works, fries and a Pepsi.

"Is there a drugstore anywhere around here?" he asked the young lady. A pretty thing she was too.

"Yes, but it's closed by now. Doc Townsend might have what you need. He keeps stuff at his office for after-hour emergencies."

"Where's his place?"

"Oh, just go into town on this same road, and at the only stoplight, take a left. You can't miss it. It's a big two-story house on your right, painted some kind of light purple color. He's got a sign out front."

"Thanks, little lady," Brad said giving her one of his dazzling smiles. If he didn't have bigger fish to fry, he'd be talking to her a little more.

"Oh yeah, honey." He was really pouring on the charm now. "Do you know where a road called Skunk Cabbage Bog is?"

The girl turned all shades of red. "Yes, it's not far from my house down the mountain in Roaring Valley. Just stay on this road out of town until you come to Shaw Road, turn left on it and go two or three miles. Your road will be on the right. It's not really a road. It's not much more than a path."

"Do you know who lives down it?"

"Nobody that I know of. My boyfriend and I drive down it to where the locked chain is across the road. We park there sometimes. One evening late, we walked on down the road and found a deserted cabin. But we couldn't get in. The doors were locked."

Realizing she already said too much, the waitress returned to the diner to fill his order.

Stupid blond bimbo, of course she parks with her boyfriend. All women are tramps.

After Brad ate, he drove all around the town looking for a room to spend the night. His wound needed dressing. He wanted a pain pill, but he settled for a stop at the liquor store. That place was the only good thing he'd seen in town. Then he remembered the blonde at the diner.

With a fifth of Jim Beam in the seat beside him, he went in search of the doctor's place. He still wanted some pain pills and he knew a shot of penicillin wouldn't hurt him.

On the way, he stopped at a service station. It was closed, but luckily the door to the men's room on the outside of the building was unlocked. Brad got the rest of the sheet strips and switched on the light of the bathroom, shutting the door. He hoped no one would drive by and notice his car and the light.

He unwrapped the bandage and looked down. Sure enough, the injury looked red and blotchy. He needed penicillin.

‣ ✤ ‣

Leroy Hanks had been the deputy sheriff at Spartan for nearly five years. Everybody knew he hit the bottle every once in a while, but nobody knew where he got it because no one ever saw him stop at the liquor store. At nearly ten o'clock on Friday night, Leroy needed a drink. Heading out of town to his supplier's house, he saw the car parked at Willis' Service Station. The bathroom light was on, probably some teenager and no need to check it out. He wanted that drink.

Hadn't something come across the wire last night about a black Ford? That was way down in Jonesboro though. He really should have driven down to the old Hampton cabin today like the sheriff had told him to do, but he had too bad a hangover to drive that far. He'd run down there tomorrow and check things out.

‣ ✤ ‣

Brad found the two-story house with the doctor's sign at ten minutes till eleven. There was a light on upstairs, so he pulled past the house and turned around in a driveway. He parked a block or so down the street. He opened the whiskey bottle and took his first swig. Then he just sat there and drank while he waited for everyone to go to bed.

The squealing of tires woke Brad. Looking at his watch, he saw it was twenty-five minutes after three o'clock. The Jim Beam bottle in the seat beside him was three-fourths empty.

Oh well. It was probably just as well that he passed out. He needed to sleep, and now it looked like the coast was clear with the good doctor speeding away on a call.

After the doctor's car was out of sight, Brad left his car and slipped through the darkness to the front door. When he turned the knob, he found the door unlocked. There was a tiny lamp on a desk that gave him enough light to see. No medicine was there in the waiting room. Opening the door to the right of the desk, he glanced around but didn't find anything useful there either. The door marked "Exam Room 1" was on the other side of the room. When he opened that door, he saw that the room's interior was much bigger than the other room. By the glow of the full moon through the two long windows, he saw the white metal cabinet in front of him.

When he reached to pull the handle, the door wouldn't open. Swearing, he reached into his pocket and took out his knife. He loved that blade. It had on it every tool a person could ever need, including a thin twirling cork-screw; the tip of this would work just fine. Sticking it in the lock, he had the door open in a second without even damaging the lock. Too bad it hadn't worked on Granny's door.

Rummaging through the medicine bottles, Brad saw the penicillin pills and put them in his pocket. Then he saw one marked Demerol. That one went in his pocket too. He closed the cabinet door, examining room door, and front door behind him as he sneaked back through the illuminated night to his car.

He needed to find a pop vending machine for liquid so he could swallow the pills. He thought about washing them down with the Jim Beam, but knew better. He had a big day ahead of him and had to be in control. Couldn't let the dames get the upper hand again.

As he steered away from the curb, he never saw the dark clad figure with the Indian black eyes watching him from the shadows of her upstairs window.

Pulling back into the same service station he used before, Brad slid out of the car seat and felt in his pocket for the quarter. The pop machine lit his face with its blue light. He hit the Pepsi button, and the glass bottle made a loud rattling noise as it rolled out of the machine. Stooping down to get it from the slot, he saw a metal gas can just beyond the machine. It felt at least half full when he picked it up.

Again talking out loud to himself, he said, "I just might need this. Never know when a man might want to start a bonfire."

⁂

With Ann and Millie leading the way, all four of the cabin dwellers ran to the front living room window together. Pulling the curtain open a bit more, they peeped out. Sammy was clinging to his mama's leg and whimpering.

"I don't want to see Daddy. He'll whip me for running away. I know he will, I just know it. Maybe I do want you to kill him, Grandma Ann." Sammy cried, remembering all the pain his daddy had brought to him.

Millie knelt in front of both her children.

"Sammy, don't cry. Grandma Ann and I won't let Daddy hurt you, okay? Do you remember what to do? If I say run, go out the side door, down through the bottom, and into the bog where Sadie found the bowl. Do you hear me? Sammy, do what Sadie says, understand?"

They both nodded their heads.

"Hello in there! Is anybody home? Daddy wants you to come out and play. Come on, Millie. You've not played with me in such a long time. I've missed you."

Ann still couldn't see Brad, but it sounded like his voice was coming from behind that man's electric company truck.

"Millie, come on now. You get on out here and come by your-self. Come to the side of the truck. I'll be waiting for you. I've got a surprise."

A few minutes passed and Brad spoke again. Millie could really hear the fury rising in his voice now.

"Millie, I won't tell you again. Get out here, now. I'm counting to ten, and then I'll be lighting the fire. I've got gas poured all around the entire place. If I strike the flint, it will go up like a cracker box, and you'll all burn to death. It would be a shame for our sweet little children to never see their poor old daddy again, and Lord knows I'd probably grieve myself sick over all of you. It's nearly driven me to suicide being away from you all these months. Now come on out. I just want you back."

Millie knew better than to believe him. Brad never grieved over anything or anyone in his life. He didn't have real feelings like other people, only anger and a penchant for control.

"Grandma, I've got to go out there. I can't let him set us on fire, and he will do it too."

"Okay, Millie. You go out the front door and I'll sneak out the side one and try to get a shot at him. Keep your distance, talk to him, stall while the children run to the bog. Okay, let's go."

"Sadie, Sammy, remember—stay in the bog until Grandma or I come for you."

Kneeling down, Millie hugged her children as tightly as she could and Ann knelt down and put her arms around all three of them.

"I love you both," Millie said through tears, "more than life, and I love you too Grandma."

Outside they heard Brad counting. "One, two, three . . ."

"Here we go. Let's do it," Ann said.

As the women rose, they locked eyes. Each drew strength from the other. No more words were needed, none except a whispered breath to her children.

"Run Wakanda and Honiahaka! Run like the wind."

Millie opened the front door at the same time Ann opened the side one, pushing the children out in front of her.

Slowly Millie stepped through the door. "I'm coming, Brad. Don't light the fire." She kept talking to him, trying to distract him from the side of the cabin. I'm sorry, Brad. I promise I'll make it up to you. I'll never leave you again." She went on and on.

"You bet you won't, " Brad said under his breath. He was kneeling where she couldn't see him.

As she walked around the side of the truck, he grabbed her legs and pulled her to the ground. Millie didn't know what had hit her when he roughly placed the smelly rag over her nose and mouth. Brad had also stolen one of the doctor's bottles of chloroform. She blacked out almost instantly.

"One down and three to go," he said out loud.

Out the corner of his eye, he saw his brats running down the hill. He'd deal with them later. They'd be no problem. Now, Granny was another story. He had a score to even with her. Reaching down he touched the tender spot on his side.

"What the hell?"

He cocked his head toward a loud noise. Sounded like a bear growling. "Yeah, right, probably some wild hog or something," he said out loud, squinting into the woods.

Sadie heard the Liwanu of the bear. She wasn't scared at all. "Come on, Sammy," she said. We're almost there."

        ❦

By the time Doc picked up Marty, it was almost eleven o'clock. Grandmother Nyoaka said not a word as they drove the few miles down the mountain. Marty was always talking, so Doc just listened and tried to slow down the roaring in his head. When they were almost to the Skunk Cabbage Bog turn, Nyoaka spoke.

"Take me to the pull-off on the Blue Ridge Parkway to the shortcut into the bog. Then you can get Marty to his truck."

"Grandmother, are you sure? I don't feel good about you walking that far in the woods alone."

Nyoaka said, "I have walked the path many times. I know it well, and I will not be alone."

Lewis didn't see any reason to argue with her. He knew how stubborn she was. It was always her way or no way.

"Okay, Grandmother. I'll walk down the hill behind the cabin and meet you at Grandfather's grave." Then he sat quietly as he listened to his grandmother's chant.

"Run, Wakanda and Honiahaka, run like the wind." Over and over she repeated herself.

In a minute Lewis pulled over on the parkway. Before he came to a full stop, his grandmother was opening the door and on her way into the woods toward the bog.

"Grandmother, be careful!" He never saw her move so fast.

She didn't answer him, but kept repeating her chant. "Run, Wakanda and Honiahaka. Run like the wind."

* 🦋 *

Sadie and Sammy ran as fast as they could through the pine grove. When they made the clearing, Sadie was relieved. She knew the rock was just up ahead, and for some reason she knew they'd be safe if they got there.

When the rock came into sight, on it sat Nyoaka. Sadie wasn't surprised, and Sammy was too scared to wonder why.

"Daddy's back. He's at the cabin. We've got to help Mama and Grandma." Sammy was talking as fast as he could as he ran into the old woman's arms.

"Now, now little one. All is well. The guardian spirits are in control. Sit—we must wait and pray." Nyoaka pulled the children down with her on the rock. "Pray, pray . . ." she said to them.

"Sammy, look. It's one of the bog turtles, right there beside you," Sadie said.

"I don't care," Sammy said. "I want my mama."

Then Nyoaka spoke. "It will take all our guardian spirits to fight this evil one, even mine, the turtle."

With Millie knocked out on the ground, now Brad could deal with Granny. He gave Millie a swift kick to the side as he stepped over her.

"Stupid woman. Thought she could leave me."

He heard the snap behind him and turned quickly. He didn't want Granny to get the upper hand . . . again. Brad stumbled backwards against the truck, trying to get his gun in position.

The massive black bear was only a few feet in front of him. Brad got off three shots at him before his giant paw smacked the gun out of his hand. The bear's claws dug a bloody trail into his skin. Remembering the bottle of chloroform he left on the truck's running board, he quickly reached down and threw the powerful potion in the bear's face.

While the bear growled and swatted at his nose, Brad stooped down and searched for his gun. The bear went ambling blindly up the hill.

* ❦ *

Lewis sat still as he watched his grandmother hurry out of sight. Then the roar began in full.

> *Grandmother Nyoaka makes her way through the woods. Twice a gun fires, its explosions vibrating through Lewis's brain stem and ricocheting through his body. He feels the pain in his left arm as the third shot blasts through him. Then a powerful, acrid smell permeates the damp mountain air. It isn't the gunpowder but something stronger, more potent. His eyes sting and pinch shut. All goes dark. Is he blind?*

"Doc, you all right? Hey Doc, what's the matter?"

Marty's voice finally broke through. Lewis opened his eyes, thankfully able to see again. Not answering Marty, Lewis threw the gear stick into drive and gunned his car toward the cabin.

* ❦ *

"Touch that gun and I'll shoot you between the eyes," Ann challenged Brad.

Slowly he rose to a standing position, his gun at his feet. Granny's gun was pointed right at his head.

"Don't move, you snake."

Walking toward the ground where Millie lay, Ann spoke her name. "Millie, Millie, wake up. Come on, honey."

Bending down, but with her eyes still fixed on Brad, Ann touched Millie's face, smoothing the hair back out of her eyes. She could feel the pulsing in her neck—she was alive.

"Damn shame she's so clumsy. Must have hit her head when she fell down," Brad said.

"What did you do to her, you wicked son of a bitch?"

Ann rarely swore, but right now she couldn't care less what she said or did to him. Yet Sammy's words again rang clear and true—*the Bible says you're not supposed to kill . . .*

During her hesitation, Brad took his opportunity. He still held the chloroform bottle behind his leg. He hoped there was enough left in it to do the trick.

Before Ann knew it, a burning sensation was blazing in her eyes. She fired the gun, not knowing where the shot had landed. Then she was out. Brad had struck her in the temple with the empty chloroform bottle. The Ruger dropped to the ground along with Ann.

Brad stooped down and picked up both guns, sticking one in each front pocket. He shouldn't need these anymore. He could handle his two weakling young'uns. They were all he'd really come after, now that he thought of it. Millie had gone against him too many times. It made him furious to know he couldn't control her. He was done. The brats were still young enough to mold the way he wanted them, or at least the boy might be.

Grabbing Millie by the foot, he dragged her into the cabin. Drops of blood dripped off his hand onto her pants, and the pulling wasn't doing his injured side any good either.

"The old gal has done gone and got fat. Can't stand a fat woman," he spoke out loud while thoughts of the blond at the diner danced in his deranged head.

By the time he'd hauled Ann into the cabin and piled her in the floor beside Millie, his side was throbbing. He'd busted his gunshot wound open, and it was bleeding again, but not too much this time, just enough to make a small stain on his shirt.

Looking back at the women lying crumpled on the floor, he said, "See you in hell, ladies, along with all the other scum women." Probably he should throw the daughter in there with them, too, but maybe she'd be a little help with the housework and cooking, at least until he could move in another brainless female.

With an arrogant laugh, he stepped out the door, shutting it behind him. He didn't mash the button in to lock it.

At the corner of the house, he picked up the gas can and poured what was left on the dried boards of the cabin. Back at the truck, he took up the rag he used to put the chloroform over Millie's face, and then he brought out his favorite lighter, the one that usually lay beside his recliner at home. He clicked the flint, letting the flame shoot through the white cloth. Fire. He loved to watch it take command over whatever got in its way. He loved fire. It was just like him—always taking.

Pitching the rag into the pool of gas at the bottom of the boards, he slapped his hands together as if his actions were nothing more than brushing off cracker crumbs.

Now for the babies . . . once he found them, they could come back and watch the cabin burn.

Heading down the hill in the direction he saw the brats go, first he walked. Then he ran as he called for them. "Sadie, Sammy, where are you? Come to Daddy. Me and Mama are waiting for you, it's time to go home." He kept repeating this to himself over and over as he followed the path with their small footprints pressed in it.

* ❦ *

"I'm scared. I hear him, he's getting closer." Sammy put his face into the folds of Nyoaka's shawl.

"It is well, little one, all is well," Nyoaka repeated soothingly to Sammy, stroking the back of his head.

"Maybe we should go. Daddy says Mama is waiting for us."

"No! Mama said wait here for her and Grandma, no matter what. Don't you remember?" Sadie said to her brother, grabbing his hand in hers. "Look, the turtle is still sitting there."

This time Sammy did at least look over at it.

Nyoaka spoke. "Did I tell you who my guardian spirit is?"

"No," Sadie said.

"As a young girl, I chose to do as the young braves did. I went into the woods close by here on the other side of the creek where the mountain of rock stands."

"Yes, I know that place," Sadie said.

"I was there for two days and three nights. I sat alone. I had many dreams and visions, but nothing came to claim my spirit, not until the dawn broke the morning sky on the third day."

Pointing to the turtle Nyoaka continued. "One of these tiny little turtles was with me. I couldn't and didn't want to believe that my guardian spirit was a weak little turtle. I wanted something big and powerful, like a mountain lion, or an eagle. Oh! To be able to soar high over the land, seeing everything and use my powerful talons to protect myself, and the ones I love! All these days and years, I have pushed the turtle away from my thoughts, but today I know it is he who lives in the bog, the one who carries his home on his back. He will be the one to lead me to my everlasting home, he who is small but brave. Look at him now as he stands by us. It is a strong spirit that counts, not so much one's size or strength."

Sadie was totally absorbed in what the ancient woman was saying. She couldn't help but ask her, "Do you really believe that the turtle will guide you to your everlasting home?"

"I believe many things, Sadie. I believe the air that moves the leaves is there even though I can't see or touch it. I believe everything on this earth has a purpose. I believe in the spirit that I hear, in the whisperings in my ear, and in the tugging of my heart. I have read the book of the Lord through many times; it's all in there. In Chronicles 16:26, God's word says: *"For all the gods of the people are idols: but The Lord made the heavens . . ."*

"As long as you know God is the maker of everything, whether you call His helpers guardian angels or guardian spirits, as long as you believe, believe in the One who made everything . . ." Nyoaka's voice trailed off to a whisper.

＊ ༄ ＊

"Sadie, Sammy—I'm getting tired of this hiding game. Come out my little darlings."

Sadie could hear her daddy's fine words, but also knew his tone of voice. He had a slap waiting for each of them.

"All is well little ones. Stay with me. Believe, Sadie, believe," Nyoaka whispered just as their daddy came into sight.

"Well, there you are. Come to Daddy."

Sammy never raised his head from Nyoaka's shawl. Sadie looked her father over. His hand was bleeding; there was a red stain on the side of his shirt. He was dirty and his shirt hung out of his pants, not his habit. He always looked neat. But what she noticed most were his eyes. They didn't look the same; they were like two black balls of coal.

"Where's Mama?"

"She's up at the house, all packed and waiting for us."

Sadie knew that wasn't true. Mama said they would never go back home to Daddy, and Mama didn't lie. Then she saw the smoke.

Brad was almost within arm's reach. He didn't acknowledge Nyoaka at all; it was as if he didn't even see her.

When Brad got close enough, he grabbed Sammy's arm.

Sadie could hear Nyoaka softly speaking, "Stay with me. Hide your face, little one. Sadie, keep believing."

Sadie closed her eyes just before she felt the sting of her daddy's slap.

* ❦ *

Over the bog came a dark mass of clouds; the bright day was suddenly extinguished. Sadie could see her daddy standing a distance in front of her, and there was Blackie coming toward him. Brad first stepped back slowly, but then he was running, frantic to escape the wild animal.

Brad ran first toward the cabin, but when Blackie cut him off, he had to turn into the bog. Sadie had never gone that way before, for it had always been too wet and murky. She watched until her daddy and Blackie were almost out of sight. Then she heard the howl of a wolf, a blood-curdling cry. Sadie could just imagine it lunging at her daddy's throat. The bog came alive then. Crows squalled and everywhere noise was drowning out any sound she might have heard from her daddy.

Sadie looked over to make sure Sammy wasn't watching. His head was still turned as if still in the folds of Nyoaka's shawl; but Nyoaka had vanished. The turtle was in her place. Yes, he was right there instead of where Nyoaka had been a minute before!

Then in the sky, above the place where Blackie and Daddy had fallen out of sight, a host of apparitions appeared. It seemed there was a filmy glaze over Sadie's eyes, but she could see an old Indian man with gray pigtails falling over his chest—then a flash of another Indian, a woman this time—and a white man who looked a lot like Doc Townsend. The old Indian man took the hand of the Indian woman. Then there was another Indian man coming toward them holding the hands of a beautiful, young maiden and a small female Indian child. They all took one another's hands, and then three more figures came into sight. A young white woman and an Indian brave walked hand in hand toward the group, and then from the other side of the circle a young child came toward the couple. When the young white woman and Indian brave saw the child, they ran as fast as they could and scooped her up in their arms. Sadie could see tears streaming down their faces. They must be the couple Grandma Ann had told her about, the distant cousins. Then there was Nyoaka walking to join the group. She took the little girl's hand.

What Sadie saw next made her gasp. It was two other men. One looked exactly like the picture of her mama's daddy—her Grandfather Jonathan—and the other one looked like Grandma Ann's husband Jake. The grown men grabbed each other in a huge bear hug then joined the clan. Holding hands, they moved to form a circle around her and Sammy. The ones who were standing over the bog were floating above the dark water.

The wind began to blow and lightning struck. Sadie wiped her eyes and tossed the hair back out of her face. She saw her daddy running back through the bog with Blackie still close behind him; they were coming toward her and Sammy. When she thought he would be upon them, Sadie didn't waver. She held Sammy's hand tighter and looked her daddy in the eye as he approached. When he got to the circle, he suddenly stopped as if seeing the ring of people for the first time. He bellowed a wicked scream and his face contorted as he spat and swore at the circled group, moving from one to the other, damning them, with every breath swearing that he'd take every one of them to hell with him if they didn't let him through the circle. Then with a whisk of light and a roar sounding like the Liwanu, the arm of Blackie fell across the phantom of Brad Madison and he was gone.

Sadie turned to the sound of her mama's voice in the distance. Was she dreaming? Had her daddy slapped her out? Then, looking all around, she saw them. The circle was still united. They were all still there except for Blackie and her daddy.

~ Chapter Twenty-eight ~

Doc Townsend's car slid sideways into the path marked Skunk Cabbage Bog just as they both heard what sounded like a gunshot.

"Who'd be hunting this time of year, Doc?" Marty asked.

"I don't know."

Once they stopped behind the black car and truck, Doc and Marty jumped out.

"Guess we'll have to walk in. Looks like Ms. Burke's got company."

Doc Townsend didn't like the feeling he had. He knew it well; there was trouble. And then he smelt smoke and started running.

"Come on Marty, hurry."

Jumping over the chain gate, they raced down the path. When the cabin came into view they could see the flames climbing up the wall on one side.

Marty ran to his truck, opened the door, reached in, and took out the fire extinguisher. Lewis ran to the front door. The knob turned and he saw the women right away. The air was clear with no smoke inside yet. Ann was closest to the door, so Lewis carried her out first, way into the front yard. Then he went back for Millie. She was stirring but was too groggy to stand by herself. Lewis threw her over his shoulder, and out she went to the spot beside her grandma. When he looked toward Marty, he saw the fire was almost out. Marty had it under control.

Lewis saw that Millie was coming around, so he turned his attention to Ann. She had a huge purple knot on the side of her temple and she smelled of chloroform.

Back inside the cabin, he fetched the bucket of cool spring water and a cloth.

Outside, Marty was still working on a few smoldering embers while Millie sat, trying to shake the fog out of her head. Doc dipped the cloth and placed it over Ann's knot. She stirred. Her eyes were red and puffy.

By now Millie could focus on what was going on. Rising to her knees, she held her stomach. Brad's kick had left an awful bruise. The way it hurt, it was probably a cracked rib.

"Grandma, wake up! Where are Sadie and Sammy?"

Ann mumbled. "The bog. Brad."

"Oh, my God! He's after them." Millie stood and swayed on unsteady feet.

"Marty, come here. Is the fire out?" Doc said.

"Yes, just sort of went out by itself. Didn't even have to use the extinguisher."

Doc said, "Keep dipping this rag in the cool water and putting it on the knot on this lady's forehead. I've got to help Millie find the children."

"This is my Grandmother Ann," Millie said. There was no time for further introductions.

Trying to sit, Ann said, "Just give me a second, I'm coming too."

Marty noticed Doc had called Mrs. Burke by a different name. He just guessed Millie was short for Mildred. Maybe they knew each other better than he thought.

Holding Millie and Ann's hands, Lewis led them toward the bottom. They went as fast as the women's trembling legs would go. Marty followed, ready to catch either of them if they stumbled.

All kinds of horrible thoughts passed through Millie's mind. She knew what Brad was capable of, and he had her precious children.

"Sadie! Sammy!" Millie called.

* * *

"Miss Nyoaka, may I open my eyes now?" Sammy could still feel her arms around him, her fingers stoking his hair.

"You can open your eyes. It's okay," Sadie said.

He leaned forward almost tipping into the bog when he saw Nyoaka wasn't there to support him.

"Where's Miss Nyoaka?" Sammy asked, looking around.

Sadie didn't answer. At the edge of the rock, the turtle was still there.

Then they heard their mama calling. She and Grandma Ann, Doc Townsend and Marty came into view.

There in front of Millie, sitting right on the rock where she'd told them to stay, were her babies. And all around them were many other people. Ann and Doc Townsend saw them too.

Ann was the first to speak. "Jake? Jonathan?"

Millie saw tears streaming down her grandmother's face. Then in disbelief Millie softly spoke as her eyes recognized the two men. "Daddy? Grandpa?"

The two men left the circle. Taking Sadie and Sammy's small hands, they went to join Ann and Millie. All six embraced. Then Jonathan stepped back, took Millie's face in his hands, kissed her on the forehead, and said, "Everything is right now. My spirit can rest." Then he was gone, and so was Jake, but not before he smiled at Ann. The men vanished in the mist of the bog.

Then Lewis walked toward the other images, first to his mother, Morning Glory, and then to his father, Dennis.

Dennis spoke, "My son, why have you burdened yourself all these years? You could not stop the wrongs that were done on the Trail of Tears, nor could you save us from harm. It was our time to depart this earth. There was nothing you could have done to stop it. Be at peace."

Then the two parents kissed their son, one on either cheek, and disappeared. That's when Doc saw his grandmother Nyoaka coming to him, holding the hands of the two old Indian men.

"Lewis," she said, "this is Wahya, my father, and Tomeka, my grandfather; the ones you've seen in your dreams. "They," she said, pointing to the females beside the men, "are Tomeka's wife and daughter, the ones who died on the Trail of Tears. They have something to say to you."

Nyoaka stepped back, and the little girl came forward and spoke. "You were not there to help us on the Trail. You must not carry any guilt. You now are to take these other children." She looked at Sadie and Sammy. "You must create a new world for them, a fresh, untarnished beginning. The past cannot be changed but the future can. Go forward. Love this family and let them love you. There is no more time in your life or theirs to cry. The trail of all our tears must end here."

Lewis stared at the last three standing in the breaking circle, a white woman, young brave, and small child.

The little girl who had spoken nodded toward them. "Today is the day to right wrongs and reunite those who have unjustly been separated. These three are now united, becoming one, just like you will be with your new family. Knowing all things happen in the Creator's own season, we waited patiently on this time of reuniting. The wrongs have now been set right. Now our guardian spirits can lead us home."

Then they were all gone, Grandmother Nyoaka included.

❧ ❦ ❧

As if he hadn't seen a thing, Sammy spoke, "Mama, Daddy grabbed my arm."

This snapped Millie back to reality. With her tear-streaked cheeks she turned to Sadie. "Where did your Daddy go, Sadie Girl? Was he with you?"

"Yes, Mama. He was here."

Millie noticed the imprint of a hand on Sadie's cheek. Oh yes. He'd been there all right. "Where did he go?"

"I'm not sure." Sammy piped in. "Nyoaka made me close my eyes and hide my face in her dress."

"Grandmother," Lewis spoke softly. "She was here. Where did she go? Where did grandmother go?"

Sadie answered this time, "We're not sure of that either."

"I'm going up the path toward the parkway to look for her. Are you guys all right?"

Sadie and Sammy nodded their heads, and Millie answered, "We'll go with you."

Marty dragged along behind them as if he just awakened from a deep sleep. The last thing he remembered was coming down the hill behind Doc and the two ladies.

Not far up the path, Lewis saw Nyoaka crumpled on the ground. He ran to her. He flipped her from her side to her back, putting his ear to her chest. "She's not breathing."

He lowered his mouth to hers, trying to breath life into her.

Sadie closed her eyes and prayed aloud softly, "Please God, let her wake up. Don't let her die, please God."

Doc worked and worked on his grandmother as Millie watched. Sammy hid his face in his mama's pant leg this time. Sadie continued to pray.

Lewis really couldn't believe it himself, but Nyoaka took a long deep breath and in a minute opened her eyes. She turned her head, looking from one face to the other.

To her grandson she spoke in a soft faraway voice, "You are all safe. That evil one will never harm you again. You, Nita, my grandson, I saw you stand by your parents and grandfathers. I heard what the young girl, your cousin, and your parents said to you. Did you hear them, and do you understand?"

"I'm not sure about anything right now, Grandmother."

"Wakanda will talk to you. She was there. You will help each other to realize the truths."

Looking now to Sadie, Nyoaka spoke to her. "Wakanda, you have lived up to your name well. I believe you'll know for sure in your many moons ahead from where the power behind your magic comes. You have seen that good finally wins in the end— don't ever forget that. It may take many seasons of changes for you to grasp all this, but it will come to you in time. You will grasp the understanding. Your intuition is even stronger than your grandmother's. Practice it wisely. The magic? Everyone has a bit of it if they believe."

Falling to her knees beside Nyoaka, Sadie laid her head over on Nyoaka's shoulder. Taking her hand, she saw the black, charred burns. Doc saw them too.

It was a few minutes before Sadie could speak. "Why did Daddy win all these years? Why did the spirits let him be so mean to us for so long?"

Stroking Sadie's hand, Nyoaka answered. "It is written in the Lord's book that not all of our days will be happy and carefree. We have burdens to bear and many troubles to carry, some our own, some we bear for others. It is these troublesome times that make us better and stronger people. If not for the past sufferings, you would not have been able to stand up to your daddy today. The guardian spirits were here, but they worked through your strength. Your innocence and belief gave them the power to overcome a terribly wicked person. The Lord's book says that sometimes it takes a band of angels to do His will."

Turning now back to Lewis who was kneeling on her other side, Nyoaka spoke again to him. "Now, Nita, my grandson, you also fought the battle of a true warrior. You have walked the Trail of Tears for our people long enough, carrying their burdens in your own heart. It is now time for you to live your life. This young girl and her family," she looked at Sadie, Millie and Sammy, "will help you heal, as you will help them. You will bring joy, love and laughter to each other. Too many tears have already been shed. There will still be troubles and heart break, but you will continue to fight as the true warriors you are. Your love for each other will sustain you."

Now looking at Millie, Nyoaka spoke once more. "You, too, have lived up to your name, Camarin. You have protected your young as powerfully as you knew how. Also you, Grandmother Hania," Nyoaka said, looking at Ann, "continue to be the true spirit warrior you are."

Looking back to Millie, Nyoaka continued, "As I have already said to you, the second evil will come back to you, but you will be brave and you will fight. When you are tired of the struggle, you will battle even harder. My grandson needs you and has waited on you for far too long. Stay with him."

"Honiahaka, little Sammy, you will not hide your eyes forever. One day you will look back and remember this day. You will need to be strong and brave as the wolf you are named after. You will learn many things from my grandson and your heart will be as his, pure and humble. You and Wakanda will not sow the evil seeds of your birth father. You will walk in the ways of the one who made the heavens, the true, the one and only Guardian Spirit."

Sadie closed her eyes, as did Nyoaka. She could see the turtle sitting on the rock with Nyoaka beside him. And Blackie? He was again trudging up the hillside, ever watchful, always waiting, ready for yet another war against the evil one.

~ Ten Years Later ~

*T*o me, Sadie, it is so good to be back, home to the mountain, and the cabin. I remember all those years ago, the mysteries that happened down in the bog. Back then I tried to explain everything to Mama, Grandma Ann, Doc Townsend, the sheriffs . . . and poor Marty, he still doesn't have a clue. Daddy just vanished. The officers looked at me like I was crazy, or something worse. But not Doc, Mama, or Grandma Ann. They had seen enough, so they believed.

The officials searched the bog for a week and never found so much as a shoe. Of course there were no bear signs either. Quicksand swallowed him up, the sheriff said. Mama, Doc, Grandma Ann, and I knew better.

Sometimes I doubt myself though. Did Daddy knock me out that day? Did I dream it all? But every time I think that, I see Nyoaka holding Sammy, and the turtle beside them on the rock. Then I see Nyoaka's hands blackened by the cabin fire, a fire she wasn't even close to, a deadly heat from which she saved Mama and Grandma. Some things are just not for us to understand. Like Mama had said coming up the mountain that first day, sometimes there is magic.

I wish Nyoaka was still alive so I could talk to her more about what I saw that day. Why did all those people show up: Grandpa Jake and Jonathan, Tomeka and his wife and daughter, Wahya and our distant cousins with the little girl who'd been taken away from them, and Doc's mama and daddy, Dennis and Morning Glory?

I know what she'd tell me though. She'd say the Guardian Spirit wanted to re-unite us. He wanted and still wants all of our hearts to be at peace. He wanted us to know the other one was all right, and that the future could be better.

I guess Blackie could have taken care of Daddy all by himself, but we wouldn't have found the stillness if we hadn't seen our families. Our Guardian Spirit sure is awesome to love us that much.

The background check Sheriff Amos did on my daddy turned up some awful things. It seems he wasn't who he'd told my mama he really was. He'd been in and out of some really bad foster care since he was found as a small boy abandoned in an alley. I reckon now—*reckon?* See how I've picked up some of that fine North Carolina drawl? I guess I *understand* now where he learned all his cruelty. I'd like to say I've forgotten all about him, but I haven't. I'm working through it though.

We didn't go back to Texas. Daddy's body was never found. Mama waited the legal seven years to marry Doc Townsend. We lived with Grandma Ann until we were able to do some updates on the cabin. We put in a bathroom and modern heat, pumped water up from the spring, and did a little cosmetic stuff here and there, but it's pretty much the same. We stayed right here till they got married, and then they moved into the lavender house. I was in my sophomore year at Carolina by then and Sammy was almost a teenager. We still spend weekends here together when I come home.

I go down to the bog and collect snake root. I mash it up in Wahya's medicine bowl; it makes a fine soothing tea for Mama, Grandma Ann, and me. Doc Townsend's taught me plenty, sometimes too much, I think. When the pines whisper and the animals' eyes are on me, there's so much talking in my head. I guess that's part of the gift Nyoaka told me about. I'm still trying to figure all that out too.

Sammy and Doc Townsend are as tight as any blood father and son could ever be. I love him too. How could I not? We fought the battle together. He's proven himself many times since. Been awful good to all of us, especially Mama.

Nyoaka was right . . . again. The other evil one came back . . . the cancer. Mama's had five more tumors removed in the past ten years. But every time, she and Doc just hold hands and pray together. It took Mama a long time to open up and let him in her heart. I guess she was more torn up on the inside than any of us could see from the outside. I guess I am also, but I'm working on that too.

Grandma Ann is still living down the mountain. She practically stayed with us fulltime those first few years till she got afraid to drive up and down the mountain. Now we go visit her every chance we can.

Grandma Ann and I both now believe that guardian spirits and guardian angels are the same thing,

I've come back home here to the cabin to live. I'm a biologist . . . and a writer. I got a job with the State to study the bog turtles; they're almost all gone now. I'm going to try with all my heart to use the whisperings in my head to save them, but whatever happens, I know there will always be one bog turtle left, sitting right there on that rock. And Blackie will be up there on the hill waiting just in case I ever need him again.

Wakanda

Guardian Spirit

In the howl of a lonely winter's wind . . . It is there.
The sound swallows up the cold night air.
Under the frozen river's current
Or across the dry, barren way . . . It is there.

Dwelling in the eagle, turtle and snail
Under a rock, over the mountain, up a tree.
When the invisible breeze flutters a window curtain
And the smell of smoke burns your eyes . . . It is there.

It is there when your attempts fail
And when your tries become successes.
When the road is long, when it is short,
When you are well or sick, small or big . . . It is there.

In the whisperings of your head . . . It is there.
At the tugging of your heart
To your left, to the right,
Up ahead or just behind . . . It is there.

Pulling you up to carry you through
Holding your hand, taking you from despair to the light.
It is there . . . Crying as your pain becomes His . . .
Do you believe It is always there? It is there.

~Sadie Madison

~ Sarah Martin Byrd ~

Born at the foothills of the Blue Ridge Mountains, Sarah Martin Byrd learned early on that to succeed, you must work. She learned this from her overachieving father who drove her to excel at all her endeavors.

Since age fifteen, through two careers, she has written stories, poems, and articles. After many strokes of the pen, she retired to compose full-time. *Guardian Spirit* is her first published novel. She also enjoys writing children's books and has finished three.

Sarah likes stories that have grit to them. Life isn't always a bed of roses, so she writes the truth. In forming her characters, she takes bits and pieces of different people she's known or imagined through the years and forms personalities that readers may not always like but will be able to connect with or be fascinated by.

The author resides, still, at those foothills with her husband of over thirty years. Aside from her books, her best friend is her daughter. Sarah's granddaughter also occupies many happy hours of her days.

She hopes you enjoy *Guardian Spirit* and will be inspired to find your own magic.

~ A Note from the Author ~

I hope you have enjoyed getting to know Millie, Sadie, Sammy, Grandma Ann, Doc Townsend and Miss Nyoaka.

The world looks at Brad, Millie, Sadie and Sammy and sees a normal, yet private small town family, just like millions of others in this country. But what people can't, or won't see is the truth. Behind closed doors, none, but those who dwell there feel the pain . . . the agony . . . the degradation of living with an abusive, unstable person.

In *Guardian Spirit* we see what the vicious cycle of abuse can do to a family. No one should have to continue in a relationship that involves suffering. None deserve to be abused. You may think things will get better and the children won't be harmed. But believe me, the kids are the ones who will remember the most, and the getting better usually gets much worse.

On the following page, you will find a short list that I've compiled of very helpful websites and some useful phone numbers. Please use these resources to get help for yourself, and especially for the sake of your children.

God Bless,
Sarah

Anonymous and Confidential Help 24/7
National Domestic Violence Hotline
www.ndvh.org
1.800.799.SAFE (7233) 1.800.787.3224 (TTY)

The Red Flag Campaign
The first statewide public awareness campaign to
address dating violence and promote its prevention.
www.theredflagcampaign.org/index.php/
dating-violence/red-flags-for-abusive-relationships/

Links and help aids for Abused or Battered Women
Domestic Violence Shelters and Support *(local and regional)*
www.helpguide.org/mental/domestic_violence_abuse_
help_treatment_prevention.htm

New Identities for Domestic Violence Victims
ssa.gov/pubs/10093.html

Help for Teens
"Love Doesn't Have to Hurt"
www.apa.org/pi/families/resources/love-teens.pdf

Safe Horizon
Moving victims of violence from crisis to confidence.
www.safehorizon.org